GIFTS
OF
ELYSIELLE

Inner Origins Book Three

ELLIS LOGAN

An Earth Lodge® Publication
Roxbury, Connecticut

Published in the U.S.A. by Earth Lodge®
Cover Design by Maya Cointreau

ISBN 978-1944396336

"Keep your face always toward the sunshine and shadows will fall behind you."

- *Walt Whitman*

"The sun is singing its love into me."

- *Rob Brezsny*

"When men meet foes in fight, better is stout heart than sharp sword."

- *The Völsunga Saga*

CHAPTER 1

I should have known better. This was never going to work. There just wasn't any way.

I checked the special countdown app I had going on my phone. Five days, six hours, and thirty-two minutes left until my Choosing. Less than six days until my birthday, the day when I could officially Choose the Light and unlock my full fae potential.

No big deal.

Everything was going totally perfectly, really.

My ex-boyfriend was still a dark fae. We still didn't have a solution to stop the anti-serum, a virus that blocked the light in people and either sent them into deep hibernation or turned them into mindless slaves. And we still didn't know exactly how I was supposed to help the Light win its war against the Dark.

But hey, no worries, everything was peachy.

1

Over the last few weeks, people had been telling me not to stress out, but here I was, stuck in a tiny little white room, with lots of options and not one clear choice. No perfect fit, anyway.

"Siri, have you made a decision?" someone called from outside the door.

I was getting really tired of people asking me that.

Seriously.

I puffed my cheeks and blew a strand of hair out of my mouth, taking in the chaos of the room before I looked at myself in the mirror, clad only in Aeden-issued silk undergarments.

"Siri?" another voice repeated, sounding out of patience.

Well, I wasn't happy, either.

"No," I called back, not bothering to hide my irritation. "I can't decide."

I looked in the mirror again, taking in the fresh bruises on my ribs and legs from this morning. When I turned, I could see a small cut that was already starting to heal on the back of my shoulder where someone had sliced me with a small dagger.

You would have thought I'd been tortured at the hands of the Dark, but it was actually some of my closest friends who had done this to me. They'd spent the morning trying to attack me, and now they had put me in this room.

Suddenly, the door was yanked open from the outside, letting in more light and a whole lot of fresh air.

"Amber! What are you doing?!" I grabbed a piece of fabric off the chair next to me and tried to cover myself. Amber rolled her eyes and stepped inside, closing the door behind her.

"What's the holdup?" she asked. "You've been in here forever."

I looked around the cramped changing room and kicked at a particularly offensive dress that lay crumpled on the ground.

"I can't find anything I like. This is torture. Can't you guys just pick something for me?"

"Nope, sorry." Amber grinned. "You don't have to get something here. We can try another shop, Siri. Don't worry so much. We'll find you the best dress in all of Elysielle for your Choosing. We still have five days."

"Five days?" I slumped down on top of the clothes in the chair and groaned. "I hate dresses. I hate shopping. This sucks."

Amber laughed and ruffled through the things on the floor. She picked out my training clothes, then handed them to me. "Put these on. I think you need sustenance before we shop anymore."

"Gods below, finally something we agree on." I hugged my pair of grey linen capris and coordinating armless shirt like old friends.

She left the room and I heard her talking and giggling with Claire in hushed tones outside the changing room. Traitors.

We'd arrived in Elysielle three days ago to make arrangements for my Choosing ceremony. Originally it was supposed to happen at my grandmother's estate in Ireland, but with the Shades on the warpath everyone agreed that Aeden was the safest place for me right now.

I hated that, being told what was best for me. As if I couldn't take care of myself. In less than one week I would be eighteen years old. A legal adult both in Aeden and throughout most countries in the world above. I pulled on my clothes roughly, annoyed about the way everyone had been coddling me lately. As if I was an infant. As if I wasn't about to become one of the most powerful fae on earth in the last millennia. And here I was, trying to find a dress. Didn't we have more important things to be doing?

I knew that we did.

This morning, we'd all been training – Mom, Alec, Amber, Ewan, Claire and Mialloch – like we had every morning for the last two weeks. Bran had been absent, work calling him away after breakfast, but the rest of us had been working on krav maga techniques after warming up with some tai chi. I'd been teaching Mialloch some knife-fighting techniques when a messenger had barged into the room.

That's how I'd wound up getting tagged by mistake, not paying attention as I spun around at the interruption. I knew I'd never hear the end of that from my mom later at dinner.

The messenger had dragged both my mom and Alec away on "urgent Light Guard business," saying only that there had been a development. I knew what that meant. The Shades were up to no good again.

So why was I here, stuck trying on dresses? I was the one who was supposed to save the world. I was the one in the prophecy. Shouldn't I have been at the meeting? My father's guards had enjoyed ignoring me when I'd tried to tell them just that, barring me from his temporary headquarters in Elysielle. One of these days, I really needed to get Dorian in the training room with me for a little sparring. So far, he'd ignored all my invitations to get knocked out.

That's okay. I was nothing if not persistent.

CHAPTER 2

I stalked out of the changing room. Amber and Claire were nowhere to be seen, so I continued through the quiet store past the racks of diaphanous, gauzy material and exited into the street.

Yet again, I was struck by the alien visual cacophony of the city. Every building was uniquely carved and bedazzled, like some ball-room dancer had gotten her hands on an award-winning architect's designs at the last minute. No two buildings were alike, nothing matched, and yet somehow everything complemented each other. The city was like a giant fractal – when you approached it from far away it presented a collage masterpiece of color and aesthetic design, but the closer you got to it, the more detail you found. Within each facet, you would find twelve more intricacies. It was like a giant Gaudí installation, but infinitely more complex. In fact, my grandmother had informed me just the other day that Gaudí had been part fae, too, although he had never been to Elysielle. I guess some things were just in the blood.

Tearing my eyes away from the red and purple balconies shimmering in the warm rosy sunlight, I turned to see my friends waving at me from an outdoor café down the street.

I rushed to join them, just barely avoiding being jostled by a troupe of street performers. Amused by the group's antics, I turned and walked backwards a few steps, watching them retreat from view.

"Hey, watch it!" A thin, reedy voice rasped at me. I spun around to just miss stepping into a boy's lap where he sat cross-legged on the stones drawing with chalk. All my training kicked in and I vaulted over him instead. Of course, that meant that now my hands were covered in chalk, and I'd messed up part of his drawing.

"Look what you did!"

"Oh, man, wow, I'm really sorry. I totally didn't see you there."

"Yeah, that's kind of obvious," he muttered petulantly. "Now I'm going to have to fix that whole section."

He waved his hand and we both surveyed the damage. He'd managed to draw an incredibly realistic 3D view of a rock well, complete with a massive opening showing the moon and the starry night sky I'd always taken for granted. Looking at it, you felt like you would fall straight into the sky.

"This is amazing," I said, kneeling down beside him. The boy seemed near my age, maybe just a year or two younger. His dark skin was clear and glistening, warmed from mahogany to a mulberry hue under the Aeden sun, making his azure eyes stand out in stark contrast like heat lighting in a midnight sky. Long, thin dreads twisted on top of his head in a wild, messy knot secured by several colored pencils. "The moon looks just right. But what are these constellations, here and here?"

"I don't know, I just copied them from some of the Ancient star charts, see?" He held out a couple pages for me to look at, seeming torn halfway between distrust and curiosity. "But how would you know if I got the moon right, anyway?"

"Well, I've seen it enough times to know, I think. I grew up above below. This is actually my first time in Elysielle." I stuck out my hand. "Siri Alvarsson."

"Brenin Mirro. Are you really from topside?"

"Yeah," I smiled.

"That is so cool. All the things you must have seen. I wish I could travel above below, but my mom says no way."

"There's a lot to see, but it's not so different, not really. Besides, your mom's right. Things aren't going so great right now for us up there. Wait a couple years before you try to travel, hopefully by then everything will have worked itself out."

I didn't want to crush his hopes, but honestly, there might not even be a world to travel to in a few months. Who could say? He seemed like a nice kid. I was glad his mom was keeping him out of trouble.

8

"Huh. Yeah, well, thanks for the chat, but I still have a lot of work to do on this before it's done," he dismissed me in a huff and turned back to his art.

"Well, hey, look, I feel really bad about messing up your piece. Why don't you take a break and come hang out with me and my friends for a while, get hydrated before you get back to work? We've all been topside, you can ask us whatever you want."

"Really?" His eyes lit up as he tilted his head to the side, considering.

"Yes, really. You know what, I even have my phone on me, you can check out the pictures I have stored up on it. They should give you some good art ideas." I stood up and held out a hand to help him up.

"You're an artist? You have paintings of Midgard?" He accepted my hand and rose, dusting himself off. Standing, I could see he wasn't much taller than me, and wearing loose clothes and pants that were just a little short for his gangly frame. Maybe he was even younger than I thought, since he was obviously still growing.

"Ugh, no," I laughed. "I draw a bit, but I'm no artist. Don't worry, what I have is even better. Come on." I linked my arm in his and dragged him over to Amber and Claire, who'd been watching the whole exchange with amused grins.

"Hey guys. This is Brenin. He's an artist, and I've promised him we can answer all his questions about the world above. Brenin, this is Claire and Amber."

Amber smiled and eyed him over her menu, while Claire patted the seat next to her. "Here, Brenin, have a seat."

"Okay, yeah, thanks." He looked around at us all in awe. "So you've all been to Midgard? Is that really true?"

"Yes," Claire answered. "This is actually my first time in Aeden, and Siri's second. Amber's a Light Guard, so she comes and goes all the time."

Brenin's eyes got round. "No way. You guys are messing with me. No way you're a Light Guard!"

Amber dropped her smile and leaned forward menacingly. "You wanna test that theory? You think I'm what, too small? Maybe too girly?"

I punched Amber in the shoulder. "Cut it out, Amb. He's just a kid." I turned to Brenin. "Amber's definitely a Light Guard. You might have heard of her uncle, Mitch Slaight?"

Brenin paled and looked quickly back at Amber.

"Yeah," she laughed. "You might want to choose your next words more carefully."

"I'm sorry, I just thought...I've never met anyone who's been above below, and now I'm meeting three of you? It's just a little hard to believe."

Amber narrowed her eyes at him.

"But I do! I believe you! Geez. You guys really know how to make a guy nervous, you know that?"

We all cracked up and Brenin smiled at us sheepishly. Amber waved the waiter over and ordered a tasting round of all their best juices and a giant sampler platter of fatishchets, an Elysielle specialty that reminded me of sweetened spring rolls.

"So, shoot," I said after the waiter had left. "Ask me anything you want to know."

"Are the plants really green up there? And does the rain really turn to white, fluffy ice? And what about the humans? What are they like? My friend Kylis says he heard that they are all really dangerous and wild, like monsters, and that's really why we're not allowed up there. He says that's why fae-human hybrids have pointy ears and funny hair sometimes. He says they're like animals."

"Wow, really? That is so not true! You can tell your friend Kylis that humans look just like us." I told him, thinking of Alec and understanding a little more of the kind of teasing he must have endured as a kid in Valhalla "In fact, from what I know, most fae have human DNA in them. Some have a little more, and it can cause some funny traits to pop up, but no one's an animal or a monster. But yeah, humans do fight sometimes. Just like how the Light fights the Dark – there are good guys and bad guys, and of course everyone thinks their side is the good side."

"Huh." Brenin chewed on his lip, mulling that over while I continued.

"The sun is yellow and the grass is green in Midgard, most plants are, at least their leaves anyways. Except in places where it gets cold and snows. We call that winter, when the water turns to ice and snow. That's when the leaves turn orange and yellow and drop off the trees."

"The trees die every winter?" Brenin looked horrified.

"No, no, they just sleep." Claire said kindly, "Spring is beautiful. Everything wakes up again and the trees get covered in bright green leaves and flowers. It's my favorite season. We have flowers that only bloom for a few weeks in the spring."

"I heard about that, too, how you guys have sessions."

"Not sessions, seasons," Amber laughed.

Brenin blushed and I explained. "In the fall, some places get colder and the leaves fall off the trees. In winter, everything is quiet and cold and snowy. In spring, farmers plant their crops and nature wakes up again. In summer, it gets hot like here, and everyone goes to the beach and plays outside a lot. And then the farmers harvest their crops and it's fall again. That's how the seasons work. Unless you live in one of the places on the equator, where it's more like here, hot all the time."

"I'd love to see all that," Brenin said wistfully. "I draw from copies of old books we have at the library here, but it's not the same. And I never know if I'm copying something that another artist made up, or if it's really accurate."

"Oh, hey, that reminds me!" I pulled out my phone and scrolled through to the photos gallery. Even though there was no signal down in Aeden, I still carried it around so I could listen to my music. Now, I thanked the gods that I wasn't into taking selfies. Most of the photos were of architecture and places I'd hiked, trained or snowboarded.

I showed him the phone. "I told you I had pictures. Check these out. Just use your finger to swipe through the photo gallery."

I didn't think it was possible, but the kid's eyes got even bigger. He tucked himself back in his seat, poring over the images.

The girls and I eyed each other, trying not to laugh. Claire shook her head and sighed, reaching into her bag.

"When you finish up with that one, you can look at mine, too."

"Sure, thanks," he said absently. I wondered if he'd even heard what she said, so complete was his absorption in the device.

The fatishchets arrived and the girls and I tucked into the food. Shopping made me ravenous, even more than training. Must have had something to do with the stress, I thought to myself and shrugged. The waiter came back and placed glass flights in front of us with four small glasses each, all containing different juices. After being in Aeden, I could see where my mom had gotten her preoccupation with fresh juice from. It was so totally genetic. Now I found myself craving juice regularly, whether they were sweet and fruity or iron-rich leafy purple smoothies.

I took a small sip of each juice in my flight, and settled on my favorite combo, a brilliant azure concoction of berries and cala. The grass had a sweet, almost vanilla taste to it, and always amped me up for the rest of the day. So much, in fact, I had to be careful not to have any after lunchtime, or I'd never fall asleep that night. I knew the girls planned to get back to shopping soon, though, so I eyed the tiny glass and wondered if I should order more to see me through the afternoon.

Finally, Brenin looked up from my phone. "These are amazing. Claire, can I see yours now?"

"Sure thing," she smiled, and tossed him her phone. He nodded his thanks, catching the phone and grabbing a couple fatishchets to munch on while he scrolled through the pictures. While we ate, Amber and Claire started discussing where we should go next.

After a while, Brenin looked up from the phone. "Who are all the men in these photos? Are these all fae who live above? They all look fae."

Claire turned bright red. "Oh! No, um, those are just, you know, random guys."

"You mean they're humans?"

"Mostly, yeah," she nodded, tucking her short curly hair behind her ears. I swear, her cheeks were redder than the brilliant crimson streaks lightening her brunette locks.

I leaned in and gave Brenin my best stage whisper. "Claire's got a thing for hot guys. She likes to stalk them and take their photos."

"I do not!" she protested loudly. Several of the other diners looked our way and she leaned across the table.

"I do not," she hissed.

Brenin leaned back and quirked an eyebrow, holding up the phone so we all could see the picture. A handsome blonde sunburned tourist was inspecting the goods at a market stall back in Egypt. The shot was clearly taken without the guy's knowledge.

"Well, fine, that one, but-"

Brenin's other eyebrow shot up to match the first as he scrolled back and held up another shot of a tight group of sun-kissed Middle Eastern soccer players horsing around.

"Oh come on, I was covering that game for the school paper-"

Brenin's smile broke out in full force and he flipped past a couple more pictures, showing us a handsome student in winter dress, standing in the Long Room at Trinity's library studying a book. Amber and I lost it, cracking up loudly.

"That was just a couple of weeks ago!" I pointed at Claire while I cackled. "You haven't changed a bit! You are so totally boy crazy."

"I am not," Claire sniffed and put her chin in the air. "I just appreciate a fine form, that's all."

Amber and I laughed even harder, Brenin joining in loudly.

"Wow," he said, gasping for breath, "I thought my sister was bad, she draws the same guy all the time, but this totally has her beat!"

"Oh, shut up," Claire huffed. "What are you, like fourteen? What would you know?"

"I just turned sixteen, thank you very much. And I know more than you think," he said, waggling his eyebrows at her.

"I, I...Whatever. I think I need to use the bathroom." Claire got up and rushed into the building, no doubt to cool her cheeks while the rest of us dissolved into another fit of giggles.

CHAPTER 3

Two hours later, Claire was still exacting her revenge.

"Just one more, I swear. This piece is perfect."

I glared at her and she winked at me, the glint in her eyes rivaling the flash of the diamond gemstones in the silver torque she held up for my approval.

After our meal, we'd left Brenin to making his art and hit three more stores before finally finding a dress we all agreed on. It was ridiculously short, which Amber loved. It had a flouncy skirt, which Claire said was a must to temper my boyish attitude. And it was simple and gray, which I required. My one vanity: I loved the way gray brought out my silver eyes. Plus, the color had a soothing effect on my mood. And there was always the added bonus that it matched everything else I owned. The top sported clean asymmetrical lines that showed off my toned arms and shoulders, while also featuring one of my favorite Aeden fashion specialties, a truly hidden and supportive built-in bra. Now, Claire was trying to lure me in to buying matching jewelry.

"Forget that," Amber waved her hand dismissively at us. "You can't wear a necklace with that dress, it'll totally ruin the lines. These are what you need."

She held up a pair of long, dangly earrings that shimmered as they swayed. Each massive diamond stud anchored three long silver chains dripping with tiny diamond and emerald slivers.

"I know you've been trying to incorporate more green into your outfits, so..." She watched me, trying not to laugh.

"Shut up," I muttered, and grabbed the earrings from her hand.

Until a couple months ago the only green things I'd owned were a pair of Doc Martens boots and a couple concert tees, but lately I'd added a few more moss and grass hued pieces to my small wardrobe. So what if it also happened to be Alec's favorite color?

I held the earrings up to my ears, admiring the way they caught the light. Months ago, I never could have imagined holding stones this precious. Now, I was in Aeden, where diamonds were plentiful and DeBeers had never run any marketing campaigns. Down here, diamonds were just another pretty rock, not something to die over in a mine.

They certainly were pretty.

"Yeah, they're okay." I shrugged, not willing to give Amber the satisfaction of winning me over. I fingered the delicate silver chain around my neck, an heirloom handed down to me through my grandmother from Tyr. I hadn't taken it off since the day Jade had given it to me. Wouldn't the earrings clash with the necklace's tiny, dangling arrows and a pale blue stone?

"Perfect, I knew you'd like them," she said smugly, taking my lukewarm response as approval. "Which is why I also picked out these."

She held up an amazing pair of emerald green boots made of a shimmery material that looked like a cross between vinyl and crocodile. I knew it was neither. No one in Aeden wore animal products, and vinyl was simply too hot. I grabbed the shoes and inspected them. The material was softer than it looked, and seemed to be made out of the same breathable material as some of the flight safety jackets I had seen people wear when they road gravicycles. Amber, of course, never wore one, and neither did I. I mean, who needed a flight jacket when you were riding a golden jetski through the air? I doubted it would do any good in a crash, at least not if you were going 200mph the way Amber and I did.

The boots had two inch platforms that came up to a narrow ankle cuff of silver, and then flared up to mid-calf. A hidden zipper ran up the back of the boot.

"Not bad."

"Try them on," Claire urged.

I grunted and leaned over to put them on. They fit like a glove.

"Why do I even need shoes? Everyone goes barefoot here."

I actually loved the boots, but who was I to ever go along with something easily? It's not that I had a problem with authority, per se, but being told what to do always chafed a bit. And my question was valid. In the months I'd spent in Aeden, no one had ever worn shoes in any of the city buildings. In the sand dunes and the forests, sure, but not in the homes or offices. Most fae went barefoot on the sidewalks, too. Fae floors were almost always covered in cala grass, and everyone walked around barefoot. The blue grass had energizing properties that helped fuel fae immune systems. It was used in a lot of fae cuisine, but just walking on it had amazing benefits.

"Not at Choosings, they don't," Amber said matter-of-factly. We may be more relaxed here, but when it's time to dress up and party, we know how to accessorize. Besides, wherever there's dancing, there's no cala. The grass would be ruined."

"Huh." I walked to the mirror and looked at the boots, turning to see them from different angles. I bounced up and down on my toes, testing the cushiony treads. "They are super comfortable. I think I could even run in these."

"Or dance," Claire offered, like it was novel idea.

"And they're green," Amber winked.

"And they're hot," Claire cajoled.

I rolled my eyes at them both in the mirror. But who was I kidding? These boots were so coming home with me. I might even officially retire my Docs for these.

Five minutes later we walked out of the store with the boots and the earrings, plus some matching arm bangles for me and a new jacket for Amber made out of the same material as my shoes. The jacket was purple, replacing the one she'd permanently loaned our friend Rose the last time we had all been in Montreal together.

Hopefully, this jacket came with better karma.

The night in Montreal had not ended well, coming to a tragic end with the death of my friend Holly, an innocent darkling. Because of what had happened that night, her brother, my ex, now hated me and all Light fae with a vengeance. Rowan had turned Dark because of her death, and he blamed me for everything. He didn't care that it was the Dark who had caused our car to crash in the first place. That it was the Dark who had chased us, who had tried to kill and capture all of us. In his mind, none of it would have happened if he hadn't met me.

The worst part, for me? He wasn't wrong. That night, the Dark had been after me. They didn't care who got in the way of their mission, who they killed or hurt. Mikael Morrigan, their leader, was obsessed with ending the war with the Light once and for all. He wanted to take over the world, dominating humans and fae alike, because he thought he knew what was best for everyone. Like any good narcissist, he believed that no one else could be trusted to make the right decisions. Only he could. Only the Morrigan. So morals be damned. Freedom of choice be damned. The Morrigan wanted control, and he was convinced that I was the one who could give it to him.

Lucky me, right?

Yeah, right. My bloodlines had come together in just the right way to give me some special powers. Some abilities, no one even knew what they might be, since they hadn't manifested yet. That wouldn't happen until after my Choosing. But already I had a pretty good way with healing, and I could get glimpses of the future. I was an earth fae, too, so I could see lights in the dark, even auras, and I could do some cool tricks with plants and animals. But world domination? Nah. That really wasn't my thing, you know?

So yeah, I knew it wasn't really my fault, everything that had happened with Holly and Rowan. I hadn't asked to become Dark target numero uno. I had never wanted anyone to get hurt. I hadn't asked for any of this.

I told myself that every morning in the mirror.

My friends reminded me daily.

But it didn't matter. My inner martyr still insisted on harboring the guilt.

I shook the thought off, like I did hour after hour, day after day, and pushed it back into the tiny holding cell in my mind that I'd created special, just for it.

Today was not the day. Now was not the time to wallow in guilt, no matter how much a small part of me wanted to revel in the dark, sad feeling.

Today, was a good day.

And I had the new shoes to prove it.

CHAPTER 4

By the time we made it back to our hotel, I was ready for a run. We headed to our rooms to drop off our bags, agreeing to meet back in the lobby in fifteen minutes.

The second I arrived in my room, I knew it was going to take longer than that.

"What are you doing in here?" I asked, striding over to the couch by the window.

Lying back with his feet propped up on the arm, Alec lifted his arm off his face and opened one eye to peer at me lazily. One side of his mouth quirked up in a smile, activating the dimple in his left cheek and setting off a minor chain reaction in my belly of heat and fire.

"About time you showed up," he drawled. "Where have you been?"

"Shopping, again. But look!" I said, shaking the bags above him in excitement. "We finally found everything I needed."

He reached up lightning fast and pulled me down on top of him, sending the bags crashing to the floor around the couch.

Suddenly, we were nose to nose, green eyes twinkling up into gray. "I'm glad you found what you were looking for," he said quietly.

"Me, too," I smiled back at him, lowering my head to brush my lips against his. The slight touch flooded me with feelings of both yearning and completion, passion and comfort, and I sighed into his mouth as he pulled me closer. His chest rumbled and he deepened the kiss. As always when we touched, the surge slammed into me.

Not every fae would experience the surge in their lifetime, and some people thought it was just a myth, a fairy tale. When two fae were truly compatible, body and soul, that's when the surge would come into play. As an earth fae, I could see the auras, the colorful energy field that surrounded all living beings. Fae auras were naturally bigger and brighter than humans, since we had more light contained in our bodies, keeping us healthy and giving us abilities and longer-than-average lifespans. But when two people had the surge, their auras expanded and grew towards each other. I'd seen it firsthand that night in Montreal, when Alec and I were dancing together. It was an amazingly beautiful sight, our auras swirling around each other and creating an energetic connection that allowed us to feel everything the other person was feeling. I liked to think of it as telempathy. I couldn't hear Alec's thoughts, but we had a level of connection that brought us closer than I'd ever imagined wanting to be to another person.

I wouldn't have traded it for the world.

Right now, I could feel his satisfaction at just having me in his arms. I could feel how relieved and happy he was, being able to release the boredom and the worry.

Wait, what?

I pulled back and brushed his unruly black hair back from his forehead and stared at him, watching him to open his eyes.

"Why are you worried?" I asked.

Alec groaned.

"Aw, come on, no fair," he protested. "Can't I just enjoy you for a minute?"

"No," I laughed, swatting him as I sat up next to him and he scooted over to make room. "What's up?"

"Nothing, really."

I raised an eyebrow at him.

"Yeah, okay, fine. We're getting some weird reports from above below. The Dark have gone really quiet, which can't be a good sign, and every facility we've hit lately has been cleared out before we get there. We don't have any concrete news, just...I don't know. Everyone is getting jittery with your Choosing coming up and no progress having been made on a cure for the anti-serum yet."

"Yeah, tell me about it," I huffed, the reminder bringing me down. Alec saw my mood shift and reached out to rub my arm, instantly lightening my mood as feel-good comfort vibes flowed through me. "Oh! I almost forgot, Claire and Amber are waiting for me in the lobby, we're supposed to go running. You wanna join?"

"Of course," Alec nodded. "You know I live to chase you."

"I don't know if I'll ever be able to outrun you, even on my best day. It's embarrassing."

"True. But that doesn't mean I don't like watching you try."

He leered at me and I laughed. "Alright, give me a minute to put this stuff away."

I picked up the bags and stowed them in the closet, grabbing my sneakers and following Alec to the door. We headed back down the hall to the lobby and saw the girls waiting for us on the chairs by the door, Amber tapping her foot impatiently.

"Finally!" she said when she saw me. When she noticed Alec behind me she grinned. "Now I know what was taking you so long."

I pretended to glare at her and she chuckled, flouncing away out the double doors. Claire rushed to join us and we all followed Amber outside.

"Same trail today?" I asked.

"No, I was chatting up the concierge and he mentioned another park on the other side of the city. He said it's just ten minutes away by trolley."

What Amber called a trolley I considered more of a monorail. It certainly didn't remind me of the vintage trolleys I'd seen when visiting San Francisco. Made from the same golden alloy as the gravicycles and the buildings of Valhalla, Elysielle's trolley system seemed to also be powered by a strange mix of gravity and fusion energy. The exquisitely delicate rail arched over the city's main streets, aerodynamic cars whizzing underneath below the rail. The transportation system was as graceful and beautiful as it was fast.

We hopped onto one of the sleek machines and sped soundlessly over the city streets below. Even from above, the architecture of the city was stunning. The organically shaped constructions looked more like jeweled animals or beasts prowling below, sometimes nestling against one another in gentle companionship, other times surging towards each other in conflict. Nothing appeared out of place or incongruous, and it was clear that the artisans of Elysielle let no detail escape their notice. When they designed their homes and workspaces, they worked in concert with the environment around them. Even after several days in the city, I was constantly amazed by the beauty that surrounded me.

"Are all the cities in Aeden like this?" I whispered reverently as Alec's arms came around me from behind.

"Nothing is quite like Elysielle," he answered, understanding exactly what I'd meant as we watched the city speed by. "But most of them are more similar to here, than like Valhalla. The architects of Elysielle are highly sought after, and their work has helped shape all the cities in Aeden. Valhalla is different. The seven towers have stood since the beginning of time here on Earth. They have never changed."

"Right. Mireia and Mialloch both told me that story. You really believe that those towers are all part of the original ship that brought the Ancients here when they fled their own star system? That it just decided one day to orbit our Sun, opened up, and the tree of life created Aeden's sun and terraformed the entire planet?"

"It's as good an explanation as any, don't you think?"

"I guess," I said doubtfully. "It's just so...so far away from what most human religions talk about."

"Well, maybe the 'word' of god was the word of the captain giving the ship the go ahead. Maybe seven days was really seven years, or seven hundred. But you know, there are so many legends above below that talk about how the earth was populated by star people, or people who climbed down from the skies. And even more legends about how the world was terraformed on the back of a turtle from the waters of the ocean. Did you know that under the world tree, under all of Valhalla, there is an entire hidden complex? Only the council is allowed down there, but we are taught in school that it is shaped like a bowl, that it is the base of the star ship that brought us here."

"So?" I asked, not getting Alec's point.

"The illustrations I've seen look a lot like a turtle shell flipped over on its back, even to the point of being armored in hexagonal gold plating shaped like scales." He paused a beat, letting that sink in. "Anyway, that's what the ship was supposedly like, a giant, thick cone, rounded on the bottom, pointy on the top. Each of the seven towers formed a piece of the cone's shell, and housed the people journeying on the ship. All the points, wrapping together in a twisted spiral to point the way to our new home. To bring us here."

He paused again, and then whispered quietly so that no one else would hear, "To bring you and me, here, to each other."

I blushed, and wrapped my arms tightly around his, drawing him more tightly to my back. The trolley chimed in warning, letting us know that the final stop was approaching. Out the window, I could see this part of the city was sparsely populated, giving way to a vast forest at its gates.

"We're here," Amber announced as the car came to a stop and sank to the ground alongside a final golden trolley beam.

Alec and I separated, following the others outside. When I stepped onto the ground, the stairs retracted and doors slid closed behind me. The car rose soundlessly and sped off back towards the city, leaving us in a lush purple wood surrounded by towering trees. The air was cooler here, the ground shielded by the direct rays of the warm red sun above that never stopped shining.

"Great, now what? How are we going to get back to the city?" Claire groused. "I am so not running all that way."

"Don't sweat it," Amber laughed, nudging her with her shoulder. "The trolley runs on an automated schedule. It comes back every fifteen to twenty minutes, according to the guy at the hotel."

"Thank the gods," said Claire, looking up at the sky in mock prayer.

"Right well, let's go, no rest for the wicked." Amber trotted off into the woods following a tiny trail into the shadows.

"As if," Claire whined. "What about rest for the weary? Can I get some of that?"

She looked at me beseechingly and I just shook my head. "Come on, lazy bones. Let's go."

I grabbed her hand and dragged her with me after Amber, Alec following behind as usual. I tried not to think about him looking at my butt while I ran. Then I tried not to think about how much I'd rather be looking at his butt while he ran.

Finally, my brain quieted down. Claire and I settled into an easy, quiet rhythm. After a while Alec passed us and she looked at me with chagrin.

"You going to ditch me, too?"

"Not a chance. I'd never catch him, anyway."

The terrain began to climb. For a while, we were silent. Our feet made hollow thuds against the deep forest loam and the red sunlight refracted in lilac rays through the leafy canopy above, turning our skin to pale shades of violet and mauve.

For all her talk about hating to run and exercise, Claire had been working really hard for the past few weeks. I think everything that had happened in Ireland and Vermont had really shaken her. More than once, she had made it clear that she didn't ever want to be caught unprepared again. Today while we ran she practiced sending off small bolts of lightning towards the larger boulders. Or at least, she tried. Most of the time the sparks fizzled out just inches from her fingertips, and one time she just missed catching my hair on fire.

Finally, she collapsed onto a fallen tree trunk to catch her breath.

"Argh! I don't get it. Why is this still so hard for me? The more I move around or the more dangerous the situation, the less I can control it."

"You just need more practice Claire," I tried to reassure her. "You'll get there, you'll see."

Of course, I didn't really know if that was true. But it sounded right, didn't it?

"That's not enough, Siri. I need to get it to work all the time. I need my power to be there for me when I need it. If I'd had it back in Falls Depot, Miko never would have died. I could have blasted Rowan before he ever tried to splash you with his goopy emo hate-bubble, and Miko would still be alive today."

"You don't know that. I thought I had it handled. If anyone misread the situation and messed things up, it was me, not you. I don't think any of us were ready to believe that he'd really gone Dark. Only Miko understood what was happening."

31

"I guess. Still, I wish I was doing better at this than I am."

"Hey, we're all under a lot of pressure right now. Use this time to relax. Stop thinking so much," I shook her lightly, teasing her with a giggle.

She smiled at me and rolled her eyes. "Fine, let's go see if we can hunt down Amber."

Claire started to rise, then startled as something fell to the ground with a large thump behind me.

"Looking for us?" Amber grinned saucily, cocking her head to one side as she placed a hand on her hip and Alec dropped silently from a tree behind her. "Come on Claire, let's see if you can catch me."

Claire groaned as Amber sped away, but she gave good chase and pounded off into the woods.

"How about me?" Alec started backing away into the wood. "Ready to try and catch me, too?"

"Oh, you are so on," I warned him.

He took off and I clicked into parkour mode, seeking out the fastest way through the trees to reach him even as he drew away. It wasn't going to be easy, but I was sure I could catch him this time.

CHAPTER 5

Okay, so fine, I never did catch him. I spent several minutes dashing through the trees, trying to close the gap between us, but it was like trying to hold water in your hands.

Totally futile, and in the end, you always lost what you were trying to hold on to.

After another hour of running, we'd all decided to call it quits and headed back to the city. I only had a couple days left before my Choosing, and I knew my grandmother wanted everything to be perfect. That meant approving menus, tasting appetizers and desserts, picking out flowers and music. And, most importantly, it meant I had to referee Jade and my mother.

Despite how similar they were, they always seemed to disagree on everything. They'd been butting heads for as long as I could remember, and, apparently, far longer than that. I swear, whenever they did agree on something, one of them would change their mind just out of spite.

You'd think maybe that would have worked in my favor, maybe they would have both thrown in the towel and said, hey, let's let Siri decide.

But no.

Apparently Choosings in the fae world were a bit like high school graduations or quinceañeros. It was a chance for proud parents (or grandparents) to show off their progeny and gloat over how awesomely their genes had come together. Even Bran had gotten in on the action, and rumor had it that his parents would be joining the party, too.

It was almost enough to make me want to take back all the times I'd yearned for a dad, for a complete family unit.

Almost.

I knew other kids who'd had absent parents. I'd commiserated with them in school – somehow we'd always managed to find each other in a crowd, like we had abandonment radar or something, an innate sense of when someone else was hiding a big hole in their heart. But Bran didn't really fit the bill. I mean, he hadn't even known I existed. It wasn't his fault he hadn't been there for me. He had tried to find my mom after their short affair, but he hadn't known where to even start looking.

Some of the kids I knew weren't so lucky. Their dads had just given up on them, moving away and not bothering to ever pay child support or remember birthdays. And there were the forgotten children, the ones whose parents were present, but they were too busy working or getting their hair done to fit their offspring into a social calendar.

And, of course, there were the kids I met like Rowan, whose parents were truly terrible people, or just plain evil. Parents who hit their kids or spent all night drinking and trashing the house. Parents who never got out of bed to make their kid a ham sandwich for lunch or take them to a baseball game.

Bran was so much better than anything I could ever have dreamed up.

Now that we'd found each other, I had exactly the kind of dad I'd always hoped for. Someone who cared for me, but wasn't overbearing. Someone who wanted to know the details of my life, but allowed me to have my freedom, too. Funny, caring, easy to talk to – he was all those things.

I knew he would have liked to have been there for me as a child, but he was content with what we had now. Not to mention, of course, the fact that I came as a package deal with my mom. My birth had been a happy side effect two teams working together on an undercover black ops mission. Well, that and the surge. My mom and dad hadn't been able to tell each other their real names while they were fighting the enemy together, but they had recognized the bond between their fae spirits instantly. After the mission was over and their teams went separate ways, it had taken them eighteen years to find each other again.

A lifetime for me, but only about 583,000,000 seconds for them.

Which was why, when my parents spoon-fed each other cake for the ten thousandth time, I was able to remember how much I missed Alec whenever he was away, and kept myself from visibly cringing or throwing my own spoon at them.

It was not, however, enough of a deterrent for my grandmother.

"That's it," she exclaimed, throwing her napkin on the table. "Freddie, you switch places with me this instant. That's right, get up, you come and sit here between me and Siri."

My mother smirked but did as she was told, valiantly holding in laughter as Bran coughed into his own napkin to hide his own amusement.

"Don't think I can't see you laughing over there, young man. Think about what kind of example you are setting for your daughter."

"Aw, I think they're cute," I drawled.

My mother beamed at me and I stuffed some more cake in my mouth to keep from laughing.

"Nonsense. I can see that we shall have to go over the seating arrangements for the reception again. There is no way I will have you two fawning all over each other in front of everyone."

"Mother, really," my mother finally protested.

"No, not one word out of you. You think it's so cute, watching you two? Think how you would feel if Alec started hanging all over Siri in front of you."

My grandmother's pointed accusingly at me, as if to make her point, while I struggled not to choke on my cake.

"Grandma!" I gasped as I reach for my water. Honestly, why did she have to bring me into this?

"Don't you 'Grandma' me, young lady." Jade wagged her fork at me while my mother looked at me like I was some confounding insect that might suddenly hatch from its casing. She still hadn't quite wrapped her head around Alec and I being together, and we'd been doing our best not to do anything to remind her. Now as she frowned at me, it seemed all our good work would be for nothing.

"Don't argue with your Grandmother, Siri. She's right, I'm having a hard time believing my baby has already found the man she wants to spend the rest of her life with."

I groaned.

"Do we have to talk about this now?" I pleaded.

"Well, as long as we've already started, I-"

My mother was cut off from finishing her sentence as our server descended upon the table brandishing several more flavors of cake on dainty floral platters. The man twirled his long, dark braided queue of hair in one hand while he listed the ingredients of each newly delivered option.

I don't think I had ever been so happy to see buttercream in all my life. One option looked especially amazing, a chocolate molten lava cake oozing deliciously onto the plate, magically capped with rich vanilla frosting and sugared berries.

By the time he was finished, my mother had either forgotten about our conversation, or decided to let it go for the moment. I wagered it was the latter, but I was grateful for even a temporary reprieve.

I reached for the chocolate berry confection before me, ignoring the other platters, and dug in. Yes, it was amazing. No, I wasn't going to try any more of the other cakes.

Like Alec, this one had me from the moment it walked into my life.

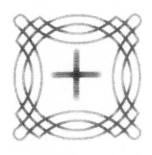

CHAPTER 6

The morning of my Choosing arrived loudly, with much fanfare.

Well, maybe not fanfare exactly, but I was bombarded first thing in the morning by Claire, Amber and Auroreis. All three of them leapt into my bed and started bouncing, jolting me awake from a very nice dream while my mother threw open the heavy-duty light-blocking shutters to let in the ruddy glow of Aeden's ever-present red sun. When Auroreis began to tickle me, I decided I'd had enough and kipped up onto my feet. Of course, Amber was quicker than I was and swiped my legs out from under me, forcing me back into the bed, which resulted in an all-out glima wrestling war.

A loud whistle pierced the air and we each froze. I had Claire pinned with her arm twisted up behind her shoulder blades, while Auroreis and Amber both hung from my back.

I looked around, trying determine the new threat, and saw my mom grinning wryly at us.

"How about we don't damage the goods just yet, okay girls? At the rate you're all going, one of you is going to have a black eye before breakfast is even served."

Auroreis scrambled off the bed while Amber flopped down against the pillows, looking as if she'd been lying there innocently the whole time. Trusting that they were not planning to regroup, I released Claire's arm and slid down onto the pillows next to Amber.

"And then?" I asked.

"And now we eat." My mother turned back to the door and ushered in two young men wheeling service carts.

"Mom!" I yelled, pulling a sheet over myself. I was so not decent enough to be in the room with a couple of random boys. The silk camisole I wore was great for sleeping, but not so much for modesty.

She shrugged her shoulders at me in a half-hearted apology with a quirk of her lips and walked the boys out of the room after having them put the carts by the table in front of the window.

"Here, I think you'll appreciate this." She pushed back the silver tops of the carts to reveal several platters of fruit, crêpes with cream and honey, and several pitchers of smoothies.

She moved back as we crowded around the table, oohing and aahing over the breakfast buffet.

I grabbed a warm chocolatey nut drink and a plate of crêpes before I settled down on one of the cushy dining chairs. I brought my cup to my lips and inhaled the rich aroma. A quick sip burned my tongue, searing

my nose with the smell of acrid smoke. Two cars nearby were on fire, crumpled together from a collision,

39

their brilliant gas-driven flames illuminating the deserted street in the night. The windows of the shops lining the sidewalk were dark. At first, I thought they were closed, but their open signs hadn't been flipped for the evening.

Abandoned, then. Not closed.

Where were the firemen, the police? Where were the victims of the crash?

I knew right away that something bad had happened here. Something dark.

I ran down the street, glancing in shop windows, looking for any sign of life. Taylor's Mercantile. Sookie's Somethings, Crafts and Trinkets for All Ages. The Cuppa Café. All empty.

A lone blinking light flashed red at the intersection and I paused, getting my bearings. The street signs read Taylor and Main. A glimmer of movement caught my eye and I turned down Main Street, hurrying to follow a small elderly woman in a simple housedress.

"Wait!" I cried. The woman continued on her way, not varying her pace. I caught up to her quickly, blocking her path. "Are you okay? What happened here?"

She looked at me quizzically, a blank smile on her face.

"Happened, dear? Why, nothing. I'm just out for my evening stroll."

"But where is everyone?"

"I wouldn't know, dear. I'm just out for my evening stroll. That's none of my business." She patted my arm and walked around me, continuing on.

I didn't understand.

And then I did. Hysterical laughter started up behind me, the rasping tone setting off alarm bells in my brain. I whirled around to see Mikael Morrigan lounging against a streetlamp, tears running down his face as he laughed with abandon.

I stalked towards him and he straightened, wiping his face with the back of one hand. "Thank you Siri, I really needed that. I haven't laughed that hard in years."

"What do you want?" I ground out.

"Why, nothing, nothing at all. You're the one that drew me into this vision, with your fear." He gave a slight sniff. "Delectable."

I shuddered with revulsion while he leered at me appreciatively.

"I should thank you, really, for bringing me here. I have big plans, you know, and now you've shown me how well everything is going to work out."

"You call this working out? What did you do to this town? To that woman?"

"I haven't done a thing." He raised his empty hands as if to show his innocence. "Yet. Don't worry about that old human. She certainly isn't worried. That's what I've been trying to show you. That's why you need to join me. Once I have my way, no one will ever worry again. Not even you."

I punched out at him and dropped him to the ground.

"Give me one reason why I shouldn't end you right now."

The Morrigan looked at me happily and burst into another round of laughter.

"You can't! This is a vision, remember? Poor little Siri, so angry, and so naïve. Let me help you. I can show you how to really channel that rage."

I stared down at him. Was this guy for real?

"I will never join you. Never." I punched him in the face and leapt off of him, shaking my head in disgust. Even if the punch didn't really hurt him, it had been satisfying. In real life, he would have been knocked out. In the vision, he just continued laughing, the sound grating on my nerves, invading all my senses. I set off running down the street.

"That's it, Siri, run! I'll catch up to you soon, have no worries."

His teasing words angered me even more, making me think of that poor woman, and I kicked a stray stone down the street in frustration, sending it flying into a shop window. The sound of glass breaking stirred something in me and

brought me back to the present. My fisted hand was dripping, cold liquid mixed with crimson blood running down my legs. Shattered glass covered my lap.

"Siri!" My mother rushed to me, gently taking my hand while I just stared at it numbly. "What happened?"

Auroreis handed her a napkin and they both began picking the glass off of me, wiping my skin. So much for my chocolatey breakfast, was all I could think.

Mom dabbed at my hand, inspecting several gashes the shards had made in my palm.

"Well, there's no glass in the wounds. Siri, you want to tell us what happened?"

"I'll go get some bandages," Auroreis said quietly, slipping out of the room.

I blinked and watched her go. My mother was looking at me with that special mixture of concern and frustration that only a mother can give you, like they want to wrap you up in a hug and shake you all at the same time. But what was I supposed to say? I looked away, and saw Amber and Claire watching me with resignation, like they already knew what I was going to say. But how could they? How could they know that I had seen the beginning of the end? Whatever they were imagining, I knew it was much, much worse.

"What did you see?" Amber asked me in a low voice.

"See?" my mom asked. "You think she had a vision? Siri, is that what happened? Come on, baby, talk to me. Just tell me what's going on." She stroked my hand and smiled at me as if she was afraid I'd break at any minute.

Poor mom, she'd been out of commission most of the time that I'd been having visions, and she'd certainly never seen me after a really vicious one. Claire and Amber knew better. Amber leaned back in her chair, arms folded, simply awaiting the bad news like a soldier who knew she was about to be sent off to war, while Claire smiled at me, hopeful as always.

I took a deep breath, and when I exhaled the vision poured out of me in a tangle of words. The town, the fire, the woman. The Morrigan, the running, the threats. I left out the punching and my own anger, because I wasn't quite ready to own up to that. Somehow, the violence the Morrigan had incited within me made me feel dirty. It didn't matter that I could rationalize it. It didn't matter that it felt justified. On some level, I knew it wasn't right, that fighting him was just a symptom of me sinking to his level. Not a punishment. Not a defense. But a sign of weakness within. A symptom of my own darkness.

43

"We should call Bran right away," my mother said decisively when I had finished. "If this is really happening, he needs to know."

"I know," I agreed. "But..." I trailed off as Auroreis walked back into the room with a jar of lavender-tinted ointment and a roll of bandages.

"But what, sweetheart?" my mom said absently as she took the medicine from Auroreis and began smoothing the cooling balm across my palm.

"Can't we just wait? Not forever, but until tonight at least? If we tell him now, he'll probably spend the rest of the day talking with the Guards, going over intel and arranging new missions...I just...It'd be nice to have him here for my Choosing."

"Oh, honey, I'm sure he wouldn't miss it no matter what's going on."

"Maybe, but he wouldn't really be there, you know? He'd be in his head, going over details." My mom finished wrapping my hand and exchanged a look with Amber. They both knew I was right, but my mom didn't look like she thought waiting was a good idea.

Claire spoke up in a quiet voice. "Siri's visions are always of the future, right? How much difference could waiting a few hours really make, anyway?"

"Please, Mom?" I implored.

My mom sighed heavily. "Alright. We can wait. But you know Bran is going to sense something is up the minute I see him."

She was right. Since they shared the surge, the second he held her hand he would feel her concern as if it was his own.

"Yes. And you can just smile, and tell him you promise you'll tell him everything. Later. I mean, he's going to see this," I held up my wrapped hand, "I can't exactly hide it. Tell him I cut myself when I tried to pick up a glass I dropped, and it just shook you up."

"Fine, fine." She threw up her hands. "I'll do it. But only because I love you and you deserve to have the perfect day. As soon as the reception is over you are sitting with Bran and telling him everything you saw. In detail."

I rolled my eyes. "Trust me, I'm familiar with Dad's interrogation techniques. Knowing him, I'll probably have to go over the whole vision five times, until he feels like he was there himself."

"Good, just so it's settled." She picked up her juice and glared at me suspiciously over the rim. "You know, lying seems to come to you a lot more easily than it used to. Don't make a habit out of it."

Mom was back. I grinned at her, shrugged like the teen I was, and said the one word guaranteed to frustrate her more than anything.

"Whatever."

CHAPTER 7

I stood outside the theatre, waiting. My hair spiraled in whimsical twists around my head like twisted wheat, delicate tendrils artfully escaping the emerald pins that held my updo in place. Amber had been right about a necklace ruining the lines of my dress, so I had wound my grandmother's chain around my ankle under the green boots. I felt sophisticated, mature and sexy all at the same time, like I'd just stepped off some fashion runway in Paris or Milan. It was a new, heady feeling. I wondered how I would feel in another thirty minutes, after my Choosing was complete.

My mother and father stood on either side of me, waiting for the music on the other side to stop. Once it did, my father turned to me.

"Are you ready?" he asked. He looked me over with concern, eyes narrowing as they roamed past my hand and returned to my face. He knew something was up, but my mother had been as good as her word and put on a smile for him, waving aside his concerns.

"Completely," I smiled up at him. It was totally true, too. Since the moment my powers had begun to emerge, the Morrigan had been urging me to choose a side. He thought if he scared me enough, threatened me enough, I'd cave and join the Shades. But everything that had happened since my first vision had made my decision clear. There was no other option for me except to Choose the Light. My parents were Light. My boyfriend was Light. But that wasn't it. The more my powers had allowed me to see and hear and connect with the earth, with nature, with the animals, I'd realized the truth of the matter.

People lied all the time, even to themselves. It was possible that the Light wasn't really any better than the Dark. But the plants and the animals saw deeper truths. They heard everyone's innermost thoughts. They knew what we all were thinking and feeling. They knew who treated them well, and who didn't. And their verdict was clear – the Shades had severed their connection to the earth and their inner light so thoroughly that the distortion in their souls was virtually complete. Only a miracle of the Light could bring them back, and I'd come to accept that miracle might be me.

The heavily jeweled double doors swung inwards, and a sea of faces awaited me. Hundreds of people I had never met before waited patiently within. Many of them were smiling, while others whispered behind their hands to each other while they examined me. Me, the child of prophecy who would either doom the Light or bring the Dark back into the fold. Me, an above-worlder who'd brought back a cure for the anti-serum, but not enough for everyone who would need it if the Morrigan had his way. Me, the daughter of the Commander of the Light Guard and the girl who'd dated a darkling.

I'm sure they wondered how much of it was true. I'm sure they wondered if I really was all those things. Hell, I wondered it myself, all the time.

47

My mother squeezed my hand before linking her arm through mine, and I squared my shoulders, threading my fingers through my father's hand. It was time. I plastered a bright smile on my face and walked down the aisle with my parents.

Funny, but I hadn't ever imagined anything like this. Even my own wedding, I'd rather thought would be an informal impromptu affair at city hall, or on a deserted beach. I'd never imagined myself walking down an aisle of any kind. Especially not with a father I'd never expected to meet. Hoped, yes. But believed? Not really.

But here I was. The huge domed theatre was round, its ceiling painted with extrasolar nebulae and stars. The design reminded me of Shakespeare's fabled Globe playhouse, which I suppose might have actually been designed to resemble the one in which I now stood. The idea startled me and I stumbled.

My father caught me smoothly, so quickly that I hoped no one had noticed my misstep.

Who was I kidding? There must have been over a thousand eyes on me right now. Oh well. It wasn't the first time I had made a fool of myself in front of a bunch of people. I was sure it wouldn't be the last.

I grinned up at my dad and looped my arm around his waist, still holding my mother tightly. We were almost to the stage. Someone had placed a set of stairs at the end of the aisle so that I could ascend more easily. In the rows to my right and left I saw all my friends – Amber and Claire, Alec and Ewan, Mitch, Mialloch, Airmed, my grandmother. And others. Dorian, Mireia, Benit.

At the foot of the stair, my parents released me and moved to sit in a pair of empty seats between Jade and another couple.

I took a deep breath and mounted the steps. One. Two. Three. Four. Five, six, seven and there.

Two young women stood before a table in front of me, each of them simply dressed and completely identical to the other in face. Twins. Funny, but they were the first twins I could remember seeing in Aeden. One wore white, the other a muddied gray. Their blonde, straight hair was pulled back into simple, low ponytails. They seemed too pure somehow to wear makeup, but they each wore large circles of greasepaint around their eyes to match their dresses. White to white, gray to gray.

I strode to the table, remembering halfway there to put a little sashay in my walk. As Amber had said "think catwalk, not gangplank." According to her, my walk needed to be a little "less krav maga, and more Marilyn Monroe." It wasn't difficult in these heels.

There were five items on the table. A bowl of silvery Aeden water, a tray of clipped cala grass, a small porous looking stone, a lit candle and a silver mortar and pestle. I had no idea what I was supposed to do now. None of my friends had been willing to share – Choosings were shrouded in mystery and steeped in tradition. No faeling ever attended a Choosing before their own time.

I placed my hands on the table and looked at the girls. "Hey." I grinned lopsidedly at them.

"Siri Alvarsson Le Fay," they began in unison, speaking as one without hesitation, "you come to us on the day of your Choosing, a faeling untested and new."

"Hardly," I muttered under my breath. The twins continued on as if they had not heard me. Maybe they hadn't.

"Today, we awaken your powers, your birthright, and you embrace your future by Choosing your present. Who you are, who you will be, who you have always been, will

49

rise tonight. Your powers have always been within you. Now, tonight, you will align the elements both outside of you, and within."

"We begin with light, just as life here began with the activation of Anansanna, our red sun."

The white twin held up the flame above her head while the dark twin crushed the cala in the mortar.

"The living energy which sustains us, heals us, just as the light sustains and heals the world. Fire to life, we come together to birth reality."

The gray twin held out her bowl, and the other set the blades of grass on fire with her flame. When the cala was fully charred, she returned the flame to the table and took the bowl from her sister. Devoid of emotion, she began to mash the soft stone into the grass.

"The earth we stand on is made of the same star-matter as our own bodies. We brought it here with us from another world, and here we birthed it anew."

She turned to her dark twin and held out the bowl, while the other poured the silver water into it. Instantly, the ingredients began to swirl together, as if stirred by an invisible spoon.

"The water of life brings us together, reminds us of the past and brings our intuition forward to guide us into the future."

The twins turned to me, each holding the bowl by its rim, and ordered me to drink.

I thought it would be gritty and bland, but a myriad of tastes bloomed on my tongue. Heat and soft sweetness. Vanilla and brimstone. Coriander and pine.

The last surprised me, bringing Alec to mind and   I turned to seek him out in the audience. The violet ring in his eyes flared, and his aura lit up around him in a wash of rose and cerulean blue. I gasped, and he moved his head slightly, urging me to turn back to the twins.

I tried to concentrate, but all I could do was think about how insane it was that I had been able to see his eyes, his colors, from so far away. That I had been able to smell, no, taste, him from that distance. But I had no time to think, because the twins had resumed their synchronized speech.

"And now, you must Choose. Will you serve the Light or chase the Shadows within you? Will you choose to shine your inner light and blaze brightly, or wallow in the sliver of Darkness we all hold within? Do you Choose the Light? Or the Dark?"

Was there really a choice? I couldn't fathom making but one decision.

"The Light. I Choose the Light."

The moment I spoke, it was if a thousand fireworks went off inside me. I felt the elixir I had drunk light up in answer to my words, setting off a cellular reaction within me. The power of it stunned me and dropped me to my knees. Behind me, I heard a collective gasp. I didn't care. Inside me, I could actually hear neurons firing, nerves igniting and entire galaxies going supernova. I looked up at the twins, searching for answers, for rescue from this exquisite torture and was met with wide eyes in blank faces.

Clearly, this was something new, even for them.

An agonizing heat flared in my left ankle and I cried out, immobilized with pain. Footsteps pounded on the stairs behind me and arms gathered me up. Even before I opened my eyes, I could smell him.

"Alec?" In his arms, the pain ebbed somewhat and I was too relieved to be embarrassed that he was cradling me like a child in front of hundreds of people.

"Shh, it's okay. I've got you," he whispered into my ear and then turned to address the stunned crowd in a formal tone.

"The Heart of Life has risen. We thank you all for bearing witness, and hope you will join us this afternoon for feasting and dancing in the Hall of Shimmers."

He stalked off the side of the stage, carrying me through dark halls into a small dressing room. He settled me into a chair and held my face in his hands, peering into my eyes.

"My gods, Siri. You scared the crap out of me. Are you okay?"

I gulped and nodded, even though I felt anything but okay.

"My boot," I said, pointing at my left foot.

Without pausing to ask, he removed the shoe and we stared.

My heirloom necklace was now a plain silver chain laying cool against my skin. Underneath the metal danced shimmering blue marks of arrows, glittering tattoos upon my flesh around a vibrant red seven-pointed sunburst that glowed like a fresh brand.

"What the-" I started as the door crashed open and my friends and family flooded the room.

"Siri!" My mother rushed forward and hugged me. "I was so worried. Thank goodness you are alright."

Everyone else just stared at me as if I had grown two heads.

"What?" I asked. "Lemme guess, people don't usually collapse at their Choosing?"

Amber snorted. "I thought I was the only one here with a flair for drama, but you...well, I think people are going to be talking about this for a long time."

"It was just so intense. I didn't expect..." I trailed off midsentence, unable to finish my thought and stood up, pacing awkwardly with one shoe off. Even now, I was finding it hard to focus, hard to think in a straight line. The pain in my ankle had receded, but I felt like a million volts of energy were coursing through me. I could understand now what Emilie and Rowan had meant when they'd said the newly awakened powers felt like they might bubble up out their skin. I'd never felt so alive, or so twitchy.

My grandmother looked at me keenly and narrowed her eyes. "What's happened to your boot?"

"Oh that, well, um...I don't quite know." I looked at her sheepishly. "I seem to have ruined your necklace."

"Stop fidgeting and stand still. What do you mean, my necklace? That's just a plain chain." She gasped and knelt at my feet, tracing the marks on my skin. "Tyr's necklace did this? It marked you?"

"Merged, more like," Alec said, sounding none too happy about the fact.

My father knelt beside her and examined the markings. "I've never seen anything like it. I don't like it," he growled. "What does it mean?"

"It means," Alec said quietly, "that she really is the Heart of Life, like I said before. You all saw it, I know you did."

"Heart of Life. What does that mean?" I'd never heard the term before, and I wasn't sure how I felt about it being applied to me.

"It's from the Song of Light, the legend that talks about how this world was created, and how one day it will need to be healed." Amber explained, as if I should know what she was talking about.

"Okay," I drawled, "but what does that have to do with me? I've heard about how you think I'm part of a prophecy that might save or end the light, and I've heard the story about how the fae created this planet and all life on it. Why haven't I heard about this 'Heart of Life?' before?"

"I guess you never heard the song the way it is sung to our young ones," my father murmured. "Every faeling learns it at school."

I looked at my mom and Jade, and they shrugged. You'd think descendants of Tyr would have kept up with the oral history of the family, since we figured in the prophecy and all, but I guess some things had been lost to the fae who chose to reside in Midgard, outside and above the world of Aeden. Claire looked clueless, too, which wasn't a surprise since this was her first visit to Aeden.

Amber sighed and cleared her throat. Looking pained, she closed her eyes and began to sing a slow, eerily beautiful tune.

In a world before time

Our star was dying

Our world turned cold

While oceans boiled

The Heart of Life

Our Queen so wise

She built a hive

So we could rise.

Through stars we flew

Escaping all we knew

Till Heart opened ship

Triggering creation

Ending the trip

With earth, our station.

A ship in place

Like an island in space

The seven towers

Bloomed to flower

The Heart of Life

Sang to wife

The red sun exploded

Our world encoded

Red queen giving birth

To home, our earth

In peace we'll live

In love we'll give

And when dark returns

The fate who earned

Blood Tyr and Faye

Will light the way

The Heart of Life will rise

Soft, strong and wise

To save or shade Aeden

And begin again.

Amber finished and did a little curtsy while my brain struggled to process what I'd just heard.

"Okay, so I'm the fate who combines Tyr and Fae blood, right? And now because I Chose the light, everyone thinks I am this Heart of Life?"

I looked at Amber for confirmation and she just nodded, looking rather apologetic.

"Who even wrote this stupid song, anyway?"

"Your ancestor, Skuld Norna first sang it, actually," Bran said.

"Oh. Well, it's all a bit circumstantial, isn't it?" I lifted one shoulder and attempted to lighten the mood with a laugh.

"Not anymore," Alec said, placing his hand on my back. I could feel that he was trying to reassure me, but behind that emotion I picked up something else. Fear? No, that wasn't it. Awe?

"Something surprised you," I stated and knew instantly I was right. "What?"

Amber shuffled her feet and my parents looked at each other.

"Anyone? Alec?"

He glanced at Ewan and a look passed between them.

"You should be the one to tell her, mate," Ewan urged.

Alec ran a hand through his hair, sending his carefully styled coif flying in every direction. I swear, it was like I could see each individual strand, practically count them. I loved the way it always looked like he'd just woken up or gotten out of a fight. Tussled, tousled, it was all the same to me. Practically blue it was so black, thick and soft. Right now with my vision heightened I could see the light refracting off every strand, glimmering in a rainbow of hues. It was wrong what they said. Black was supposed to exist as a color because it contained no light, no colors, but I could see every color in the darkness of his locks. I wanted to run my fingers through it right now. I wanted...But wait. Weren't we supposed to be talking about something?

I raised my eyebrows at him, frowning as I tried to focus on the present moment.

"Right, well, I can't speak for everyone here," he was saying, rubbing the back of his neck and then fidgeting with his hair again. "I'm not sure what other people saw, you know my vision is better than most people's...When you Chose, you lit up like nothing I've ever seen before. It was like you went supernova. I swear, I thought I saw galaxies shoot out of your body. Your aura flooded the whole room."

"Wow, really?" Claire stepped forward eagerly. "I saw this warm red light surround her. For a second she looked like the red sun."

"Anansanna," my grandmother whispered. "She glowed with the power of the red queen."

"The Heart of Life," Alec said matter-of-factly.

"Oh great. Now I'm a character in Wonderland. Perfect," I muttered under my breath. I looked around the room. "Did everyone see it?"

Everyone nodded.

"Awesome. Does anyone know what these marks are about?" I pointed at my ankle and no one seemed to know what to say. "Okay, this just gets better and better. Now what?"

My mother took a deep breath, always a precursor to some big, deep thought that I wasn't ready to hear, but Amber beat her to it.

"Now? What else? We show off those awesome boots of yours, we dance and eat cake."

CHAPTER 8

Although I'd been involved in much of the planning for the reception, I'd never actually been to the Hall of Shimmers. My grandmother had thought it would be more fun for me if it was a surprise, and between the planning and my training obligations, I'd been happy to have one less thing to do. So the first time I entered the hall, could I help it if my mouth gaped open?

Jade elbowed me in the ribs with her elbow, speaking to me out the side of her mouth.

"Stand up straight and stop gawking. You look like a tourist."

"I am a tourist," I protested mildly and returned to gawking.

It wasn't just a room, and "hall" didn't do the place justice. The entire place was a work of art. Shimmers didn't begin to describe what the walls were doing. At first I thought the Hall was circular, like the theatre, but that wasn't quite right. The walls had angles, and looking around I thought I counted seven. The massive panels were encrusted with brilliant gemstones to form what was probably the most expensive mosaic on the planet. Some of the stones seemed to fluoresce under the lights, which hung as dripping crystalline chandeliers. The prisms hanging off the lights cast rainbows throughout the room despite the low mood lighting, so that stones glittered and shone like so many stars in the sky.

The mural itself was exquisitely done, and seemed to depict much of the story from the Song of Light. A world in darkness where a sun was dying, an exodus in a golden ship that resembled a stately pinecone, the opening of the ship near our yellow sun, the birth of the tree of life and Anansanna, the creation of Earth and the enlivening of humanity. The last panel segued seamlessly into the first, suggesting the circle of life and death, endings and beginnings.

"So beautiful," I murmured.

"Yes. Yes, you are." Alec caught me up from behind and kissed my neck. I realized with a start that everyone else was already moving through the room towards the dinner tables, and wondered how long I'd been staring. Embarrased, I flushed. Too late, I noticed that people were beginning to stare, not at the walls, but at me.

"Should we sit?" I asked.

"If we can get there," Alec laughed. "I think that might be easier said than done."

I looked around and noticed several groups of people heading towards us.

We started walking, and only made it about ten feet into the room before the first group caught us.

"Congratulations." "I've never seen anything like that-" "Thank you for bringing back a cure for my uncle."

Everyone wanted to shake my hand, wish me well, congratulate me. After a lifetime of wandering with my mother, being on the receiving end of so much positive attention was a foreign experience. I understood that most of the people meant well, but I quickly started to feel overwhelmed. Alec, on the other hand, seemed to have been made for this. Graciously acknowledging the well-wishers while he brushed them aside, he helped me pass through the crowds until we reached our table.

My mother looked at me apologetically. "I'm so sorry, Siri, I should have stayed with you. I wasn't thinking of how everyone else would be reacting."

"Nonsense," Jade huffed. "The girl is going to have to get used to it sometime. Better to get it done with all at once."

Amber nodded in agreement. "Yeah, by the end of tonight we'll have them all seeing that Siri is just a normal girl, trying to lead a normal life."

Claire snorted. "Good luck with that one." I had to agree. I imagined that seeing me light up like Rudolph's nose and fulfill some ancient lullaby wasn't going to fade from anyone's mind anytime soon.

Bran stood up, pulling out my chair and pointing to a slightly older-looking couple on my left.

"Siri, I'd like you to meet my parents, your grandparents. Yvain Le Fay and Kalila Norna, may I introduce your granddaughter, Siri Alvarsson."

Yvain stood and bowed deeply, kissing my hand while I stammered, "It's so nice to meet you, sir."

"Oh, Yve, stop acting like an Ancient." The woman with untamable amber hair exactly like my own gently pushed him aside and drew me into an embrace. She might have been older, but she was deceptively strong, holding me tightly against her.

"Welcome to the family, Siri," she whispered tearfully in my ear. "I knew you were coming, but I didn't know when. Bran never let on that he had met someone, so I'd imagined that you still had yet to be conceived. I am so sorry I wasn't there for you when you were young."

"You knew I was coming?" I looked into her eyes and felt a tug of recognition stir in my mind.

"Of course, my dear. That, and other things. I am sorry I could not be there to ease your transition when you needed me most. But I look forward to getting to know you now."

I smiled back at her, knowing instantly that we were going to get along just fine.

"Me, too, Kalila."

"Please, call me Lila. Everyone does."

She patted my shoulder and I moved to sit between Yvaine and my father, while Alec sat between Claire and Jade. At my grandmother's nod, servers descended upon the tables bearing great platters of food, colorful arrays of steamed vegetables and spicy bean fritters, fresh fruits and bottles of violet sparkling wine. The last thing I actually felt like doing was sitting still and minding my manners, but the wine lit up my taste buds and the food seemed to ground me a bit.

My leg started bouncing up and down under the table involuntarily. After a few minutes of quiet conversation around the table, my grandfather reached out and clasped my fingers. I jumped in surprise, realizing that I had been tapping out the beat to Prodigy's Firestarter from my head without knowing it.

"You've got the Choosing jitters, my girl," he laughed heartily and took a sip of wine. "I still remember my Choosing like it was yesterday. I don't think I'd ever felt so alive. Well, that is until I met your grandmother over there." He lifted his glass to her and winked.

"If everyone feels that way, why have a reception afterward? Shouldn't we just go straight to dancing, or running, or, or, I don't know, something?"

"That's a good question. I suppose we do it because that's what we've always done. And I am told there will be dancing, soon enough. But if you would like to walk, how about I take you around the room and introduce you to some of my friends?"

Making small talk with strangers? Oh gee, yes, please, sign me up. That sounded like so much fun. Not. But he looked so hopeful, so dapper and sweet like a well-aged Harrison Ford, that I couldn't really see any polite or kind way out of it.

"Of course, Grandfather, I would love that."

"Wonderful," he said, looking delighted. We excused ourselves from the table and began making our way around the room.

In the end, I was glad I'd agreed to accompany him. The dancing didn't start for well over an hour, and my grandfather was adept at keeping us moving, never spending more than a couple minutes talking to any one person. Walking would never compare to running or dancing, not in my book, but the activity helped keep me from jumping out of my skin. I don't know how he did it, but somehow he managed to extract us from conversation politely each time, so that everyone looked honored and pleased when we left. Talk about life skills. Maybe he should be tutoring me, too.

When we'd almost completed the circuit, we came to a table with Mialloch and his parents. The men stood, shaking Yvain's hand. Absently, I wondered whether he had done Iron Palm training, the Shaolin practice of slapping a bowl of rice or water day after day to accustom the hand to abuse. We must have shaken a couple hundred by now, and his back would surely be aching after bending to kiss so many women's hands. Everyone seemed to know Yvain and he had a kind word to say to each of them, always asking about family members, remembering what their favorite pastime was or where they worked. He had a way of making everyone feel important and appreciated.

"Hello Raev, Mialloch. Sasho, so lovely to see you again," he bent and kissed Mialloch's mother on the cheek. "May I present my granddaughter, Siri."

"A pleasure," I murmured, shaking their hands. Maybe it was time I started some of that Iron Palm training myself. Mialloch's dad, Raev, had a grip like an iron vise. Mialloch nodded politely at me and I shook my head at him, giving him a hug. "Mialloch, it's so great to see you. You should swing by the table and introduce everyone to your parents later."

He hugged me back stiffly, his gold and silver arm cuffs digging into my back. I released him and laughed, smoothing the front of his crisp white linen shirt.

"Ah, but now, look! I've wrinkled your shirt," I teased.

"I see you and my son have made fast friends," his mother said with a frosty smile. "Although, perhaps, not as closely as we would have hoped."

Mialloch coughed, turning an impossible shade of red. "Mother, please."

"No, it's okay." I put a hand on his arm. "Your son is a very fine man, Sasho. I should thank you for allowing him to tutor me all these months. I've learned so much from him, and he's become one of my closest friends on the planet."

"Indeed?" his father asked, a calculating look flaring in eyes. Uh-oh. Double matchmaker alert.

"Oh yes, and Alec's too. It's been sooo great helping them get reacquainted." I looked at him innocently, knowing all along that Mialloch's father had never approved of him having a friend that was half-human. "Isn't it wonderful when old friends can reconnect?"

"Ah, young Alec Ward. Yes, I believe he has been acting as your bodyguard these last few months, correct?" his mother said disdainfully.

"Bodyguard. Bestie. Boyfriend. Whatever." I said airily, waving my hand while she sputtered on her wine. "Speaking of, I'd better get back to my table, my grandmother seems to need a word with me."

I wasn't making that last part up. Jade was glaring at me and had just beckoned imperiously with one finger.

"Come along, grandfather. I'm dying to have some of that cake they're serving now. It was ever so nice meeting you both, you must be so proud to have raised such a charming, generous son."

I winked at Mialloch, who was clearly struggling not to laugh, and linked arms with Yvain. As I directed him back towards our table, he leaned down so he could speak in my ear.

"Not that I'm complaining, I've never particularly liked Sasho, but what was all that about?"

"Didn't your son tell you? He and Raev thought that Mialloch and I might hit it off and pair up. To be fair, though, neither of them knew I was already involved with Alec. When Alec and Mialloch met up with me in Montreal a few weeks ago, we all thought they were going to kill each other. I guess they had a big falling out years ago because Mialloch was on track to become a Council member like his dad, and Alec was mixed blood."

"Ah. Yes. Sasho has never been the most tolerant of women. Her mother was killed and tortured by humans above below as a witch, so she has a somewhat tainted view of their species."

"Oh. Oh wow. I didn't know that. That's horrible." Now I actually felt a little bad for sticking it to her like I had. But then I saw Alec, watching me from his seat, and I set aside any feelings of guilt. "But Alec is different. She should have known that. He used to be Mialloch's best friend."

"And now?"

"Now I hope that they will continue repairing their friendship. So far, I think it's going pretty well." And it was. Minus the occasional flare of insecurity on either side. They hadn't fought at all in over a week.

"Hmm. You really are a healer, my dear, and most definitely Tyr-brave to stand up to his parents like you did. I think you are going to do great things." He patted my arm and smiled at me indulgently.

"Because of the Song of Life?"

"No, because you're you."

CHAPTER 9

Finally, the harpist gave a nod to the twelve-piece band and they took the stage, playing an upbeat ethereal waltz. Couples made their way to the open dance floor at the center of the room and began to whirl in concert. I gazed wistfully at their brilliant gowns and starched linens. I'd never seen people dance like that in real life.

Some of the women wore otherworldly creations, gauzy fabric swirling about their feet, while others wore more conventional ball-gowns or modern, minimal club wear like my own. The men also wore a variety of garb, some in starched white linens that made me think of India, others in brightly colored tails and tailored vests. In Aeden, it seemed the only formal dress requirement was that it suited you and looked well-made. The speed of the dancers increased with the tempo of the music. I wondered how they managed to spin like that without getting dizzy.

"Shall we dance?" A husky voice brought me out of my reverie and I looked up to see Alec bowing low in front of me. I placed my hand in his and stood.

"Alright, but fair warning, I've never waltzed before."

"Nothing to it," he winked. "Just mirror me, and keep your eyes on mine. I'll lead you through it."

We reached the floor and he placed a hand around my waist.

"Ready?"

"As I'll ever be," I smiled.

He kissed me lightly on the cheek and looked me in the eyes. "Remember, just follow me."

"I thought that was your job?" I teased.

"Not this time. See if you can keep up," he dared me.

The waltz had entered a slow phase again, so at least I'd have a chance to acclimate to the motions, I thought. Alec began moving forward, so that I had step backwards to accommodate his presence. And that was how it progressed, his body leading me around the floor, always advancing, pushing the boundaries. I'd never realized the dance was such a show of dominance, of interest, on the part of the man. No wonder the waltz had been considered outrageous when it first came about. It wasn't just about the touching, although there was that. It was about the man's interest, about making his intentions known. Showing his desire physically, always intruding upon the woman's space, pressing in.

I wouldn't have wanted to dance it with someone I didn't like, but with Alec, it was delicious.

The awe I'd felt coming from him had receded, to be replaced by the most complete feeling of acceptance and respect I'd ever experienced. And desire. Yeah, there was that, too. But somehow, without words, our relationship seemed to have progressed to a new level of commitment and mutual support. There was no backing down from this. The way he had come to my aid on the stage had evolved out of an instinctual need to be with me, but it had also been a declaration of our relationship that anyone with two eyes would be able to decipher. And, of course, there had been plenty of eyes on us at that moment. Even now, I could feel the intense scrutiny of the other couples on the floor. Even among the colorful dancers, all eyes were on us.

I chuckled, thinking of Sasho and Raev among them.

"What's so funny?" Alec asked.

"Nothing really. I just met Mialloch's parents a few minutes ago. I'm afraid I may not have made the best impression."

"Were they rude to you?" His hand tightened at my waist and he looked around, trying to spot them through the other dancers.

"No. Sasho made it clear that she didn't like you very much, so I sort of told her just how much I do."

Alec let out a bark of laughter. "You what? Oh, Sasho must have loved that."

"Yeah, well. I guess after tonight the cat's really out of the bag, huh?"

"What do you mean?"

"Well, now everybody knows we're, you know, together. I hope you don't mind."

"Siri, I will never mind anything that has to do with you. You should know that by now."

"I do. I just kind of like to hear it once in a while. Or every day." I pretended to think for a moment. "You know, every day isn't bad."

"Okay, deal. Every day then. For forever." He stopped and pulled me to the side of the floor, closing his arms around me to deliver a sweet, chaste kiss. I knew he was on his best behavior in front of my family, but the promise contained in the strength of his lips would have knocked me to my knees if he hadn't been holding me up. I was grateful not to have to suffer that indignity twice in one day in front of this crowd.

Just as we were drawing apart, Bran walked onto the band's platform with my mother.

"Good afternoon folks, I'd like to thank you all for joining us in celebrating my daughter's Choosing. As many of you no doubt noticed, she seems to have a bit more energy to burn off today than most faelings," he paused as everyone in the audience laughed, a few people let out loud whistles and Amber cheered "Yeah, Siri!" Then he continued. "Not many of you know this, but Siri started developing mature abilities several months ago, so we had a feeling something like this might happen."

People at the tables started whispering among themselves, probably speculating on just what my powers entailed and where Bran was going with his speech.

Me? I just hoped he'd hurry up and finish so that I could hide under a table somewhere soon.

"To that end, we asked her friends to make up a compilation from her own music library for us to dance to. I'm sure it will be a little different from what most of you are used to, excepting a few of the younglings among us this afternoon, but I do hope you will stay and enjoy the rest of the festivities."

My mother smiled and handed what looked like Amber's phone to a man in the band. He walked over to the large speakers and begin to plug in the phone, but stopped when Bran held up a hand.

"First, however, I do have another announcement to make. The last few months have been a terrible and exciting time for me. I've come up against some of my biggest challenges this year fighting the Dark. But I have also had the utter joy and pleasure of finally meeting my daughter, and reconnecting with her mother."

He turned to my mom and held out his hands. She took them, blushing. She was used to working security behind the scenes or teaching seminars on how to kick butt, not holding hands in front of a room full of people.

"Frederika Alvarsson you are my one true love and I want everyone to know it. Will you marry me?"

My mother squealed – squealed! – and leapt into his arms, wrapping her legs around his waist.

"Yes! Of course I will."

And then the kissing started.

"Oh gods," I muttered to Alec. "Do you think they even remember they're on stage?"

"Don't worry, I'll take care of it." And then to my utter amusement and dismay he shouted, "Hey Bran, get a room!"

I could hear my grandmother groan in embarrassment behind me at our table, even above the catcalls and laughter that filled the room. Bran lifted his head and saluted us, walking off the stage and out the nearest exit, still carrying my mother. Geez, what was it with Alvarsson women being carried today.

Right on cue, the music started; the funky beats of Fatboy Slim's "Praise You" came on. It couldn't have been a better choice, celebrating life, love, the hard times and the good. Most of the older couples started leaving the dance floor, while I gave Alec an excited look and grabbed his hand.

"Come on!" I shouted. "You owe me another dance!"

"Do I?" he protested weakly, letting me drag him out to the dance floor. Almost immediately we were joined by Claire and Amber.

"Where's Ewan?" I yelled in Amber's ear.

"Getting another drink. He's talking with Mitch at the bar, says he needs more fortification before he'll dance with me."

"Aw, just tell him you guys can do lasair. That's like dancing, and we all know he's got the moves for that."

"Now there's an idea," she laughed.

Mialloch came on the floor, accompanied by several other people who he quickly introduced. A couple of the girls seemed to know Alec already and gave me hard looks, as if I'd stolen their candy. Before I could wipe the plastic looks off their faces, more young fae overran the floor, most of them appearing to be anywhere from 15 to 30. Of course, I was sure some of them were even older than they looked. Someone bumped into me and I turned. Brenin stood there looking both more dapper and taller than I remembered, but he still had wild hair that rivaled my own and looked like he needed to eat more spinach. Like me, his hair was in an updo, albeit a more mannish samurai knot.

"So, I hear you stole the show earlier."

"Didn't you see?"

"Nah, too young, remember? So, you going to tell me what happened?"

"Nice try, faeling," Amber laughed as she clapped an arm on his shoulder. "There'll be plenty of time for that later...Like, two years later." She cackled and spun away, dancing her way into the middle of the crowd.

Claire giggled and took pity on Brenin, grabbing his hand and pulling him along with her, following Amber into the fray.

Alec shrugged and leaned in close. "So. Are you really going to make me keep dancing to this crap, or can I go get myself fortified now with Ewan?"

"Bah! You men are useless," I exclaimed and playfully shoved him away. "But don't blame me if I find someone else who appreciates my moves."

Alec was back in my face in an instant, nostrils flaring even as he smiled. "Not if they know what's good for them."

"Neanderthal," I grinned and pushed him again. "Now be a good boy and go fetch Ewan. I want to see you both back here in twenty minutes."

"Ten," he promised, the dimple piercing his cheek while his eyes flashed purple, and he was gone.

I turned to follow my friends into the crowd and smashed into one of the girls who'd come with Mialloch.

"Ooops, sorry, I didn't see you there." She glared at me without saying a word and pushed past me. I kept going, too, talking to myself while I walked. "Huh, guess not everyone is into the whole Heart of Life thing, that's cool."

"Hey girl, who you talking to?" Amber snagged me as I almost passed her by.

"Me? What? No, nothing, I was just talking to myself."

I had to be. Because I was standing in the middle of a street again, and there was no one, I mean no one, around.

I was alone.

73

Crap.

I gazed around, trying to see if this was the same vision as before, but I didn't recognize anything. I jogged around the corner and stopped dead in my tracks.

There it was, the same damn car, burning.

Polluting the air, not that anyone seemed to be alive in the town to care.

This wasn't good. Whenever visions repeated themselves they seemed more likely to come true. So if this was true, I needed to remember the details. If I knew where I was, maybe I could stop it. I looked down the street, trying to etch the details into my mind. Blue street signs reading Taylor and Main. Hand lettered boards above stores: The Cuppa Café, Sookie's Somethings, Taylor's Mercantile.

I repeated the names over and over in my head, trying to commit them to memory.

Once I felt satisfied with my efforts, I did something I'd never done before. I intended to return to the present

and I did. One minute I was on a deserted smoky street and the next I caught myself mid-stride on the dance floor. I don't think I'd missed a single beat. While my visions usually felt like they took minutes, this one seemed to have taken only an instant.

No one had noticed I was gone. I didn't feel nauseous. I didn't have a headache. I wasn't disoriented. Was it a side effect of the Choosing, this improvement in my ability? A bonus if it was, though it didn't matter now.

It was time to have a conversation with my dad.

Chapter 10

"You had the same vision twice?"

"More or less," I shrugged, watching my dad as he paced around the small room.

We'd gathered in a small dressing room off the hall. Mitch, Claire, Amber, Ewan, Alec, Jade, my mom. I'd waited until Alec rejoined me on the dance floor before sending him to collect my parents, figuring they deserved some private time to be mushy and celebrate their engagement. Now, though, their attention was fully on me.

With so many people packed into the room, there was barely room to breathe, let alone pace. Everyone was leaning against walls or sitting down trying to make themselves small. Trying to give my large, angry and concerned father extra room.

"Twice?" he asked for the third time in a row. I raised my eyebrows in question at my mother, hoping she'd put an end to this. He'd been pacing for several minutes now, most of it in silence. She just made a face, like I was on my own. Great, it was up to me to calm him down. Honestly,

I'd never seen him like this. He was usually so calm and level-headed. I wasn't sure what to do with him now.

I'd taken him and my mother to the dressing room, planning to have a small, private conversation with them. He'd listened in stony silence while I related everything I could remember of both visions, and then left the room, barking out orders to several of his Guards, and then marched back in to watch as everyone filed in. And then the pacing had started.

"Geez, Dad. Yes, twice. And it's too consistent. As much as I had hoped this could wait until the party was over, I think you need to start looking into it right away. Those street names, the shops. There has to be a way to pinpoint the location and get a lead on the Shades. Maybe we can head off the vision before it happens."

"Wouldn't that be nice," Amber grimaced.

"What, don't you think we can?" I asked.

"Like I said, it'd be nice," she shrugged.

"Still, we obviously have to try," declared Ewan. "Sir, with your permission, I will go back to Valhalla immediately and talk with Mireia, see what she can find out about possible matches for location."

Mitch pushed away from the wall and rolled his neck. "Good thinking, Ewan. I'll accompany you. Alec?"

"Of course, I'm in." My heart dropped to my toes at the thought of him leaving again, but I knew there could be no other way. It was what he did.

My father shook his head ruefully. "Remind me, who is the Commander here?"

"You are, sir." All the Guards in the room stood at attention, watching him warily while the rest of us just

76

smirked and rolled our eyes (the standard Alvarsson protocol for situations like this.)

"Glad to hear it." My dad looked us all over and rolled his own eyes. Apparently he'd been spending too much time with my mother. "Mitch, Ewan, Alec, we'll leave in three hours. That should give us enough time to wrap up here without causing any worry among the guests. Alec, I want you to find your father and tell him to join us, too."

"My father, sir? He's here?" Alec sounded one part excited and two parts nervous. He saw me watching him and leaned back against the wall again, trying to act nonchalant.

"Yes, of course, I invited him myself. He's at the table near the bar, with some of his lieutenants. I'm surprised you didn't see him." My dad clapped his hands together. "Well, I guess that sums up about everything we need to do."

"Um, not quite," I raised my hand. "What the hell am I supposed to do? Hang out in Elysielle and wait for another vision?"

"No, not at all. Airmed is here, and she's already asked to spend some time with you this week, teaching you some of her healing methods. With this new threat popping up, I think that is a wise course of action. Maybe you guys can figure something out that our scientists have missed."

"Okay," I said doubtfully. Spending time with Airmed wasn't really high on my list of to-dos. I highly doubted we would be able to crack the antidote for the anti-serum.

"What about me?" Amber spoke up. "I'm a Guard, too, you know."

"We know," Mitch and Ewan spoke up at the same, clearly wishing the opposite was true. Men and their silly need to protect everything without a penis. As if not having one somehow made a woman weaker. I never got how having balls became synonymous with being tough. Um, hello, sensitive target area? Whatever.

Bran coughed and stepped up to Amber, whose hands were fisted and was clearly gearing up for a fight.

"Amber, I know you are a great Guard, but you're still green compared to the others. Besides, I need you here, with Siri. I need someone I can trust to stay with her."

"What about Alec?" she whined. "And how am I supposed to not be green when I'm always left behind?"

"All in due time, Amber. Alec has been working these teams already, he knows the drill. Besides, I don't trust him to keep watch on Siri 24/7, at least, not until they are married. Or I'm dead, whichever comes first."

"Hypocrite," Jade coughed into her hand, which set the rest of us laughing. Good old Grandma. She usually acted so prim and proper, but underneath it all she was a firecracker. And she sure knew how to surprise a room with those well placed verbal-bombs.

"Okay," said Bran, ignoring her. "So it's settled. Everyone, take some time to enjoy yourselves before we leave. And don't forget to eat well, it's a long ride back to Valhalla."

"I'll have the staff pack up some bags for you all," my grandmother said and slipped out of the room.

Everyone started to file out of the room. Alec stepped in front of me and held out his arm like an escort. "Well, gorgeous. How would you like to meet my father?"

I threaded my arm through his and we walked through the hall, finally stopping in front of a table of tough looking men and women. I knew they were Light fae, but honestly, if I'd seen them on the streets of any human city I would have steered clear. You could see the warning signs in the way they moved, or didn't move. Every person at this table was an elite killing machine. They were eating and drinking and laughing like everyone else in the room, but there was an aura of tension and power among them that radiated coldly through the corner of the room. One man stood out from the rest, watching us with cold fathomless eyes. As we approached, he placed his cup down and smiled, yet it did nothing to warm my heart.

"Alec," he nodded, standing.

"Father, it's good to see you. Ambrose, Cleo, Sewenesh, Ryker." Alec acknowledged the rest of the warriors at the table and they each held up a glass, watching us with interest. "Siri, I'd like you to meet my father, Flynn Ward. Father, Siri Alvarsson Le Fay."

Flynn's deep purple eyes flashed a brilliant shade of violet as he shook my hand, and I felt bombarded by emotions for an instant. Approval. Sadness. Anger. Dismay. I fumbled for a greeting and removed my hand, taking up Alec's. Instantly the emotions receded to be replaced by longing and love.

"So, this is the one?" Flynn looked me up and down, no hint of what he was thinking in his face. "Congratulations on your Choosing," He raised a glass to me.

"Thank you," I stammered.

"You made quite an impression on everyone today. Both of you." He raised an eyebrow at Alec. "I hope your union will bring happiness to you both. Gods know there hasn't been any in the Ward family in years."

Alec fidgeted, mussing his hair as he ran a hand through it. Can you say awkward?

"Union?" I coughed. "Um, yes, well, we haven't announced any plans officially yet, so..."

"Didn't you?" he smirked. "Every fae in the room saw my son go to you on that stage. Trust me. It's official."

Flynn had all of Alec's good looks, and the worst of his manners. I could only begin to imagine what it had been like growing up with this shell of a man. Surely it was devastating to lose your wife and daughter so violently, but seeing the way this cold, aloof man behaved, my anger rose. Alec squeezed my hand, sensing what I was feeling.

He wanted me to smile, to let it go. That made me want to slap the grin off his father's face even more.

"Your son is amazing. I can't imagine how hard it must have been for him growing up without his family. He is such a good, caring man. I hope you are proud of him."

Flynn's eyes flared and then softened just a bit before the light in them shuttered again. "I am," he muttered. "I just hope that his attachment to you doesn't cause him more heartache. In my experience, love is just another weakness in a Guard's armor that the Dark can stab right through."

"Father," Alec growled in warning.

I placed my hand on his arm. "No, it's okay, Alec." I looked at Flynn with pity. "You're wrong. Love is not a weakness. Your fear of it is. In fact, you sound like a Shade. I'm surprised you bother to strap on your gear in the morning. What bother fighting the Dark at all?"

Flynn advanced and glared down at me, but I stood my ground. Alec had told me that from the moment they came to Aeden, his father had poured himself into his work with the Light Guard and Alec had been left to study and train on his own. Alone. Twelve years old, and utterly alone. No wonder Alec had doubted I could really love him. His father had wounded him so deeply with his absences, building walls around both their hearts. The thought of him trying something now filled me with anticipation. Ever since my Choosing, I'd been filled with energy that was just dying for physical release. The wild side of me itched to get my hands on him, give him a taste of how he'd hurt the man I loved.

"I bother, young lady, so that bleeding hearts like you won't have to," he sneered. "So that no one else comes home to find their families dismembered and beaten."

"You think you're scaring me? Without love, what's the point? You're just an empty shell," I taunted, poking him hard in the chest. "You don't deserve a son like Alec."

"How dare you? I died that day. The only reason I still live and breathe is to protect my son, his friends, all Light fae from enduring what I did."

"But who protected him from you? Alec didn't die that day. He needed you. He still does." I looked him over with pity. "Someday, maybe you'll remember that."

One of the men at the table whooped with amusement, and started clapping, while the woman to the left of him elbowed him in the ribs. Surprised, I looked at him.

"Woo, girl, no one's ever spoken to Captain Ward like that and lived to tell about it. You've got brass balls."

"Stuff it, Ryker" the woman next to him said, shushing him.

"That's right," I said, standing taller and winking gratefully at Ryker. He'd diffused a lot of tension at the table with his outspokenness. "I do."

I looked at Flynn again, who was staring at Alec like a mystery he'd just uncovered.

"Love isn't a weakness, sir," I said again, this time more gently. "I'm sorry if we've started off on the wrong foot, but I hope we can get to know each other better so you'll give me a chance to show you that."

He regarded me skeptically, but shook my hand again. "I suppose I can do that. For Alec."

"For Alec," I agreed, giving him the full force of my smile. After that, everyone relaxed a little and Flynn invited us to sit down. Not wanting to push our luck, we gracefully declined, noting that we still had a few more people Alec wanted me to meet. Alec arranged for Flynn's team to join Bran later for briefing and we walked away.

"Well, that was intense," Alec whispered to me.

"You think?" I laughed.

We made our way through the room, meeting more of my friends' family members and former classmates. This round was different from when my grandfather walked with me – this time I met the younger fae. It was interesting, how their auras shone lighter, brighter. The older generations seemed to have been tainted by the years of war with the Dark, even though it hadn't really touched most of Aeden. You could tell that their hearts ached for the unity and peace previous generations had known. The younger fae had no such heaviness. They hadn't lost their natural joy and light yet.

When we walked by Sasho and Raev's table, I had no intention of stopping, but a glimmer of long pale hair caught my attention.

"Airmed?" Dark eyes met mine and I rushed forward, bending down to hug Mialloch's grandmother. "It's good to see you. How are you?"

"I am well, young one. And you? Your energy feels much better than last we met." She eyed me critically, her gaze lingering on my ankle. "You are different now."

"Yes, I feel great."

"As it should be. And you, Alec. Give me a kiss, you handsome devil." She angled her face upwards and pointed to her cheek. Alec obliged with a twinkle in his eye. I saw her son watching our exchange with a glower and fought an impish desire to stick out my tongue at him.

"We should talk, but now is not the time," she addressed me with a regal wave of her hand. "Tomorrow, meet me by the roses in the Honey Gardens at noon. I have something I'd like to show you."

"Alright, that shouldn't be a problem." I hugged her again. "At noon, then."

"Yes. And Siri? Come alone."

CHAPTER 11

I picked my way through the streets of Elysielle absentmindedly, my thoughts on Alec and my father. Most of the guards had left early this morning for Valhalla, where they were set to convene and discuss strategy. While Mireia worked to pinpoint the location of the town in my vision, teams were being dispatched to tighten security around the world. For the first time ever, the Light Guard was working openly with the Guardians from Midgard, Light fae like my mom whose ancestors had stayed above below actively fighting to protect humans and nature. Until now, the Light Guard's top priority had always been shielding the fae community of Aeden while they generally left those who lived above to fend for themselves. Mikael Morrigan, in his quest to dominate the world with his anti-serum, had made this everyone's fight.

I was glad people were coming together. I was.

Then why did I feel so uneasy?

I thought back to Rowan, and how the fear and anger in his heart had caused him to throw away our friendship and turn away from the Light. How was Flynn any different? How were any of us any different?

I didn't want to hate the Shades. I didn't want to fight or fear the Dark. There had to be a better way. A way to bring everyone back together, a way to heal the rift between the two sides. Somehow, I didn't think blaming them, or thinking my side was better than theirs, or more enlightened then theirs, was going to solve any problems.

I sighed and turned a corner, approaching the gates to the Honey Gardens. Like everything else in Elysielle, even the entrance was a piece of art. Jeweled insects spun lazily on mobiles, swaying in the gentle breeze to dip among the kaleidoscopic collection of flowers twining through the scrollwork. Real bees of all sizes flitted to and fro above my head as I passed below the arching gates, buzzing loudly as they collected more glittering pollen for their hives.

Honey Gardens was an apiary marvel by human standards. The heritage strains of bees here had each been hand bred to prefer feeding on specific flowers. Unlike the bees I was familiar with, the inhabitants of Honey Gardens didn't just collect from every flower in the vicinity. Here, hives collected from single sources to create their honey, producing unique strains for every flower. And when I say every flower, I mean just that. Honey Gardens held each flowering plant known to Aeden, and even some that otherwise only grew in Midgard.

Some honeys were considered delicacies and went at a high price, like caviar or truffles in Europe, while others had specific medicinal or cosmetic uses.

I looked around, reading the signs, and headed for the section that was dedicated to growing roses. I had a bit of a walk ahead of me, since it was a massive, sprawling park made for workers who never slept. Happily, the bees were also bred for their gentleness. They were so docile you could actually pet them, which I did as I bent down to rest a moment and smell a flower. The bumblebee's rounded, fuzzy butt hummed under my finger, tickling the nerves there before it flew back to its hive. I rubbed my finger against my thumb, smiling, and resumed walking.

Finally, I arrived at the roses. The path was lined with bushes of every color and size, while arches of vining roses shaded pathways to the side. A gazebo at the center was sheltered by impossibly large blooms, plate-sized petals peppered with large flakes of pollen. Like the pollen, the bees here were bigger, three times the size of a normal bumblebee and sporting brilliant vermillion stripes contrasting with chocolate fuzz. I laughed, thinking this really was a "Rose" garden – my friend back in Falls Depot would go wild over the sight. Pink was the natural red-head's favorite color, although Rose didn't discriminate and liked to combine her vintage finds with a rainbow variety of accessories.

I stepped up into the gazebo and took a seat on the bench next to Airmed, who was sitting quietly with her eyes closed.

She opened her eyes and smiled at me. "Siri, hello."

"Were you meditating?"

"No, just enjoying the song of the bees. I always find I can hear more sharply with my eyes closed, don't you?"

"I suppose so," I shrugged.

"Haven't you ever noticed how people always close their eyes when they smell something? Removing one sense helps heighten the others."

"That's true, I guess I do that. I never really thought about it though. Cool."

"But we're not here to talk about expanding the senses, much as I wish we were. Mialloch told me that you have had some disturbing visions." She gave me a penetrating stare and I squirmed a bit in my seat.

"I don't really want to talk about it, if that's okay. It's just...it's all still really raw in my mind right now, and I've already gone over everything several times with my dad."

"I totally understand, Siri. We don't need to go into specifics. Mialloch relayed enough of it for me to know there isn't anything in the vision that will help us. But it does tell me that we have to try to work on a cure, before the Dark do something we can't come back from."

"But, you already used up all your Nelumbo Lux elixir from this year's harvest, and there will never be enough for everyone that might need it."

"That's true, and it can't be replicated," she said pursing her lips in thought, "but that is exactly why you and I need to work together."

"What could we possibly do that the scientists in Valhalla haven't already tried?"

Airmed's laughter tinkled like fairy bells through the gazebo, harmonizing nicely with the birdsong above and the rumble of the bees on the walls of vines.

"Oh, my dear girl, don't ever go putting all your faith in men of science," she laughed. "There are far too many unknowns in this universe, far too many miracles yet undiscovered, to assume that science holds all the answers. We are the two best healers in the fae world right now. You, dear girl, are the Heart of Life. I have a feeling that things that may have been impossible last week might suddenly be quite possible now. If you are willing to work with me."

Crossing my foot over my right knee, I rubbed my ankle, considering. Airmed eyed the red and blue markings and nodded. "See? Miracles. Everywhere."

"I don't know if I would call getting an insta-tatttoo uninvited a miracle, exactly," I grumbled.

"Pish-tosh, dearie. It is a miracle and you know it. Your ancestor Tyr is looking after you, and you have more power in your little toe than I have in my whole body. So, are you going to work with me on this, or not?" She smirked at me like a mom waiting for her toddler to apologize so he could get some cake.

"Yeah, okay. Of course I want to work with you. I just don't see how it's going to do any good."

"Then we will be the perfect team. I have a millennia of hope and experience on my side, and you have all the creative power and potential of the universe at your fingertips. We can do this. I know we can."

She beamed at me and stretched out her hand, inviting me to join her happy-fest. I grinned and took it, shaking to seal the deal.

"Alright, let's do this. Where do we start?"

"Right here. We're sitting in the middle of one of the most amazing resources for a healer. Not only is practically every plant known to both man and fae grown here in the Honey Gardens, but we have a honey for all of them. I don't suppose you are aware of the benefits of honey?"

"Um, well, I know that it's good for a sore throat...not that I've ever had one. And it tastes awesome in tea."

"Yes, both those things are true. But it also has amazing healing properties. All honeys, so long as they haven't been over-heated or processed, have anti-bacterial and anti-fungal properties. A jar of raw honey can sit on a shelf for decades without going bad. But the real interesting magic happens when the pollen the bees collected to make the honey comes from a medicinal plant, or from a particular area. Many people in Midgard use local honey to acclimatize themselves to the molds and pollens that cause seasonal allergies."

"Oh, yeah, I remember one of my friend's moms doing that one spring."

"Okay, well, did you ever hear of Manuka honey?"

"Nope. What's that?"

"It's made by bees that feed exclusively off of tea trees in Australia."

"Okay? And?"

"And, it is one of the most powerful antibiotics known to man. Not only does it fight MRSA infections, but bacteria can't develop an immunity to it, the way they do with synthesized antibiotics. Don't get me started on the folly and dangers of those," she said grimly, shaking her head.

"Right, well, that's all very cool, but I don't see how it helps us."

"Look around, Siri. The scientists in Valhalla have no idea how to super charge an antidote with healing power. They can't do it, because no one has the juice that you and I do. And you can bet that they discounted the medicinal honeys produced here before they even started. No. You and I, we are uniquely suited to working together to create something that just might work."

"Where do we start?"

"Well, there are several varieties of plants that help boost the light in the body. I think they might be useful. Saint John's Wort, it's used to combat depression and increases photosensitivity – a good indicator that it increases light in the system. Also, marigolds, dandelions and sunflowers can all have similar effects. Roses work with the heart and the emotional centers of the brain to increase receptivity to love, so that part of the garden might hold some clues, too. I have more ideas, but those are all good places to start. How about we walk the gardens, and you can tell me if anything else strikes your fancy? We mustn't discount a woman's intuition. Then we will meet with the honey master to procure samples for testing. I am thinking the right honey mixed with the right flower essences and some of our combined healing touch might just do the trick."

"It's worth a shot," I shrugged and stood, feeling antsy and ready to get to work. Alec was surely halfway across Aeden by now, and sitting around mooning was so not my style. "Let's get to work."

Chapter 12

The next couple days were spent in a haze of confectionary bliss. Other than a quick run each morning and evening through the streets of Elysielle on my way to and from the Honey Garden, I passed all my hours tasting exotic and wildly different honeys and fermentable nectars. We secured sealed pots of the most promising ones, filling several trunks to be taken back to Valhalla for our work on an antidote to the Shade's anti-serum. Under the brilliant red sun, we laid out sparkling bowls of hand-carved quartz filled with water, floating a single blossom upon the surface of each one, creating flower essences that would later be blended with the honeys.

I didn't know if any of it would help. But the work itself was healing. I was able to use my heightened earth powers to speak with the plants, determining which had the most potent effects, which flowers wanted to be used, and which would have no benefit. Surprising both Airmed and myself, we discovered I had a unique aptitude to feel the emotions of the plants. I found myself having actual conversations with the plants more than once.

That's right. I was Aeden's newest plant whisperer. By the end of the second day, I had uncovered several plants who swore their petals held powerful cures for diseases like cancer, and another that said it could unlock emotional blockages in the body, making it a good candidate for the treatment of certain kinds of autism and PTSD. We filed this information away in Airmed's journal for future use, remaining focused on the most pressing matter – finding a cure for the anti-serum.

We tried to tackle the issue from several angles. Maybe something that would preserve or shield light in the body so that the Dark's weapon couldn't take hold? Or perhaps something that halted viral evolution, so that the anti-serum couldn't become contagious? Or, maybe we needed something that blocked Dark magic, since that seemed to be part of the formula for producing the anti-serum. Every idea was a shot in the dark. We had no real idea what might actually work. So we were trying everything.

On the third day, we returned to Valhalla with our bounty carefully packed into several trunks. Alec had already left for Midgard, dispatched to a yet another medical research facility in the American mid-west where there were rumors of Dark involvement. Almost every team of Guards had been sent above, literally scouring the earth in light of my newest visions. Given the danger, Jade had sent word to Claire's parents that they would be remaining in Valhalla for a few more weeks, and invited the Brucies to visit if they could.

Mireia had pinpointed the town in my vision, Timber Valley, Montana, but Flynn's team had already reported in, saying it was all clear, at least for now. Bran had ordered the team to fan out in all directions, checking neighboring towns for Shade activity. So far, they hadn't turned up any leads.

"Maybe your vision is already changing," Amber said hopefully as she ducked to avoid a palm-strike to the face.

I shook my head, following the palm-strike with a cross-body punch and shifting quickly into a lasair maneuver, dancing around to her side as I threw in a quick ax-kick mid-twirl. "I don't think so. Something doesn't sit right. Either we're just too early..."

"Or?" she asked, sliding under my leg and jabbing me in the thigh before she popped up behind me.

I whirled and bent backwards, her fist glancing off my shoulder. "Or someone's missing something. I don't know. I guess we'll just have to wait and see." I signaled for a break and toweled off the sweat from my chest as I took a drink of water. "I should get back to the lab. They probably have everything all ready by now."

The scientists in Tower Four had grudgingly agreed to let Airmed and I use one of their labs for our research, and had promised to lend us any equipment and as much infected blood as we might need for testing our remedies. Of course, with Raev and the Council breathing down their necks for a cure, they hadn't had much choice other than to agree.

I left Amber in the training room and walked over to Tower Four, riding the winding escalator up to the tenth floor where Airmed had told me to meet her. Walking through two doors marked with a biohazard symbol, I found the healer unpacking our jars and bottles, lining them up on glass shelves while another fae watched her eagerly.

"Are you sure we cannot help you, ma'am?" the skinny man in a lab coat asked, fidgeting with his long red hair.

"You? No, thank you," she scoffed. "We can't afford to have any of these broken. Some of these honeys we can't get more of until next year."

The man looked crestfallen and sat down on a stool, apologizing, "I'm sorry, I never drop anything, I swear. I

93

just wasn't expecting you when you came in, and well, you know, you are you, so I was so excited and then-"

"I know, I know. The great Airmed lives, call the presses," she mocked, waving him off. "Well, I'm here now and this is my lab and we will do things my way. Which means no more broken beakers, even if they are empty."

"Yes, ma'am," he mumbled morosely.

I cleared my throat, and Airmed lit up. "Siri, darling, you're here! Be a dear, won't you, and help me unpack our things."

I glanced at the lab assistant and smiled in apology, going over to the second trunk and beginning to set its contents out on the counter. Airmed took the jars one by one and placed them in their proper places, alphabetized by origin flower, on the shelves.

I looked at the guy again, who was watching us with a mixture of fear and awe. "Um, hi. I'm Siri. And you are?"

"Oh, of course, how rude of me! I'm Risten Kyderis, but everyone calls me Red." He blushed an unfortunate shade of pink that clashed with his bright hair and I wondered which had inspired the nickname.

"Hi, Red. Nice to meet you."

"I'm here to help you with anything you might need, you know, cell manipulation, growing test cultures, that sort of thing."

Airmed snorted and I rushed to cover her rudeness and make him feel welcome.

"That's great! I don't know much about that sort of thing. I'm sure we'll be able to use your help. Maybe you could set up some cultures now for us to test later? We already have a few formulas we want to try out."

Red's blush faded and he looked relieved to be put to work. "Sure thing, boss," he said, saluting me. "I'll get right on it."

Airmed leaned over as he started working across the room, pulling petri dishes out of drawers and lining them up. "You sure he's up for this?" she whispered in my ear. "What if he gives us all Zika virus?"

"Nothing ventured, nothing gained," I quipped. "Give the guy a break. I'm sure they wouldn't have sent us a newbie to work with."

Turns out, I was right. Red really knew his stuff. The more we chatted over the course of the day, the more I saw how great he was at his job. Over tea, he confessed that he had next to zero elemental abilities.

"All my abilities," he said, tapping his forehead, "are up here. Science has really always been the only thing I was any good at. It turns out having a great memory, a knack with numbers and being a little OCD are all key ingredients for running a lab."

"Well, you certainly know your stuff." He did. The cultures had been prepped and catalogued, and we had over a hundred infected petri-dishes waiting for their first round of treatment.

"Between you and me, I'm thrilled to be working with you guys." He looked around, making sure Airmed was still out of the room. She'd gone to use the bathroom, but she must have run into someone she knew because she'd been gone almost half an hour. "I mean, the great Airmed? She's legendary. Makes what we do here seem like kid's play."

"Aw, come on, you guys do some amazing work. I've heard about the different vaccines and cures you've leaked out into Midgard."

"Yeah, but Airmed...she can heal without the science, without surgery. She's made people whole again just with her magic. I wish I had that ability."

I figured now wasn't the time to let him know I had that power, too, and was about to change the subject when he beat me to it.

"And you! Everyone is calling you the Heart of Life, saying you lit up the whole room at your Choosing, did you know that?"

"Yep," I said wanly. "I was kinda there, so yeah."

"How awesome is that? Do you have amazing powers, too? How does that work out for you, combining the three bloodlines together?"

"I'm still kind of figuring all that stuff out. But yeah, there are some cool powers. All the abilities I had before seem to be getting stronger."

"Like what?"

"Well, before I could talk to animals and do some stuff with plants, but now I can sort of hear what the plants are feeling, too."

"Wait, you could do stuff before your Choosing?"

"Mm-hmm." I blew on my tea, watching the steam roll off of it."

"Man, you are so lucky. It's been six years since mine, and still all I can do is heat up a glass of water."

"Water fae?"

"No, fire. It does help a bit when I am working with the cultures, I am able to help them stay at the right temperature for incubation. But anything more than that taps me out."

"I have a friend who was like you, but now he's doing more stuff," I offered, thinking of Mialloch. "Maybe you just need more time, or the right sort of trigger. You know, like for my friend, being in a stressful situation really helped him bring out his powers. Don't give up yet."

"Gee, thanks Siri, that's really good to hear. I-"

Airmed strolled back through the double doors of the lab and Red jumped up, busying himself arranging the cultures for the millionth time. I restrained a chuckle and stood, whispering in his ear as I passed, "Don't worry about Airmed, her bark is worse than her bite."

I walked over to the healer and looked down at the tray of labeled syringes before us. We'd mixed the three flower essences with six honeys into 120 different permutations, pouring our combined healing energies into each one for several minutes. Now all we had to do was add them to the numbered cultures and see what happened. All three of us donned our masks and gloves as Red began inoculating the numbered cultures, one by one.

"I can't tell if anything is happening. How will we know if it is working?" I asked.

"If it's going to work, it should set off a chain reaction right away, like the Nelumbo Lux did. When I've finished here we can start checking them out under the microscope and see if there are any changes."

"Oh," I said, feeling disappointed. I'd been expecting something a little more dramatic. A flash of light maybe? A glow? A detectable aura? I don't know. Something more magical than peeking through a lens. I liked science, but I'd rather been hoping a fae lab would be more exciting than the chem classes at home.

"Here, why don't you start from number 120 and work your way backwards, then we can meet in the middle."

I nodded at his suggestion and picked up the syringe, carefully injecting the essence into the culture. I placed the syringe into the massive biohazard receptacle by the counter and moved on to 119. Airmed watched impatiently, tapping her long fingernails on the counter while she waited.

Finally, every dish had been inoculated. Red straightened and brought over two microscopes, setting one up at each end of the table.

"Okay, let's continue in the same order. The serums should already be producing results, if they're going to do anything at all. I'll start with number one; Siri, you check 120 first, and go from there. Airmed, how about you mark down the results."

"Sounds good," she said, picking up the clipboard that listed each of our permutations. Keeping good records was time consuming, but important if we ever wanted to reproduce our results. "We've got four parameters – negative results, non-active, low positive activity and high positive. Just list off your number and the result as we go."

"120, non-active," I sighed, chucking the plate in the bio bin. "119, non-active."

"1, non-active."

"118, non-active."

"2, non-active. 3, non-active."

"117, non-active. 116, non-active."

"4, non-active."

"115, hold on I've got something...It's...Oh, no. Ew. This one is bad, really bad. Definitely negative." I wrinkled my nose and started to take it out from the microscope.

"Hold on, let me see," Red elbowed his way to my scope and peered through the lens. "Yep, you're right. This happened before when we were trying to find a cure. Every once in a while one of the cultures would start to die off."

"That's not dying. That's molding. See, there are spores in there."

"Was it contaminated?" Airmed asked.

"No, I think it's just a product of the darkness, the absence of light in the culture."

"Okay, so note to self, some cures will kill us quicker. Awesome. Great. Good to know," I said with false brightness.

"Yeah, well, let's not let this one have its way." Red picked up the culture and disposed of it carefully.

We went back to listing off dish results. In the end, not one yielded positive activity, and twelve had become festering pools of mildew.

"Well, gee, I feel better now, don't you?" I grimaced, taking off my mask and gloves after we had cleaned up and disinfected the area again. I washed up at the sinks, lathering my arms, face and neck with anti-bacterial soap.

"Look," Airmed said gently, "no one ever said this was going to be easy. Did you really expect to find a cure on the first day?"

Feeling a bit naïve, I frowned. "I guess a part of me did, yeah. I mean, you're the great Airmed. I'm the Heart of Life. I guess I thought we'd be able to do this."

"And we will. I have no doubt. We will find a solution. But it might take a while."

"What if we don't have a while?"

"Then we'll work faster. You're a natural optimist. Don't give up on us now, after the first setback."

I groaned. "Fine. You're right. I know it." I hugged Airmed and felt a quick pulse of her healing energy flow up my arms. "Thanks for setting me straight."

"Anytime, youngling. Now, why don't you go see your friends, relax with some of that 'training' you love so much. Tomorrow we'll start fresh."

"Okay, sounds good. Thanks, Airmed." I smiled and looked over at Red who was prepping fresh dishes with labels. "You should take a break, too, Red."

"I'm just going to finish these up and then I'll head home. Don't worry about me, I live for this stuff," he grinned.

"Nerd," I grinned back and waved. "Alright, see you guys later."

I walked out of the lab and headed straight outside, pausing a moment to drink in the sunshine. After watching the darkness spread through some of the cultures with such devastating effects, I could practically feel the sterilizing effects of the red sun shining mercilessly above me. It was just what I needed. That, and maybe a bucket of bleach to wash to ick factor of the lab off of me.

Airmed had suggested training, and that sounded like a great plan, but first, I needed a bath.

CHAPTER 13

Several days later, reading off the results of dish number 903, I felt like one of the negative cultures. Dirty. Infected. Festering.

Hope had literally fled the room. We'd made almost a thousand cultures over that last several days, and we only had a handful left to check. Not one had yielded even the tiniest indication of a positive result.

I puffed out my cheeks and stared at the ceiling for a moment, praying for a cure and some calm as I reached for culture 902. I had no sooner placed a finger on it when Airmed cried out.

"Red, no! Don't touch it!"

I looked to my left and saw Red, frozen in horror with his hand wrapped around a dish. A brown foam was climbing over his fingers, disappearing as it melted into his gloves.

"Quick," I yelled, "put it in the bin!"

His eyes flashed to mine and he sprang into action, tossing it into the bin along with his gloves. He ran to the sink and started scrubbing.

"What the hell! What was that?" I asked. "Are you okay?"

He didn't answer me, just kept scrubbing, but I could see he wasn't okay. A fine sheen of perspiration had broken out on his forehead, and his skin was pale.

I placed a hand on his back, planning to give him a healing boost, and gasped. Waves of nausea rolled over me, and I felt cold. So cold.

Darkness creeped in on all sides and my hand

turned to ice in Mikael Morrigan's palm. His eyes glinted like hard, cold diamonds, but his hand was soft, as if he had never touched dirt or worked a day in his life. For an earth fae, I found that strange.

"So, we have a deal, then?"

"Yes. I'll do it."

"I knew you'd come around, Siri. You'll see, this will be best for everyone. And stop looking so worried, please. I always honor my agreements."

I doubted that, but I kept my peace. This had to be done. It was my only hope. I would figure the rest out later.

I still had my hand on Red's back when I came out of the vision.

Me? Making a deal with the Morrigan? I shuddered involuntarily remembering the chill of his fleshy hand in mine. When pigs fly, I thought. I'd rather shake hands with one of those moldy cultures. Speaking of which, Red was really not looking so hot.

I started to gather my power to send him some energy when he turned to me, mouth open, a look of dread on his face.

"I don't-"

His eyes rolled up in his head and he collapsed to the floor before he could finish the sentence.

"Red!" I cried, trying to wake him. Airmed rushed over and we looked at each other grimly, placing our hands on him at the same time. We both called up our energy, I could feel it drawing power from the earth deep below the building, tapping into the life giving roots of the Tree of Life outside, and before the power could consume me I pushed it out my fingers, into Red.

The jolt should have been enough to awaken the dead.

Nothing.

Nothing happened. I shook my head, knowing it was useless.

"He's out. There's nothing we can do. Without a cure for the anti-serum, we'll never wake him."

Airmed made a face, as if she wanted to argue with me, before it crumpled and she put her face in her hands.

I left her to sit with Red while he slept blissfully unaware on the floor and went to hit the emergency intercom by the door.

"We've got a situation here," I said, not knowing if anyone was even monitoring this thing. "We need a med team from the sanatorium, and a cleanup crew to sanitize immediately."

"Okay, we're on our way," a voice assured me and clicked off, leaving nothing but static.

Twenty minutes later the guys in white coats had wheeled Red away for safe-keeping in the sanatorium, along with the other new cases of infected. Airmed had followed, promising to make sure he was treated well. Now, my dad was pacing the hallway outside the lab while we waited for the clean-up crew to finish removing all evidence of the fouled anti-serum.

The doors parted and the crew left, and I started walking through the entrance back into the lab.

"Just where do you think you're going?" My father yanked me away from the doors, grabbing my arm.

"To the lab, duh. We still have more dishes to check off the list," I explained impatiently, like I was talking to someone with a lot less brain cells. "Any one of them could be holding the cure."

"No way. Not happening. Not a chance."

"Dad!"

"No, I can't let you do this. It's too dangerous. Think about what just happened to that young man."

"I am thinking about Red! How do you think he's going to get better? You think he's going to just magically wake up? No. I've got to figure this out. The dark are planning something big." I snapped back to my vision and felt dirty, doomed. "If I don't do something now, we might all wind up like Red."

"No, no way," Bran growled. "You're not stepping foot back in that lab until we've outfitted it with new procedures. Full hazmat suits. A clean room. No risks. We don't know what happened to Red. From what Airmed said he might be suffering from something worse than the anti-serum now. Somehow, that anti-serum got through his glove, into his skin and now he's infected. It didn't go airborne, but it didn't need to be injected, either. I'm not going to take the chance that next time you are the one out cold on the floor. It's just. Not. Happening."

"I can't believe you!"

I stomped my foot, unable to help myself. I was trembling with anger. I knew it wasn't entirely his fault. He wasn't really being unreasonable. But I had just shaken hands with the dark side. I had just watched a friend succumb to the anti-serum and lose his light. I was not going to just sit around smiling while they asked me to do nothing.

"Siri, please. Just be patient. We'll have the lab in working order within a few days, it will-"

"Don't talk to me!" I screeched and walked away, storming past casual observers on the escalator.

Because it wasn't going to be okay. In a few days, I might be shaking hands with the devil. And there was no cure for that.

Chapter 14

I was still fuming in my room when the summons came. I'd snapped at Auroreis, ordering her from the room with no explanation. She'd looked crushed, and part of me had enjoyed that. At least someone had to listen to me. But mostly, it just made me feel worse. I had started running a bath when I heard a knock at my door.

"Enter," I called, expecting it to be one or both of my parents. Growing up, my mother and I had never been able to stay mad at each other for long. Whenever she had sent me to my room, she'd usually come in soon after to give me a hug and apologize, and then we'd work everything out with chocolate and a chick flick.

Instead, Barit Koelo walked in. The fit guard looked uneasy as he entered the room, like he didn't know what to expect. It didn't fit with his regular demeanor, which generally rang more surly surfer than anything else. The fit Guard was like a poster ad for multiculturalism, his warm mocha skin offset by almond shaped, moss green eyes and a curly blonde mop of hair.

"Did Bran send you?" I crossed my arms and leaned against the couch, not really interested in putting him at ease.

Never much of a talker, Barit grunted in annoyance. "Bran wants you in his office. A transmission has come through he thinks you'll want to hear."

My stomach dropped, and I hoped that we weren't already too late.

"Has something happened?"

"How would I know? I'm here collecting you. If you're ready?" Barit's frustration was rolling off of him in waves. I guess I wasn't the only one who was worried.

"Right, yeah, of course. Just let me turn off the water." I went through my bedroom to shut off the bath and rushed back to follow the Guard, who was already striding out into the hall. We climbed on the escalator and started to ride up in silence.

"So..." Barit started, shifting to look back at me. "I understand you guys had an accident at the lab?"

The regularly stoic Guard's question surprised me. He didn't usually bother talking to me, generally treating me like a kid beneath his notice.

"Yeah. Our assistant got infected. Risten Kyderis. Did you know him?"

"Thin guy, red hair? Yeah, I know him. He was a few years below me in school, friends with my sister. Nice kid."

"Yeah." Conversation dropped off. There just wasn't much to say. I didn't have any hope to give, and dwelling on Red's current state wasn't exactly inspiring.

Barit approached the doors to my father's Command offices. They were strangely unguarded for once. The golden doors gleamed, as always, a small engraved plus sign at their seamless juncture the only adornment. The Light Guard did not have to follow a strict set of laws or rules, it was simply expected to adhere to the ideals of equal justice, balance and harmony. Simple, right?

Barit passed his hand over the doors and they swished open soundlessly. Inside, the Command table was crowded, Guards sitting in every chair, and more leaning over the shoulders of the seated. Everyone was poring through maps and scrolls, conversing quietly. Dorian glowered at me, looking up from his chair, his face relaxing when Barit approached him, leaving me to survey the room.

My dad stood by the windows with Mireia in a heated conversation. He gestured back at their empty chairs, scowling. His eyes lighted on me, and his expression softened. Mine didn't. I marched up to them, crossing my arms defensively over my chest.

"Well? You wanted me?"

"It's happened."

Those two words made me forget I was mad at my father. They made me forget how sorry I was feeling for myself.

Time stopped, and suddenly I felt like I wasn't in my body anymore.

"Siri, breathe." Mireia placed her hands on my shoulders and looked into my eyes, her calmness flooding me, bringing me back into my core.

"What happened?" I asked, not really wanting to know.

"The town. The people. It happened just like you said it would. Everything was just as you described."

I looked up at my father, his cool silver eyes reflecting my own denial.

"But you said Flynn was there. They didn't find anything. I don't understand."

"Flynn and his team were in the area, they had all split up in different directions, trying to sniff out anything unusual. Alec says everyone on both teams is okay, no one was actually in the town when it happened, but all the inhabitants have been affected."

"Alec says? What do you mean? He's there?"

"Yes, we were just talking to him. I sent him there last night to help Flynn cover more ground. Right now, they are trying to figure out how the town was infected. It's not airborne, but somehow the Shades were able to hit everyone at once. Right now, we're trying to round up all the townspeople and keep them at a primary school. We need to send up a med team to quarantine the area. We're working on the arrangements now with some Light Guardians your mother knows, hoping to keep this off the human government radar if at all possible."

"I," I opened my mouth to speak, but I wasn't sure what to say, and closed it. What could I say? "What can I do?"

"I called you up here because I knew you would want to know. But I don't want you to do anything. I want you to stay here, at least until we know what our next move is. The lab will be ready for you and Airmed to get back to work in a couple days." He glared at Mireia. "That's where you're needed."

"I disagree," she said, shaping her lips into a grim line. "Your teams are turning up nothing on the ground. We need her up there. We need to know what she sees."

"And I told you," said Bran, his voice rising in anger, "that there's no way in hell I am going to send my

109

daughter up there into danger. We don't know where those damned Shades are hiding. We don't know what they are planning next. There are too many damn unknowns."

"And I told you," Mireia said, boldly stabbing my father in his rock hard chest with her finger, "that your daughter is not a child anymore and she can make her own decision. She deserves the right to see this through."

My father took a step toward her and I stepped forward hastily, wedging myself in between them to freeze my father with a glare.

"Whoa, whoa, back up there just a second. Instead of yelling at her, why don't you take a minute to calm down and try talking to me for once? Ask me what I want to do."

"I already know what you'll want to do," he scoffed. "And it's out of the question."

I rolled my eyes. "Really, Dad? Really? Because all I want to do right now is talk to Alec."

"I said no. I'm not letting you...Oh. You want to. Oh." He pushed his pale silvery blonde hair back with both hands, and took a deep breath. "Okay, yeah, alright, you can do that."

"Great. Thanks, Dad," I drawled. Parents. They thought they knew everything, but mine could barely keep it together in a crisis.

I stalked over to the table and peered at my father's water bowl. "So, um, how do we get him on the other end?"

"He said he was keeping the line open, so he should be nearby. Just hold the bowl and concentrate on who you want to talk to."

"Right, I remember." I put my hair up in a loose knot on top of my head and grasped the fine crystal bowl in both hands. I closed my eyes, thinking of Alec's brilliant green eyes, the way that fine purple ring would flare when he looked at me, the way he always seemed to drink me in like a glass of water in the desert heat. I imagined a bowl glowing, chiming on the other end, singing with my need to make a connection. Nothing.

I sighed, knowing he was busy, knowing the devastation that surrounded him in that small, sleepy town. I'd seen it before. I didn't need to see it again. My father didn't know it, but I had no desire to ever step foot in that town. I never wanted to be anywhere near it. Because if I was there, if my visions were true, then I wouldn't just visit the town. I would meet the Morrigan. Maybe not there. Maybe not right away. But I would meet him. And I feared what I might agree to if I did.

But now was not the time to think of the Morrigan, not unless I really wanted to conjure him up in the waters. That, I definitely didn't want to do.

I turned my mind back to Alec. I thought of him as I had met him on that first day, months ago at Vala's. The way he had leaned against her doorjamb, watching me with that insufferable grin on his face, his inky black hair looking effortlessly mussed, like he'd stepped straight out of a manga comic. The way his body had felt minutes later, after he'd nimbly flipped me to the ground and pinned me with his hips. He'd cocooned me with vines from the earth until I'd conceded defeat.

That day, I'd discovered two things.

One? The hottest guy I'd ever seen could spar better than I could. Two? Real magic existed, and I didn't just mean the fact that he could call plants up out of the earth to do his will. No, I meant magic like they talked about in Disney films, pull at your heart strings kind of magic, love

111

at first sight kind of magic. Because this guy? This guy made me want to climb up on furniture and sing at the top of my lungs. At least, when I wasn't itching to smack him.

And right on cue, just like that, his face shimmered into view.

"Alec? Oh my gods, you're there! Finally! I've been calling you forever."

"Yeah, I know, I'm sorry about that. I was checking out an apartment above the hardware shop, found a kid in there playing Minecraft on his tablet. I had to get Ambrose to take him to the school, find his parents. Not that the kid seemed to care at all. I swear, Siri, what they've done to these people, it's like rounding up sheep in a pen. They have no will of their own. It's like, whatever they were doing when the anti-serum hit, they're still doing it on autopilot. I don't know what would have happened if we hadn't been here. It's a miracle you had those visions."

"I wouldn't bet on it," I grumbled.

"What?"

"Nothing. Never mind. So, um, have you guys found anything else?" He must've had his bowl of water on the hood of a car, because I could see the blue sky up above, the corner of a building in the view, while Alec stood above peering down.

"No, nothing. At first we thought maybe they had sprayed over the town, but some people were inside when it happened, so that seems doubtful. We're thinking maybe they dosed the town's water supply, but that's a longshot. We really need that med team from Valhalla, soon. We've set up a couple roadblocks to town, but we can't keep this under wraps ourselves. Any news on that from Bran?"

"We're working on it," my dad said over my shoulder. "Several teams should be joining you over the next 12 hours."

"Okay, great, thanks Bran." Alec's eyes flicked back to mine. "How about you? Any headway on the vaccine yet?"

He'd tried to keep the hope out of his voice, but it was there. I felt terrible to be the one to squash it.

"No. Nothing. We had a really bad accident in the lab. We're going to take more precautions, but it means we can't get back to work for a few days."

"Oh," his face fell. "That sucks. Is everyone okay?"

"I'm alright, but this guy Red got infected." My voice caught, and I pushed through the pain. "He's in the sanatorium now."

"Oh. Wow, that's awful. I'm glad you are okay though. If you were hurt, I..." he glanced past me, and I glared at my Dad, making him give us some privacy. "Well, I think I'd go a little crazy, to be honest. I wouldn't be able to handle being here, knowing you were hurt." He smiled, trying to make light of it, "so stay safe down there, okay? We kind of need you to do that, you know? I need you to."

"Yeah, yeah, Heart of Life and all that. I know." I laughed, going along with his teasing. Clouds began to roll into view, shading Alec. "So is there anything else you can tell me about the town?"

"Not really. It's kind of a mystery. I mean, it looks like one minute everyone was fine and normal, and the next it's like a switch got flipped and turned everyone onto their 'zombie' setting. It's totally creepy, to be honest. I'd rather be fighting any day."

"Wish granted," I heard a cold voice say. A flash of light blinded me, illuminating the water like a nuclear glowstick just as a crack of thunder on Alec's end sounded.

113

It was loud enough to make ripples on the water and send a tremor through the table.

The glow receded, and all I could see were dark clouds through the water. Alec had disappeared from view.

"Alec!" I yelled, practically spilling the bowl as I leaned forward to try and get a better view. But water bowls weren't adjustable; they didn't come with remotes to shift the angle. You got one view, and you were stuck with it. No zooming. No panning.

I held onto the bowl for dear life, worry building inside until I thought I would burst, not daring to lose the connection. What the hell had happened? Where was he?

Then, a face rippled into view, and everything became clearer.

Deep blue eyes stared into mine. Once, I'd seen stars in those eyes, but now they held only the cold of a dead, barren space.

"Siri," Rowan greeted me vaguely, angling his head as if he was listening to someone in the distance. "Sorry, but no time to chat now. We'll take good care of your boy. Don't worry, you'll hear from us soon."

He cocked his head to the other side and made a strange motion with his hand. The water in my bowl froze in place, expanding so quickly that fissures cracked through the crystal. And with that, he was gone.

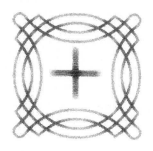

CHAPTER 15

The room went dead quiet. I let out a sob, and pushed the bowl away from me, the chill in my fingertips nothing compared to the cold dread that now filled my chest.

Condensation now turned to ice, the bowl slid easily across the table, coming to a dead stop in Dorian's hand. Silently, he picked it up and inspected the damage. All eyes were on him, on the bowl. Asking. Wondering.

"I've never seen anything like it," he said in a voice approaching awe.

His words broke the spell in the room and everyone leapt into action. My father started barking out orders. People rushed to get more bowls from a cabinet, filling them with water, trying to get in touch with the rest of the team members in Timber valley, any Guards that might be in nearby areas. Mireia hurried from the room to alert the council of this new development. People started arguing and whispering amongst themselves, afraid. Angry.

I just sat there, frozen.

Someone pulled out the chair next to me and I sensed rather than felt strong hands grip my seat, turning me roughly to face them. My knees bumped theirs, and I looked up into hooded hazel eyes.

"Are you okay?"

The shock of hearing those words come out of the mouth of Dorian Claffsson jolted me towards consciousness.

"Who did it?" he asked, gesturing toward the water bowl, thawing quickly in the warm Aeden air.

"Rowan Carey," I said, starting to shake. Get a grip on yourself, I thought angrily, and forced the tremors to stop. "A water fae."

"An incredibly strong one, by the looks of it," he scowled darkly, the expression somehow at odds with his fair coloring.

"I guess." I shrugged, not wanting to think about Rowan's growing skillset. Alec was gone. What would Rowan do to him?

"Is this the same Rowan you used to date?"

Normally, I would have expected the question to be laced with scorn, especially coming from Dorian, but there was no judgment there, only a question.

"Yes. He's Dark now."

"I kind of figured that out on my own, thanks. Do you know where he might take Ward?"

"I don't know, I mean, he works for the Morrigan now, apparently, so your guess is as good as mine. I don't think I know anything about him anymore."

"Okay." He said decisively, as if we'd figured out everything. As if we'd figured out anything.

I had nothing.

He grabbed me by the chin and looked at me, hard.

"Don't you go shutting down now. Ward needs you. We need you. You're the freakin' Heart of Life and we are going to figure this out. Together. As a team. Got it?"

I nodded, eyes wide.

"Good. Now keep it together. Be the feisty brat I've come to admire. No wimping out, okay?"

Tears pricked my eyes, not because I was hurt, but because I was surprised by the gruff kindness behind his angry words. I had underestimated Dorian Claffsson. It wasn't the first time I had done that with someone. Look at me and Rowan. But this time, I welcomed the surprise.

"Aw, crap. Don't do that. Can we get a tissue over here?" he called out over his shoulder.

I wiped my eyes quickly with the back of my hand. "No, no. I'm fine. Don't. Really." I waved away the woman approaching with tissue in hand. I swallowed, and looked around the room.

One by one, the field teams were responding. Within minutes, six water bowls glowed warmly on the table, while people talked into them with varying degrees of relief and severity. My father circled the room, listening to conversation, giving commands, moving teams around remotely like pawns on a board.

It was all a lot to take in, but I listened and was able to glean that no one else had been taken. The Shades had launched a covert attack on Alec, and left the new field base at the school alone, for now.

"They were probably just running recon," Dorian muttered, "and stumbled across your boy in a fit of luck."

The people closest to Alec had been searching several streets away when the attack came. They had seen a Humvee leaving the area, but beyond that, nothing. They hadn't even realized Alec was missing until we contacted them.

My father called Dorian over and linked him up with one of the bowls, where they started planning a new mission. Recon at the site first. Forensic searches. Finding Alec. I could only hear bits and pieces of the plans over the other conversations in the room, but I'd heard enough.

I pushed my chair back from the table and got up, walking over to stand behind Dorian. I placed my hand on his shoulder, like he was something I owned.

Dorian ignored me. They all did. At least, they did until I spoke.

"I'm going with him."

My father turned red, honestly, I could practically see the steam coming from his ears. "Like hell," he ground out.

I could see the toll those two words took on his patience. Two more might actually push him to full boil.

"I'm going."

The guy sitting next to Dorian took one look at my father's face and practically ran from the table. I smiled sweetly at my father and sat down.

"So, what's the plan?" I asked Dorian, not bothering to look at Bran.

Dorian smiled, the first true smile I'd ever seen on his face.

"We're going on a rescue mission, faeling, above and beyond." For once, I didn't want to bash him over the head for calling me faeling. In that instant, every bad feeling I'd

118

ever had for Dorian Claffsson fled my body and was replaced by pure kinship. I'd found a new friend. He was big, he was surly, and he was going to help me get my boy back.

"Perfect. I wasn't really in the mood for a solo mission, anyway."

My father threw up his hands in frustration, unwilling to take it any further in front of a crowd.

"Fine, but Dorian – you're in charge. She gets out of line, she's your responsibility."

"Yes, sir," Dorian agreed.

Bran could have ordered Dorian to leave me here. He could have commanded him to do pretty much anything he wanted. But my dad had gotten my hint. If they tried to leave me behind, I'd be on the first gravicycle out of town on my own.

I resisted the urge to do a fist pump in the air. Yeah, okay, I did a little one under the table. But no one saw. At least, that's what I thought until I looked at Dorian, who merely quirked one eyebrow at me. Some things would never change.

I raised an eyebrow at him return.

"So what's the plan, team leader?"

"Well, the town still needs extra security, and a med team. We haven't had any luck finding the Shades' bases over the last few months. Even the ones we had eyes and ears on have gone to ground. So I say we meet the med team in Timber Valley, and try to pick up the trail before it runs cold."

"Pick up the trail? How?"

"Well, part of the med team was going to include a forensics unit, so we could determine the method of

119

infection. We'll double that unit, make sure we have enough manpower to do a thorough search. We're trying to reach some Light fae your mom knows, too, a couple of elite hackers. They might be able to access some footage from the scene. Investigating the town will hopefully kill two birds with stone – give us a trace on Alec and bring us closer to a cure."

"There must be some Shades we can talk to, or follow. What about the ones at Trinity College? Cooper or Rowan's parents?"

"All gone. Everyone has cleared out of their homes without a trace. Honestly, it's been freaking us all out for weeks now."

"Then how is this the first I'm hearing about it?"

"Your father didn't want you to worry." At my protest, Dorian held up a hand. "I told him he should stop coddling you. You're not some delicate flower that needs protecting."

I snorted, and he grinned at me.

"But he wouldn't listen. Didn't tell Alec, either, or any of your friends. Knew they'd tell you first chance they got, or that you'd figure it out on your own. That darkling, Cooper? The one who helped you guys out? He's been staying with Vala for over a week, waiting for his own Choosing. Your Druid pal doesn't even know, Bran made Vala swear an oath to keep it to herself."

"That's impossible, Rose is there almost every day, unless she's boarding on the mountain."

"I heard the guy hides in a room upstairs when she visits." Dorian lifted one shoulder, looking like the idea was beyond him, too.

"Okay, so we've got no leads. Got it. Well, so when do we leave?"

Dorian started tapping his fingers on the table, like he was counting something out.

"Dorian?"

"Hold on, I'm thinking...The med team needs more time to get ready, we were talking about that before your boy called in. Our forensics team is always ready, I think they sleep with their gear, those guys are such tech nerds. That just leaves you, me, Barit. How soon can you be packed?"

"Me? I'm ready to go now."

Dorian laughed. "Yeah, okay faeling. As pure as you are, your sweat'll still stink after a day or two. Go pack a bag, keep it light but bring a couple changes of clothes. Layers, too. Montana isn't exactly steamy this time of year."

He shoved his chair back from the table and stretched.

"I've got some other business to attend to now. Bring your favorite weapons, and meet me on the gravicycle deck in three, no, make that four hours."

Before I could get a chance to thank him, Dorian was gone, walking away.

"Well, he's in a hurry," I muttered, getting ready to leave myself.

"Probably saying goodbye to his family. Dorian doesn't go above below very often anymore. Those trips are usually reserved for the childless, and the young." My father's voice sounded behind me and I turned.

"He's got kids?" I asked. Who would've thought?

"Twin boys. Born five years ago this month."

"Oh." I hadn't imagined Dorian as a family man. I hadn't imagined him as someone a person could actually love.

"He's a couple years older than Ewan. Old enough to be your father, too, I suppose."

"Ew. Dad!" No wonder he called me faeling all the time. I'd seen parents like him before. Once a parent always a parent. Change one diaper and suddenly the whole world was your child. But today, in the middle of all the horrible moments, I'd seen him laugh. Seen him smile. And I knew, just knew, that he was a good dad. Probably the kind that played with his kids every night when he got home. The kind that made silly animal noises and read them bedside stories. And now he was going above below, to face real danger.

I added Dorian to my ever-growing list of reasons why I had to stop Mikael Morrigan. My mom. Holly. Rowan. Alec. Dorian. Aeden. Humanity. Everyone would suffer if he got his way. Heart of Life or no, I'd be damned if I'd just sit back and watch it happen. It was time to rise up and meet his challenge head on. This time, I was going to take the fight to him. No more running. No more reacting, scrambling for solutions to problems the Morrigan caused. Screw that. It was time to take the fight to the Dark. Time to make them sweat.

"Siri? You alright?" My dad shook me, and I looked him in the eye with a smile I didn't feel.

"Yeah, Dad. I'm alright. Just going to go get packed up. Meet you back here in a few. And Dad?"

"Yes, Siri?"

"Thanks for not trying to hold me back." I leaned up and gave him a peck on the cheek, and he drew me into one of his great bear hugs.

"I just want you to be safe, you know," he whispered in my ear.

"I know, Dad. Believe me. I want that, too. But while the Morrigan is out there causing trouble, none of us are really safe. I have to do this. I need to."

"I know you do. You remind me a lot of myself at your age, you know that?"

"I do?"

"Yeah," he said, quirking up one corner of his mouth in a wry half-smile. "That's what makes me so nervous. Just...try to think before you act, okay? With the bond you and Alec have, I worry you might not think clearly out in the field if something happens."

"Something's already happened, Dad. Do I seem like I'm not thinking clearly?" I tried to make a joke out of his concern, but he took it as an invitation to examine me more closely.

"I don't know. Something's off with you, I can feel it. Is there something you're not telling me?"

I pushed all thoughts of my vision with the Morrigan out of my head and tried to plaster an angelic facade over my face.

"No Dad, of course not."

"Alright, I'm sure it's just my own nerves making me jumpy," he said, still watching me carefully. "But if you change your mind, if you need to talk, you know I'm here for you, right?"

"Yeah, Dad, I know," I played the teen card and gave him my best eye roll. "Now, can I go? I have to pack, and I should stop by Airmed's first, let her know what's happened."

"Yes, of course. But before you leave, I wanted to give you something." He pulled a small dagger from the belt at his hips and handed it to me. "My father gave me this the first time I went on a mission as a Guard. As of today, Siri, you are an official member of the Guard. That means you're not just my daughter along for the ride. You'll be a full member of the team. You've earned it."

"Thanks, Dad." I accepted the knife, looking at the jeweled sheath. It had a hook that allowed it to clip to a belt or a boot, and I knew it would slip perfectly in the cuff of my Doc boots. It looked old, expensive. I pulled out the dagger and saw it was lethally sharp and perfectly weighted for throwing. "It's beautiful."

"Well, don't get too excited. Dorian's still in charge of the team. Make sure you listen to what he has to say." He pulled me into another hug and mussed my hair. "Stay safe, kiddo."

"You, too, big guy."

I slipped out of his embrace and tucked the knife into the waist of my pants, giving one last wave before I left the room.

CHAPTER 16

I walked through the cala grass to Airmed's home with a heavy heart. Saying goodbye to Auroreis and my mother had been difficult. Both had been waiting in my room for me when I'd returned from the Command offices. My mother had been quiet, but the strength of her embrace had told me how reluctant she was to let me go. I was relieved when she didn't try to talk me out of it. When I said goodbye to Auroreis, I was struck by how the young girl no longer seemed like a child. This time, she didn't ask for candy and skinny jeans from Midgard when I returned. News of the Shades' latest misdeeds had spread like wildfire through Valhalla, and this time all she'd wanted was my safe return. There had been tears in her eyes as she'd zipped up my satchel, promising it would be waiting for me on the gravicycle deck.

I'd already changed into travel gear, my regular human uniform of skinny jeans and a tank top clinging to me in the sultry Aeden heat. Shoes, thankfully, could wait until it was time to go. No one wore them within the city confines, it wasn't good for the cala.

Airmed's home lay on the outskirts of the city. The houses here were made of the same golden alloy as the seven spires, but otherwise were as different as could be. Where the spires towered above everything, dwarfed only by the Tree of Life, the homes here were short, most only reaching one story, some two. Each was circular and domed, like an igloo, with round windows and arched doorways. They shimmered in the sunshine, adorning the landscape of blue grass and brilliant flowers like large dandelions in a summer meadow. Some of the homes, perhaps designed for larger or more important families, sported multiple interconnecting domes, reminding me of bubbles stuck on a wand.

The place I was going now had a single dome surrounded by multiple fountains and gardens, each host to a variety of flowers and herbs. This was where Airmed came when she was in Aeden. This was where the Nelumbo Lux had first sprouted, a once in a lifetime miracle of her healing gardens. I walked through the gardens, winding between the fountains and various focal points. There was no designated path – wherever the flower beds ended, cala grew, and cala was both grass for picnicking, path for walking and herb for healing in this realm.

I would have loved to stay longer. I had only been here a handful of times, and each time the gardens had yielded up some new discovery, some beautiful flower or healing gift, but today I had no time. I fought the urge to lie down in the grass and marched up Airmed's steps.

Before I could knock on the door, it opened. Mialloch gave me a half smile and invited me in silently. I walked in and he closed the door behind me, sighing as he swept a hand through his short brown hair. He'd shorn it off a few weeks ago, but hadn't gotten used to the new length yet. Frustrated, he dropped his hand back to his side, bracelets jangling.

"You heard?" I asked.

"I heard. I came here straight away to let my grandmother know about the town, and what happened to Alec. Are you okay?"

No, I thought. Definitely not okay. I took a deep breath and bolstered my brave face.

"I'm handling it. I just wanted to check in on Airmed before I leave. I'm going with Dorian's team to Timber Valley."

"Is that a good idea?" Leave it to careful Loch to point out the obvious flaw in my plan.

"Probably not," I shrugged. "But I'm going."

"I don't suppose there's room for one more on your team?" Loch's request surprised me, but it showed how far he and Alec had come in rekindling their friendship.

"I'd love to have you along, you know I would, but it's not up to me. And somehow, I don't think your family will allow it. It's just not safe. Bran only put me on Dorian's team because he knew I'd steal a gravicycle and go on my own."

His eyes grew wide in disbelief. "Would you really?"

"In a heartbeat. Which is about all the time I have before I have to go. Is your grandmother home?"

"Yes, of course. Forgive me." Mialloch's courtly manners kicked in and he ushered me through the house, back into the shaded conservatory where Airmed liked to spend most of her time.

Beneath a massive palm, Airmed was sitting in deep meditation. Mialloch cleared his throat, "Siri has come to say goodbye, grandmother."

Her eyes opened and shone with deep sadness.

"Siri, dear heart, come join me." She patted the patch of blue grass next to her. "You, too, Loch."

We sat with her and she clasped my hand in her own. "I am so, so sorry for what has happened. You must be experiencing the worst sort of pain right now. To lose a loved one to the dark...I know of no worse fate than that."

"He's not lost, yet."

She looked at me with pity clear on her face.

"Isn't he? Have I heard wrong then? Was he not taken by your darkling?"

"He... Well. Yes. He was. But I'm going to get him back. I'm not giving up. He wouldn't give up on me, and I'm not coming back until I've found him."

"And your parents approve of this course of action?" she asked doubtfully.

"Approve? No, of course not. My father is worried sick, and I haven't even left yet. But they know it's something I have to do."

"Hmm. Well, you are the Heart of Life. More than any other, you must remain open to following your path, for the sake of all of us. Just remember, your actions do not only affect you, but all of Aeden and Midgard combined."

"Gee, well, when you put it that way, no pressure." I rolled my eyes, trying to shrug off her concerns the way water rolls off a duck's back.

"Pressure can do marvelous things, like turn coal into diamonds. But it can also break a body. So heed my words youngling. Be careful. Be brave, but be wise." She eyed the marks of Tyr ringing my ankle pointedly. "One without the other leads only to folly."

"I'm trying my best."

128

"I know you are, sweet girl, I know you are." She gave my hand another squeeze and picked up Mialloch's hand on her other side. "Now, link hands," she instructed us.

"Before you go, I want to give you a gift. My grandson may not have the gift of healing, but he does have a certain way with patience and seeing clearly. It's part of the blessing of Air. Mialloch, I would like you to imagine that you are pouring this gift through your hands, through the circle, into Siri. I have a feeling she's going to need it. Meanwhile, I am going to focus on strengthening your aura. You've suffered a real shock, and it shows. Your energy levels are all over the place. You need to be in top form if you are going to face any Shades."

"What about me, what should I do?"

"You? You just sit there and open yourself up to our energies." I closed my eyes and tried to imagine myself as an empty cup, filling up with their gifts.

"That's it, she murmured. "Just relax, and receive. The heart isn't meant just for loving, but to be loved. The healer mustn't only heal, but be healed. If you don't allow yourself to receive, if you don't take time to nurture yourself, you will become empty and have nothing left to give."

"Is this part of your secret beauty routine?" I giggled, feeling lighter as their energy poured through the palms of their hands to wash over me like a healing balm.

"Hush, you. Perhaps someday I shall share my secrets with you, but today is not the day. But yes, self-nurturing is part of my regular practice. Now, be quiet and relax."

I giggled again, feeling giddy, and resolved to stay quiet. I put on a serious face and focused on sinking into the feelings. Fresh, vibrant energy creeped up the sides of my feet from the cala while warm feelings of comfort enveloped me on the right. The healing energy from

Airmed felt like a large, pink hug, washing away any unease I had been feeling. I doubt it was her intention, but the sensations were filling me with courage. On my left, cool energy flowed up my arm, chilling my hand, forcing my mind to slow, to take everything in, while my heartbeat slowed and steadied. I felt more assured of my course now than ever. Whatever came my way, I knew I could handle it. I just had to remember to assess, analyze and then act. That was Tyr-wise. That would assure my success.

Relaxed, assured, I felt myself slide deeper into myself, to a place beyond the sensations, beyond the energy that was swirling and merging within me, filling me up. For a moment, I had the presence of mind to realize that I was going deeper into a meditative state than ever before.

And then, I was gone.

Pure darkness subsumed me.

Yet, I wasn't lost. I felt at peace. Quiet. Complete.

I don't know how long I floated in nothingness. How long I was nothingness. But then, a light emerged from the dark, a tiny spark fathoms away. Growing brighter. Bigger. Closer. It came on fast. So fast, if I had been in my normal state of mind, I would have been worried. But I didn't have it in me to worry. I was nothing but peace. Nothing could hurt me.

The light slammed into me with the force of a thousand butterfly kisses, expanding my soul with the breath of every wind that had ever been and ever will be, illuminating my heart with a purity of being that would have brought tears to my eyes if I had any. It was the song of a million central suns at dawn. It was the song of love. It was life.

With that realization my soul began to condense, to coalesce, to pulse and to heat with that love, that life. So much so that it burned, a deep rich delicious heat that reminded me of cayenne and cocoa. I came together into a steaming mass, watching life expand outwards as if through my very will, my love of life creating more, and more. Forests sprang up below, villages and farms and waters and mountains. And the more I loved, the more the lands flourished. The beings who scampered below, they flourished as well, and the love I felt for them blended with the love I had for the lands and the trees and I scented coriander and pine on the wind and knew I had come home, home to the world that was mine and mine alone.

Without me, these lands would be dark and cold. But without them, I was nothing. We belonged to each other. They fueled me with love, and I fueled them with life-giving energy. It was a circle. It was whole. We were one.

I stayed like that a long time, basking in the circle of completion, the yin and yang of life and love.

Finally, I came to, someone's hand on my shoulder, shaking me gently.

"Siri. Siri. It's time to come back now. We're finished. Siri?"

I opened my eyes and looked at Airmed leaning towards me. I blinked. As at my Choosing, I could see her aura clearly. Beautifully.

"So bright," I whispered.

"What's that, dear?"

I shook my head, clearing my head. "Nothing, just, your aura, it's bright."

"I've pumped it up a lot, it helps me transfer energy to you."

131

I glanced at Mialloch. His was bright, too. Maybe even brighter.

"So is Mialloch's," I said.

"I didn't do anything special, other than what she told me to do," he said, looking perplexed.

"The place where I was, it was so dark. And then so bright. No. That's not right. I was bright. I was the sun."

"The sun?" Mialloch asked, looking at Airmed for answers.

"Anansanna?"

I nodded. "I think so. Yes. I was. It was...amazing. So much love. So much life. So much...everything."

"Connecting with Anansanna, what a gift. So you go to battle with three blessings, and not just two." She knelt forward and kissed me on my forehead. "But I fear you have spent too long here. You must go now. I do not have any more Nelumbo Lux, but I do have this." She pressed a tiny pot into my hand. "I have a feeling you might need it, for Alec."

"What is it?"

"Honey gleaned from the pollen of the Joseph's Coat climbing roses. It's a major energizer, and helps people heal from trauma and sadness and let in more light. If he's been affected by the anti-serum, it won't be enough to wake him, but if he's only been tortured-"

"I understand," I said, cutting her off. "Thank you. Hopefully, we won't need it."

"Yes, I'm sure you won't," she said with a smile that didn't reach her eyes. Before I could say anymore, she hugged me. "Stay safe, young one."

"You, too, Airmed. Will you be here when I return?"

"Yes, I imagine so. I fear the world above has become too dangerous, even for one living as a hermit. I'll stay here, and keep working on finding a cure."

"Thank you," I said. I released her and stood, extending a hand to Mialloch. I pulled him up and into a hug, burying my face in his chest for a moment. "Keep an eye on your grandmother, okay? Maybe you can help her in the lab. After all, you do have quite the mind for research. Maybe there's something in that big brain of yours that can help."

He laughed, his deep chuckle thrumming below my ear through his pecs. Working out with us every day had done Mialloch a world of good for his hunk factor.

"I promise, I'll do as much as I can. Or as much as she'll allow me."

"Same difference," Airmed said airily, waving his words away.

"You two are going to do great, I just know it. I bet you'll have that cure up and in replication by the time I get back." I winked at them, and headed out the door before my confidence could wane.

Because for all the beauty and splendor of the sun in my meditation, for all the warmth of my vision, I could feel a breath of darkness brushing up cold against my neck. The Dark was coming, and I wasn't sure I'd be able to fight it.

CHAPTER 17

Amber wasn't in her rooms. I didn't want to leave without saying goodbye, but I was even more reluctant to give Dorian a chance to leave without me. He'd given me a specific window of time to get ready, and I was pushing the limit.

Telling myself not to worry, I reasoned that a little run would be a good opportunity to let off some steam. I raced up the spiraling stairs of Tower Three, the escalators granting the illusion that I was a much faster runner than I really was.

Finally, I burst onto the Tower's gravicycle deck.

"I'm here!" I announced needlessly. Heads turned and someone snickered. Dorian held up his hand and the laughter cut off abruptly.

"Did you think we would leave without you?" he smirked.

"Well, yeah, actually. I kinda did."

"When I say something, I mean it. That includes agreeing to take you along on this mission. Don't make me regret my words, Ms. Le Fay."

"No! Um, of course not. I would never..."

"Aw, come on Dorkian, cut the girl some slack," a snarky voice said, punching his shoulder as they came around from behind him.

I would have known those pigtails and pearly pink platform boots anywhere. "Amber? I'm so glad you are here!"

"Did you really think you could shake me that easily? Your dad wasn't kidding about me being the only person he trusts to guard you day and night." She glanced meaningfully at Dorian and the other men on the team. "So, lucky you, you're stuck with me 24/7."

"Yeah, and that means I'm stuck with the lot of you." Dorian shook his head ruefully. "Well, looks like we're all here now. Siri, meet the rest of the team: Kye, Jonal and Mari. Everybody suit up and grab a cycle."

Mari I had met before, she was a gorgeous, impossibly thin woman with ebony skin and an emerald green Mohawk – rather hard to forget. Kye and Jonal looked like brothers with only a few years between them. Of course, being fae that could mean a decade or more in age difference. They both sported a careless California beach bum look that I was sure helped charm their way out of dangerous situations more often than not. Mari? She radiated appeal, but you could tell she'd rather slit someone's throat while they slept than bother wasting her charm on the enemy. She was a busy woman, and subterfuge wasn't worth her time.

I spotted my bag and shoes leaning against one of the cycles and rushed over to pull them on. Everyone else was already ready, and I hurried to get my laces tied.

Amber straddled the cycle next to mine and leaned down, whispering, "Relax, girl, you're the star of the show, no matter what Dorian says. No one's leaving you behind."

I took a deep breath and finished off my bows with double knots.

"Okay, ready." I said, straightening my pack across my shoulders and gripping the handles of the gravicycle.

"Okay, everyone. We're heading to the Ananzi portal. Stay in tight formation. I don't care how impenetrable everyone says Aeden is. Be ready for anything, anywhere, any time. Let's go."

Our cycles rose into the air and I leaned left to stick by Amber.

"Ananzi portal?"

"Yeah, it's the closest one to Montana that's accessible mid-winter. It comes out on Navajo lands in northern Arizona."

"Navajo lands? Not fae-owned?"

"Actually, there are plenty of fae in the tribe, though not many people know that. The families with fae blood have always worked with the elders to protect the portal. Still, these days we don't use it as much as some others, since it's gotten kind of touristy on the rez, but they know we're coming."

"Wow, cool." The rest of the team in front of us started picking up speed, so we both turned our attention to keeping up. The wind made it a little hard to have a good conversation, anyway.

Following the group, I started thinking about the last time I'd seen Arizona. Phoenix had been my home for a year before I'd arrived in Falls Depot, and I hadn't really been sorry to leave it. Sure, I'd had a few people I could call friends. But no one really close.

The city itself had been too far from good snowboarding for me to get excited about living there, although there had been some killer hiking trails nearby in the mountains.

I'd been to the area we were headed to now, just once. We'd gone on a class field trip to the Four Corners Monument marking where four states meet. I remembered that the entire area was surrounded by four massive tribal reservations –Hopi, Navajo, Ute and Zuni. I'd been overwhelmed by the beauty there. The trip had been a couple weeks before the end of school, a way to keep a bunch of juniors from getting deep into spring fever, a way to keep us out of trouble.

Perched on a rock overlooking the valley of sand and sagebrush, tears had streamed down my face without my even realizing it. Of course, the kids in class had just loved that. The day had earned me a new nickname, Sappy Siri, for the rest of the year.

Yeah, Phoenix had kind of sucked.

I decided to focus on better things. Like my gravicycle. The sleek golden machine purred between my legs as we flew over the fertile valleys below, and I needed to pay attention to where we were going. We'd flown south past the dunes of Zerssura, and then turned west where I'd never explored. The fields seemed to go on forever, interrupted only by the occasional farmstead or small village. Roads were few – most people either walked or road gravicycles, as far as I knew, and shipments of crops and goods were transported using bulkier, slower hovercraft or river ferries.

"How far are we flying?" I called to Dorian.

"About five more hours. We'll take a break when we get mid-way. If you need to stop before then, let me know."

Five more hours? I thought and groaned inwardly.

137

I checked my watch. We'd already been riding for almost an hour. The wind no longer felt quite so exhilarating. But, I suppose it was better than riding cooped up in a car. I reached into my jacket pocket and rummaged around for my headphones, carefully inserting them into my ears. I pulled out my phone and plugged them into the jack and selected a playlist of team spirit music, fight songs I'd picked out to keep me motivated when I was training.

I didn't really need motivation, of course, not with Alec missing. But as the classic strains of Queen's "We are the Champions" came on, I couldn't help feeling a little more optimistic. I would have been happier not to have to fight. For all my training in martial arts, I was definitely more of a defense girl, more of a lover than a fighter. But I wasn't sure how else to win a war.

How do you win a war without fighting? Somehow, I knew simple pacifism wouldn't get Alec out of the Shades' clutches. Not fighting would just leave the world at the mercy of Mikael Morrigan. But I felt like every time I pushed against him, every time I allowed myself to get angry, I just made him stronger.

There had to be a better way.

A simpler way.

If only I could see it.

I knew what Vala would say. That I just had to trust that everything would work out. That the path would become clear when it was time. But I was so, so sick of waiting. Since my Choosing, I'd practically been overflowing with energy and power, yet somehow I felt more powerless than ever before. Everything had gone wrong lately. So many people had suffered. The innocents of Timber Valley. Red. Alec.

I couldn't even think of Alec without fear and anger bubbling up.

Where was he now? Was he okay? Was he infected? Was he being tortured?

Mindwashed?

Pain lanced through me at the thought of him being converted to a Shade, the thing he hated most. I couldn't let that happen. I'd do anything to stop it.

I sucked in air, trying to clear the heaviness from my chest. The anxiety felt like a lump of granite crushing my ribs. I exhaled, and imagined I was a dragon breathing out fire, dissolving the stone and burning up all the toxic emotions festering inside me. Fresh air in, toxins out. It wasn't a real solution to all my problems, but for the moment, it was all I could do.

After a while, a cramp in my leg grabbed my attention and I realized that I'd been flying on autopilot for who knew how long. My butt was numb and my legs ached from remaining locked in place for so long. I double checked my safety harness and stood up, arching my back and wiggling my hips a little to get the blood flowing. Looking around, I saw Kye was leaning back, steering his cycle with his feet. Apparently, I wasn't the only one who'd grown weary of the long ride.

I looked below us and saw that we had entered a new landscape. Vast, jagged plateaus staggered above the canyons where ribbons of silvery Aeden streams shimmered. Waterfalls fed the streams. I thought of images I had seen of Victoria Falls, and didn't think it compared to this.

Large white shapes dotted the land here and there, contrasting sharply with the lush violet fields of grass. One of the animals spotted us and took off at a run, racing towards a cliff. I gasped, watching the animal race to its doom. It looked like a large horse, but bulkier. Surely it wouldn't really run off the edge?

At the last minute it gathered its legs beneath it and leapt. I cried out, and everyone in the group looked at me, worried. Unable to speak, I pointed to the horse below. But the horse wasn't dead. It wasn't falling. Impossibly, it had made the leap across the gorge to land on another plateau and was still running, herding a group of smaller white horses. The divide had to be at least 30 feet. Probably closer to 40. No horse could jump that. Could they?

Amber pulled her bike closer to mine.

"You okay?"

"Yeah, I thought that horse was going to die. Did you see that? That was crazy!"

I turned to look back at the herd of animals, and could have sworn I saw a glint of silver flash on the lead animal's forehead.

"What the-?"

Amber laughed.

"What, didn't you ever see a unicorn before?"

"Unicorn? Nice try, Amber."

"No, seriously. You want to take a closer look?"

I nodded, stunned.

"Hey Dorkian," Amber yelled. "How about that break, yeah?"

He turned around and rolled his eyes at her, but signaled to the others that it was time to stop.

We slowed the cycles and followed Amber who led us down to a lush field of wildflowers and boulders on a plain overlooking a pond-fed waterfall. Across a small crevasse, another herd was grazing.

"So unicorns, huh?"

"Yeah. Awesome, right?"

"Will they run away?" I asked, unbuckling the bike's safety harness from around my waist.

"Depends more on us than on them. But not usually, no. The people in this region have ridden and trained with them for as long as anyone knows. They're used to seeing people."

I looked at my watch and saw we'd been flying for close to three hours. Although my butt probably disagreed, I was glad we hadn't taken a break before.

I wouldn't have wanted to have missed this.

I stood up on shaky legs and did a few stretches. As feeling returned to my legs, I realized that my butt wasn't the only thing glad we'd taken a break. I looked around, spotted a small boulder twenty feet away, and hoofed it over there to use the facilities. I hadn't had anything to drink in hours, but my body still had needs. I peed quickly, unwilling to have anyone catch me squatting behind the rock, zipped up and came back around the boulder.

Suddenly I was eye to eye with a gorgeous white foal. I mean unicorn. Foalicorn? I'd have to ask Amber about that. Standing so close to the young animal I could see he was nothing like the horses I knew from above below. The foal's head was massive and boxy, strongly reminiscent of the face of a bull terrier – without the predatory canine teeth. I'd seen ancient horse fossils at the natural history museum in London when I was younger. This reminded me of those. Except unlike those small, miniature remains, this horse was clearly going to grow to become as large as a Clydesdale someday. Its frame was sturdy, but that wasn't the first thing you noticed.

I know, you'd think it was the horn, right? And, I mean, yeah – seeing a unicorn in real life was pretty amazing and its horn was impressive – about 8 inches long already, and made from a shimmery opalescent material. But no. What grabbed me was its eyes. Beyond huge, each oval eye was over four inches long and a startling shade of green. They appeared to be prismatic, like an insect's, so there was no central pupil to break up the glittering field of jade. I'd never seen anything them, and found myself lost in their depths.

"Hello," a quiet voice sounded in my head.

I looked around, and realized belatedly that the voice was coming from the unicorn.

"Hi," I smiled, putting out my hand for the foal to smell. It butted my hand, inviting me to pet its muzzle. "I've never met a unicorn before. You're beautiful," I thought.

"Thank you. We are fleet, and my name is Kaletka. You're the first person I've met, too. Have you come to select a foal for training?"

"No, no training. We're just resting on our way to help a friend above below."

"Above below?"

"You know, in the world above Aeden?"

"Ah. I have heard tales of another world with a yellow sun, but I have never seen it. No fleet has, not for hundreds of years. So, it is true then," the young unicorn mused.

"Fleet. You said that before. What is it?"

"That is what we call ourselves. What we are." He dipped his head and nuzzled my arm.

I stroked the soft fur along its neck, appreciating the way its white mane faded to deep black at the ends. "So, what sort of training do you do?"

"Each fleet is meant for one rider. That has always been our way. We live long, long lives, just as the fae. It is a good pairing. That is why we have always shunned humans – to bond with a human rider would mean bonding with one who would leave us too soon. The riders of Roumkivara have been training with us for as long as we have horse-stories to tell...But you are different, like one from the stories. Are you an Ancient one?"

"Me? Ancient?"

"Yes. You can speak with me. The others cannot anymore, not the way the Ancients are said to have. We can hear their thoughts, but they cannot hear ours, except perhaps sometimes the most rudimentary of communications. Feelings, sometimes. Words, no."

"Oh. Right. Yeah, not too many fae talk to animals anymore, I've heard that."

"But you can." He prodded me with his head, the words a statement more than a question.

"Yes."

"When you return, will you come see me again?" He pranced around me in circles, making me spin and giggle. "I think I would rather bond with you than one of the riders of Roumkivara."

"Really? You would? I've never been much of a rider."

"I would not let you fall. Together, we would be fleet. Fast. Awake." His prancing turned into a show of bucks and leaps. "Together, we would soar."

"Well, when you put it that way," I laughed. "I think I would love to come back and see you. But how will I find

143

you? And I might not make it back for a while. What if the riders come first?"

He snorted. "They will not be able to catch me unless I want them to. If you come looking for me, the others, they will let me know. Just come, and think of Kaletka, and I will find you."

"Okay, it's a deal."

"Siri! Break's almost over," Dorian yelled. "Stop petting the wildlife and come have something to eat before we hit the road."

"I gotta go," I apologized to Kaletka. "I'll come back as soon as I can."

"I know you will. We don't just read thoughts, we feel emotions, we fleet. I know you have things to do, worries to ease. But I will still be here when you have finished."

With that, the young stallion turned and galloped off, rejoining his herd. When he reached them they all began to run, thundering across the plain and leaping, one by one, across a wide crevasse to another mesa. It was as if gravity had no hold over them. They didn't stop running, crossing from plateau to plateau like so many stepping stones, until all we could see was a cloud of dust in the distance.

CHAPTER 18

After some ribbing from the others which I mostly ignored while I stuffed my face with dried veggie chips, we climbed on our gravicycles and rode into the sky. I didn't tell anyone about my conversation with Kaletka. My ability to talk with animals still wasn't something everyone knew about, and I wasn't really in the mood to add to my weird factor. After all the drama following my Choosing, I'd decided the particulars of my powers were a need to know detail – and no one needed to know. No new people, anyway. I was sure I would tell Amber all about it later. But for now, I sort of wanted to keep the magic of the day to myself. I felt like I'd been given a precious gift, and since the terrible events of the last two days, I really needed something positive to hold onto.

So instead of thinking about Red, or Alec, or Rowan, I focused all my attention on the wind streaming through my hair, imagining I was riding Kaletka across the plains. We leapt over waterfalls and followed the herd from mesa to mesa. I pretended that the rest of the gravicycles were riders on their fleet. We raced through fields and dodged trees under forest canopies.

We must have ridden for hours, but to me, on Kaletka, it seemed like minutes. Dorian held up his hand, signaling to the group that we would be descending, pointing to an overgrown glade of trees. We flew slowly beneath the wide trees, pale pink fronds of moss trailing from their limbs. We wound between the frothy ribbons, but every once in a while one would touch my cheek or brush my arm, reminding me of a cotton-candy kiss.

A dark rock cliff rose out of the jungle, not as tall as the trees, but still no less imposing. The cliff had been carved in relief to depict two huge figures with round eyes and snarling teeth. Between the figures a massive cave opening led into darkness. Cave dwellings had been dug into the rock face along the rest of the cliff.

This had clearly once been a busy portal, but now, it seemed so quiet.

"Does anyone still live here?" I asked Amber, who was riding near me.

"Yes, there are a few families who live here seasonally and help maintain the portal. I don't know if they're here now or not."

We drew closer and I saw signs of life – a rug hanging out to dry from one of the windows, a gravicycle sitting on the forest floor by the cliff. No one came out to greet us as we landed, so we focused on stretching our legs and taking a short break.

It seemed like I'd only just begun to get feeling back in my thighs when Dorian signaled it was time to move again. Grumbling as I packed my water back into my pack, I swung a reluctant leg back over the bike. I started up the gravicycle and followed the team as we flew under the watchful eyes of the giant statues, into the deep black.

Almost immediately the UV lights on our cycles switched on, and the tunnel lit up like the Milky Way on a clear night. This wasn't the tunnel near Montreal, and I saw no pretty pastel rocks glowing, only a million tiny shards of white light glimmering among the black. The effect was dazzling, and I almost missed the steep drop down into the depths as the cavern floor descended.

My keen earth vision quickly adjusted to the dim lighting, and soon I could see not only the glittering crystals but also the moist, murky tunnel walls. It was easy to keep up with the rest of the group, no matter how fast we zoomed. Like the tunnel from the Niflhelf mountain range that emerged in eastern Canada, this one seemed to plunge down into the earth below Aeden, twisting and turning time and again before it finally began to rise. Ascending upwards through the cool passageways, we flew toward the world of Midgard, into the land of humans above the fae realm below.

Never before had the words above below rung so true.

We must have descended, twisted, and climbed for close to three hours before slowing to land in a large underground hall. The ceiling was decorated with massive chunks of the same crystals, flawlessly depicting the fae creation myth of Earth and Aeden. In the middle, a huge seven-rayed sun symbol dominated the tableau.

Kya saw me staring up and paused as he walked by.

"It's supposed to represent the world tree creating the sun. They're linked, just like we're linked to them."

"Why seven rays? I don't think I've ever seen this sun symbol before."

"Actually, you see this same symbol throughout Africa. And seven pointed stars have always been associated with the fae. Most humans now think it's because we're lucky or because we came from the Pleiades, the group of seven stars, but really it has more to do with the seven towers in

Valhalla, how they worked with the tree to make Anansanna."

Dorian told us to keep moving, and Kya walked away. The art was amazing. I followed reluctantly, hoping that one day I would be able to return and examine it more carefully.

We had parked alongside a couple hundred other gravicycles, their sheer number making it clear that this portal saw a lot more traffic than the one I was used to.

Everyone on the team turned on their flashlights, although I left mine off, preferring to test out my enhanced night vision. Several smaller tunnels branched off from the cave and I only had a moment to wonder where they led before we started walking. The team was silent, no big surprise with Dorian as leader, and I felt an awkward need to break the silence. Amber, however, was up ahead trailing Dorian, so I held my peace.

We walked a long way up the steep incline of the tunnel before I finally felt the tell-tale warmth of the underground barrier. Designed to keep uninvited guests out of Aeden, the barrier would knock out anyone who wasn't Light fae if they tried to cross it.

Humans would see the barrier as an impassable wall of stone. Dark fae would see the entrance, but they wouldn't be able to breach it without experiencing a whole lot of pain and passing out. For Light fae, it was just a little uncomfortable, a bit of heat and a weird squeezing sensation, coupled with an unpleasant sense of foreboding for the uninitiated. This was my first time crossing a barrier since my Choosing, and I found it easier than ever before, the slightest breath of warmth washing over me.

The climb became more gradual, and the cool air began to warm. Almost imperceptibly at first, but soon I was removing my jacket, starting to sweat from the exertion coupled with the slightly warmer temperature. Before long, I could see a bit of light up ahead.

It didn't look like the end of a tunnel. It couldn't be, because the light moved. It swayed and bobbed as we approached, until I saw that the light was a lantern, hanging from the hand of a giant man as he walked towards us.

Dorian laughed and embraced the guy, clapping him on the shoulder. "Tiny! It's good to see you."

"And you, Dorian."

"Tiny?" I whispered behind my hand in Amber's ear. "Looks pretty freaking huge to me."

She choked back a laugh as Dorian turned to introduce his friend to the group.

"This is Taini, that's spelled T-a-i-n-i, in case anyone was wondering," he said looking pointedly at me. Right, so Dorian had super hearing. Good to know. That must have sucked for his kids. "Taini is a Navajo trail guide, and one of us."

"I've got a car ready for your group, we just have to navigate the tourists – Keet Seel is pretty swamped today."

His black eyes glittered in the torchlight like the sea at night. Dorian finished introducing us all and we began walking again.

"So, um, Taini-not-Tiny," I began, scrambling up next to him. "Does your name mean something? Other than not small?"

He grunted, though whether in amusement or annoyance I couldn't tell. "New Moon."

"Oh, because of your eyes?" I asked.

149

"No."

I waited for him to explain, but he didn't. Okay then. So much for making friends. I stayed beside him, quiet now. The walls of the tunnel no longer glittered and had taken on a lighter, grittier appearance. We walked through another barrier, this one even gentler than the first. So gentle, in fact, that I wondered if I'd imagined it, but then we emerged into a small square-cut room that had been hewn from stone, the citrine glow of daylight clearly illuminating the space. We walked through another door into a larger room that boasted rough shelves and benches dug into the walls, and then out into the harsh light of day. Looking down from a significant height, I could see water-starved pines dotting the valley before us.

"Oh wow. Are we in the Anasazi ruins?!"

Taini looked at me strangely, like he couldn't figure out if I was joking or not, but he didn't answer.

"I told you we were coming out through the Ananzi Portal," Amber rolled her eyes, smirking at me like I was an idiot.

"Um, totally not the same thing. How was I supposed to know what you meant?"

"Well, here we are. Unfortunately, kiddo, we have no time to waste." Dorian stared descending through the ruins and the rest of us followed. We hiked through the valley to reach a dusty pickup nearby. Dorian climbed in front with Taini, while Amber, Mari and I squeezed onto the rear bench seat. Once Kye and Jonal had settled down into the truck bed in back, Taini started the engine and we set off on a bumpy ride on a dirt track through the park.

Resuming our earlier conversation, I spoke to Amber in a low voice. "Okay, so give. What's up with the Ananzi portal – were the Anasazi all fae, or what?"

"Yeah, they were. Most of them abandoned their villages when the split between the Light and Dark happened. Most fae aren't into fighting, you know? So, a lot of the villagers moved down into Aeden. In fact, a lot of their descendants live in Roumkivara and some of the other nearby settlements."

"And the rest?"

"The rest stayed above below, becoming Guardians, like your mom. The ones who stayed behind never went too far, though, joining other local tribes like the Hopi and Navajo."

Taini spoke up, and I had to strain to hear his deep voice over the rumble of the truck.

"Anasazi is usually translated by white people as "enemy ancestor", but really it is a Navajo word that means the old bones of an alien ancestor. The secret is hidden right there in the word. The funny thing is, the word itself came from the name Ananzi, who was an elder of the village of Keet Seel, the one who decided it was time for our people to retreat below. His daughter stayed behind with her husband and family, along with others, to guard the portal from above."

"I didn't know that," said Amber.

Taini's mouth twitched, as if he imagined there was a lot she didn't know. He flicked his eyes to look at me in the rearview mirror before returning his attention to the road and continuing.

"Ananzi was a great traveler before he moved the people down below, and often visited other realms using the portals. That is how he knew it was time, that the sickness of the Dark was spreading throughout the fae, and that it was no longer safe here. You know, many people think that the Anasazi left because the desert went dry, but actually it was the other way around. When the

151

people were here, the water flowed and the earth gave abundant crops. Ananzi knew how to bring out the best in the land and in people – in fact, there are stories about him in other continents, stories about how he helped tribes come together and taught people how to farm."

"Wow, that's so cool. What other places did he travel?"

"He's really well known in Africa. There, Ananse is a son of the creator god, of the Sun, which of course is a reference to Aeden. But you can find other stories everywhere, if you know where to look."

I'd always been drawn to science, but hearing more about the links between fae history and human mythologies, I started to wonder if maybe anthropology wouldn't be a better way to spend my time in school. Assuming I ever made it to college.

Taini turned to Dorian. "Are you sure you guys want to leave right away? I know you said you're in a hurry, but some people are coming over later for a potluck. You all could rest up and stay over, leave at first light."

"That'd be great, but I think we should travel as far as we can before night falls. We still have a long way to go."

Taini shrugged, accepting Dorian's refusal and said he'd make up some sandwiches for us to eat on the road. Just thinking about food made my stomach growl, and I realized it was probably already past dinnertime in Valhalla. A peek at my watch confirmed it – it was almost midnight. Of course, here the sun was just starting to consider setting in the winter sky. I glanced at the clock on the dash and reset my watch to match the local time of 4:37pm.

When we got to his house, a large adobe structure on an isolated stretch of land, Taini was true to his word. While the rest of us made use of the facilities and packed our meagre belongings into a roomy Dodge Durango,

Taini filled up a cooler with enough sandwiches for several meals.

It was the last homemade food I would eat for days.

CHAPTER 19

After stopping at a motel in the mountains to catch up on our sleep, we'd driven for sixteen hours straight to Montana. Dorian, the brothers and I had taken driving in shifts. Mari and Amber didn't have licenses, so they had taken the roles of navigator and DJ, respectively. Most of us were happy with Amber's club-style musical choices, although Dorian was less than enthused. I assumed he would have preferred some traditional Viking dirges, or perhaps just some good old-fashioned rock.

It was well past sunset when we finally rolled into Timber Valley. Military-style roadblocks were already in place, forcing me to stop before actually entering the main part of town. I could just barely make out the quintessentially quaint white steeple of a church in the distance as I rolled down my window.

"This town is on lockdown, miss. Gas leak. You'll have to turn around."

I wasn't sure how to gain access – was this guy really US military? How much did he know? Was there some kind of a special handshake?

"We're with forensics," I said. The guy just looked at me doubtfully, shining his flashlight over my obviously teenage face and peered into the car. Behind me, I heard another window roll down, and turned around to watch Dorian pass his wallet to the sentry.

"Let us through."

"Yes, sir, Colonel Claffson." Feet snapped together and the guard waved us through with a salute.

"You're in the army?" I asked, glancing in the mirror.

"Marine Reserves."

"Ah." That explained a lot. I guess I shouldn't have been surprised, after all Bran had been with British Special Forces when he first met my mom. I supposed it was just another way for the Guards to stay connected with what the Dark were up to. "Do all Guards join the military at some point?"

"No," he said tersely.

"Okay then," I muttered under my breath and returned my attention to the road ahead. I knew we weren't the first team there, after all Alec's team was still in place, and I knew other operatives had been pulled in from nearby. Still, I hadn't been expecting everything to be so well contained and organized.

Several mobile trailers had been set up alongside the town green, and one of those ominous giant hazmat domes they liked to show in movies when there was some kind of outbreak. Huge freestanding halogen lamps were set up all along the streets, illuminating every corner while people walked around doing their jobs. Some people seemed to be collecting forensic evidence, scraping surfaces for samples and collecting fingerprints off cars and doors. Others were busy cleaning up the mess and devastation the Shades had left in their wake, hooking up blackened vehicles to tow trucks.

Dorian leaned into the front seat and signaled for me to park over near the dome. I pulled into an open spot and turned off the car, sitting for a moment before getting out. As much as I wanted to stretch my legs and start doing something useful, part of me was afraid to move. What would I find when I went in that dome?

I eyed the glowing structure with distrust.

"You coming?" Amber stuck her head back in the car. The rest of the team was already walking away.

"Yeah, I'm coming." I scrambled out of the car and cracked my neck a few times as I raised my arms over my head to loosen up the muscles.

"You an X-files fan?" Amber asked me with a grin, raising her eyebrows at me as she bounced up and down on the balls of her feet, walking backwards and leading the way.

"Not really." My mom had loved the sci-fi drama, but it had always been too creepy for me.

"Too bad. Today would have been your lucky day."

"Yeah. Maybe give me touch of the plague and it'll be a damn holiday."

"Oooh, touchy! Alright, Serious. Let's see what's down the rabbit hole, shall we?" She breezed past a couple of guards and opened the air-locked doors to the dome. When we walked in, a hiss of air washed over us, the smell of ozone and disinfectant filled the vestibule, and then an LED sign came on over the next set of doors saying, "Safe Entry."

No, that wasn't creepy at all.

Even Amber looked a bit subdued, shrugging at me as we walked inside. I didn't really see the point of being sterilized, anyway, since nothing could neutralize the anti-serum. But hey, it was nice that they were trying to keep up appearances.

The dome was bigger on the inside than I had anticipated. Most of the vast, empty space was lined with rows of cots for the town's afflicted. Along one side of the wall there were tables set up to make space for a makeshift kitchen. By the doors, where we were, examination rooms were curtained off and doctors walked to and fro with electronic tablets in hand. Next to the clinic, there was an area cordoned off with heavy duty clear plastic sheeting – a hazmat lab, by the looks of the masked suits inside.

"It's too quiet," Amber murmured.

"What?"

"It's too quiet," she repeated, narrowing her eyes. "Everyone is so calm. This isn't normal."

She waved her hand towards the cots and I realized what she meant. Children were sitting quietly next to their parents, staring straight ahead. Some people were lying down, but they didn't appear to be sleeping. No one was talking. No one was crying. Kids weren't playing or running around. No one looked concerned, or confused or afraid. It was the antithesis of every aid center I'd ever seen on the news.

And it definitely wasn't normal.

I saw Kye wave to us from across the room, beckoning us to the mess area.

"We're being summoned," I said.

"We're what? Oh, right." Amber grabbed my arm and led me over to the tables through the cots. A woman sitting on one bed caught my eye. She was small, elderly and utterly familiar. She should have been – I'd seen her in my vision.

I pulled my arm out of Amber's and knelt down in front of the woman. Her hands were clasped lightly on her knees while she stared blankly at the ground before her. I place one of my hands on hers.

"Hello."

"Hello," she looked up and gave me a small smile, but the light did not reach her eyes.

"Do you remember me?" I asked.

"No, should I?"

"No. I guess not. Do you know why you are here? Do you remember what happened to you?"

"I was taking an evening stroll," she said simply, like a child.

"Yes, and then what happened?"

"And then...I was taking my evening stroll. I so love taking a stroll. Don't you?"

"Yes. I love to walk."

"Shall we go for a walk now?"

"Oh. Um, no, I think right now it's best if you stay here."

"Alright. I do so love to stroll. Perhaps we can walk together later."

"Yes, perhaps we can." I chewed on my lip, remembering my vision. She had been the one human I'd seen walking around in the chaos. Maybe that meant she had seen the first team arrive? Seen Rowan and Mikael?

"I'm actually looking for some friends. A blonde boy, bright blue eyes, spiky hair? And a taller guy, black hair, green eyes? Have you seen them?"

"Siri, you really think this woman knows something?" Amber protested. "Dorian's coming over, you better hurry."

I ignored Amber and stared at the woman, willing her to answer as I repeated, "Have you?"

"Seen them? I did see some boys, yes."

"Where?"

"You're hurting my hands." She said it calmly, not acting like she was in any pain, but when I looked down I could see my knuckles were white, my fingers were wrapped around hers so tightly. I forced myself to relax and moved to sit next to her.

"You were saying? The boys you saw?

"By the old waterworks building. I was walking. It's so nice to walk, don't you think?"

Out of the corner of my eye I saw Dorian approach our little group.

"Yes, yes it is. I'll come back and take you on a walk soon, okay?"

"That would be lovely." She sighed, and looked back at the floor, retreating back into herself. It was like talking to a robot in a sci-fi movie, just before they powered down.

Beyond creepy.

"You know you can't take her anywhere, right?" Dorian's voice cut in roughly.

"Calm down," Amber said. "She's a harmless little old lady. What's wrong with humoring her?"

159

"Until we know exactly how the infection was spread through the town so quickly, we don't know what's dangerous and what's not. Don't forget who's in charge of this mission, Slaight." He turned on his heels and stalked off with a jerk of his head, clearly expecting us to follow him

"Sir, yes, sir." She mock-saluted him sarcastically behind his back.

I bit back a giggle and followed.

By the tables, Jonal handed us lukewarm bowls of soup and bread. We ate standing up, listening while another fae continued talking, catching us up on the situation. Unfortunately, as far as I could tell, they had no new leads.

No one knew how the anti-serum had been delivered. They were still waiting on lab analyses to be certain. Crop dusters and water contaminants were everyone's best guesses, but those delivery systems wouldn't have resulted in a 100% infection rate. No. Something else was going on here. But what?

The woman had said she had seen boys by the waterworks. Maybe it had been through the water after all? But then how had people on well systems been affected? There were too many loose ends to tie up, and not enough explanations.

I didn't have the patience for this. I liked science, sure, but I wasn't a scientist. I didn't want to sit around conjecturing while Alec was out there, lost to Shades.

"Where the hell is Flynn?" The words were out of my mouth before I had a chance to stop them.

Dorian glared at me for interrupting, and the scientist blanched.

"Sorry, rude, I know. But as long as it's out there – have you seen Flynn Ward?"

The man stammered, and I realized that just the name of my boyfriend's dad scared him. "N-n-no. I haven't seen him. His team has been out securing the perimeter since before I got here. I hear they've brought in a few prisoners, though."

My heart leapt. "Here?"

"No, of course not. One of the mobile units outside. They're using it as a temporary holding cell."

That was all I needed to hear. I was halfway to the exit before he finished his sentence.

Chapter 20

They weren't there.

Oh, there were Shades in the holding cell, alright. But no one that mattered. Not Rowan. Not Mikael. No one I wanted, needed, to talk to.

When I'd left the dome, Amber stuck to me like glue, catching up with me just outside the dome and shadowing me step-by-step.

A couple fae had stood guard outside the makeshift jail, barring entry until I mentioned I was on Claffson's team. I'd probably get in trouble later for using his name, but I wasn't worried about the future. Only one directive spoke to me at the moment. Find Alec. I couldn't stop the anti-serum today, I couldn't even think about it. Without Alec, the world would be a dark place, with or without a Shade invasion.

Inside the mobile unit, there were fourteen small cells, each one barely large enough for a narrow cot and small toilet. Most of them were occupied. I walked up and down the narrow hallway, eyeing each prisoner. They all had thin silver bands around their necks, but other than that they were unrestrained.

"Do we need to worry about their powers?" I whispered to Amber.

"No, they are wearing some of the finest fae/Druid tech Valhalla has to offer. Think of it as a mobile warding system. If they even think about using their abilities, the ward comes up all around them."

"But what does that do?" I asked, picking up a spare collar from a table, examining the harmless looking tech. The band was smooth and flexible, something you could wear out like jewelry and not be noticed.

"You know how the tunnel barriers can drop a Shade?"

"Yeah?" I looked at prisoners as I got what she was saying. "Oh, wow. It drops them right there? On the spot?"

"Yep. Awesome, right?"

"Come 'ere and let me put the collar on you, girlie. Betcha wouldn't think it was so awesome then." A rough looking man sneered at Amber, his fingers opened and closing like so many gnarled claws.

"You could try," she answered blithely and gave him a wide smile. "But then I'd have to kill you."

I slipped the band into my pocket. It seemed like something that should be standard issue these days for mission operatives. Who knew when it might come in handy?

I stalked up and down the hall again, inspecting each Shade more carefully. A girl who looked deceptively young wearing ripped tights, combat boots and a private school uniform, complete with the requisite tiny plaid skirt. A sinister looking skinhead. A pale guy in a suit. Several of your typical Shade thugs. Another woman dressed in black from head to toe, her dark skin and hair making her practically invisible in the shadowed corner of her cell. Another skinhead, this one with a mass of tattoos

163

around his skull and neck. A devilishly handsome rogue, dressed identically to the woman in black – that one gave me a stunning smile, as if he thought we could be best friends.

I stopped and stared at him. "Does that actually work for you?"

"Usually, yeah. Wanna let me out? Maybe take a walk?" He raised his eyebrows invitingly, making me snort in surprise.

"Not really, no."

"Carter, will you never learn?" The woman in black sighed from her cot, speaking with an upper crust London accent. "Your powers don't work anymore, remember?"

"You wound me, sweetheart." Carter placed both hands over his heart as if he'd been struck. I couldn't tell if his gentle southern twang was genuine, or an accent he put on for effect. "Are you trying to say that my handsome face and devil-may-care attitude ain't enough to win a woman over?"

"Not this one, sorry," I laughed, and walked on. Next to Carter, I saw another woman, but this one struck a chord. "I know you."

The woman looked up, glowering at me through a curtain of red hair.

"You're that woman from the portal in Canada. Gina, was it?"

"Giselle," she ground out, flipping her hair back over her shoulder. "And you are the girls who killed my friends."

"Actually, I think it was my boyfriend who did that. We just kicked your ass." Behind me, I heard Carter snicker. I guess I wasn't the only one who disliked Red. "But that does bring up my next point. How are you not dead?"

We had run into Giselle and her team of thugs in the woods at the caves near Montreal. Amber and I had fought them well, especially considering it had been two against five. But it had been Alec who'd finished them off, throwing knives with lethal accuracy and taking them all out in seconds. At least, I'd thought he had finished them off. Apparently, Red had survived.

"Back-up was already on the way. They found me and were able to repair the damage your boy did." She pulled down her shirt, proudly showing me a nasty scar right over her heart. It looked like the sutures had been made in the dark, on a bumpy road, by a child. "They stitched me up in the helicopter back to HQ."

"I can tell."

She sniffed. Apparently that wasn't the reaction she was hoping for.

"Well, enough pleasantries," I said, dusting off my hands and spinning to walk back up the aisle. "I'm looking for a friend. I think some of you might know him. Blonde. Handsome. Anger management issues?"

The young girl in the first cell snorted behind my back and I turned.

"Ah, so you've met?"

"As if I would tell you," she glared. Thick eyeliner rimmed her eyes.

"You know you lost one of your eyelashes, right?" Amber grinned and leaned towards the bars, pointing to the girl's right eye. The girl narrowed her eyes at Amber while reaching up to feel her lashes. She peeled off the lone lashes from her left lid and tossed it on the floor.

"Whatever." She crossed her arms.

"Who wears fake lashes on assignment, anyway?" I asked, truly mystified.

"Hey now, a girl's gotta look good, am I right?" Amber chided me and turned back to the girl. "I feel your pain."

The girl looked away.

"No, really, I feel it. And you know what? It's not half as bad as it's going to get if you don't tell my girl Siri here what she wants to know."

The girl looked away and maintained her silence.

Okay then. So much for idle threats.

"Look, your boss, he wants to talk to me, right?" I went back to walking up and down the aisle, looking at each Shade in turn. "Well, I want to talk to him, too. But the only one of you I'll trust is Rowan. Tell me where he is, and I will turn myself in."

"Siri," Amber warned.

"Stay out of this Amber," I shushed her. "So, I'll ask again. Where. Is. Rowan?"

No one spoke.

Then, the door opened and Jonal walked in.

"Dorian sent me to check up on you two. He wants you back in the dome, like, yesterday."

I protested, but Jonal just stared at me. Who knew a surfer could be so intimidating.

I started walking out, when Carter laughed. "I can't believe Rowan ever thought about joining you softies. He's totally in his element now."

"Bite me," I said and stormed out, leaving Jonal with the prisoners.

I was so frustrated. How the heck was I going to find Alec now? Jonal had totally interrupted my game. Not that I'd seemed to be getting anywhere, but who know what would have happened if he hadn't butted in.

"So, are we heading back to Dorkian or what?" Amber jogged down the steps of the mobile unit and stood next to me.

"No...Maybe? I don't know!" I threw my hands up and started pacing on the sidewalk. "Freakin' Rowan. I can't believe he's really working with those people. Can you believe it? I mean, that southern idiot actually said Rowan is in his element. In his element! Like he's some happy, fulfilled person now. Can you imagine?"

"Well, no. Not really. But don't you think-"

"Right, exactly. No way is he happy. He's angry and in pain, but he's hardly in his-" I halted in my tracks.

"Hold on," I said, pulling my phone out of my hoodie, "I know where we need to go."

Maybe the old lady had just been babbling. But that guy Carter had mentioned Rowan being in his element. And Rowan's element was water. I googled a map of the town on my phone and grabbed Amber's hand, pulling her along with me as I walked.

"What's the map for?"

"I think we should check out that waterworks building after all." I showed her the map on my phone. "It's just a few blocks away, on the outskirts of the center of town."

"Why now?"

"That old lady said she saw some boys go in there. What if she saw Rowan and Alec? What if they're hiding him in there?"

She scrunched up her face in thought. "I guess. But what if she just saw some of our guys scouting the area? I mean, someone that old, everybody looks like a boy, right? Plus, she's not exactly all there, if you know what I mean."

"I know. But that guy mentioned Rowan, and his element. That's water. Maybe he wanted me to figure it out."

"Sure, and maybe it's all just a trap. I mean, why else would he have told you where to go?"

I stopped to consider her words and stared at the sky, looking for answers. A sign. Something. "But he didn't, not really. I mean, if it was a trap, wouldn't he have just told me exactly where to go."

"I guess," she said, twirling one long pigtail around her finger, thinking. "Or, maybe he just wanted you to not think it was a trap."

"True...But I saw her in my vision, you know."

"Who? The old lady?"

"Yeah. She was out for a walk, just as out of it as she is now. What if I saw her because I was supposed to talk to her? What if she's the key to finding Alec?"

"I still think it's a longshot. But if a longshot's all we have, then I'm in. Lead the way, girlfriend."

I took one last look at the map, memorizing it, and put my phone back in my pocket.

"You think Dorian's going to kill us for not following orders?"

"If the Shades don't, definitely." She smirked.

168

"Awesome. Come on, let's run." I picked up the pace and we jogged down the road. Despite everything, a glimmer of hope unfurled in my chest and I couldn't help smiling as I watched our reflections sprint by the gloomy windows of the Cuppa Café.

The blocks weren't big, and before long we had reached a large brick building built alongside a reservoir. Aged bronze letters adorned the façade above the second story – Timber Valley Public Waterworks.

There weren't any cars parked outside the building, but that didn't mean the place was empty. Dimmed fluorescent lights shone through the high transom windows, giving the place an eerie, almost haunted look. I hoped the place worked on an automated system, because right now everyone in town seemed to be completely incapacitated. The town had enough problems – a lack of running water really didn't need to be added to the list.

"What now? Do we just go inside?" I asked Amber.

"Isn't that what you wanted?"

"Well, yeah. I just wasn't sure if we should scout the perimeter or whatever. They always seem to do that in movies."

"Nah. I much prefer going in blind."

"Really?"

"No. But I don't see anyone here. And the windows are too tall for us to look in. Come on, let's go around the side and see if we can sneak in unannounced."

We left the front door behind and crept into the shadows along the side of the building. Sure enough, there was an entrance. I reach for the door to open it, but Amber held me back, peering along its seams.

169

"You always gotta check for alarms, first."

"And?"

"I don't see any." She gave the door a gentle tug. "Locked."

"Great, now what do we do?"

"Don't worry, youngling, a Guard's training isn't all just fun and combat." She reached down into her boot and pulled out a small case, opening it to reveal several thin silver instruments.

"Lock picks? Seriously? That is so cool."

"It's only cool if I can do it. Give me a minute." She inserted two of the tools and started to finesse the tumblers into place, chewing on her bottom lip while she worked. "Almost...Got it!"

She gave the handle a twist and opened the door with a triumphant grin. "That's actually the first time I've gotten to do that outside of class. So glad it actually worked!"

She held up her hand and I happily gave her a high five.

"You did awesome!" We turned and peered into the darkened stairwell. The exit sign over our heads cast a disturbing red glow over the walls. My voice dropped to a whisper of its own accord. "Okay, what do you think, up or down?"

"What, you don't want to split up?" Amber whispered back sarcastically.

"Thanks, but no. I've seen too many horror movies to know how that ends."

"Like I'd leave you alone, ever. Your dad would have my hide. Come on, let's start in the basement – that's where the rats usually hide."

"And the serial killers. Don't forget them."

"Thanks for the reminder." She rolled her eyes at me and began creeping down the stairs. For all her talk about monsters, I knew Amber wasn't really afraid. She lived for this kind of thing.

I wish I could have said the same.

Every step down towards the basement level made my insides churn with fear. I couldn't help thinking that this was a really, really bad idea. Dorian would have a fit if he knew what we were up to.

Yet somehow, I couldn't make myself reach out and stop her.

I had to know if my friends were down these stairs.

There could be no turning back.

I followed Amber, step by step, into the gloom below.

CHAPTER 21

I watched with baited breath as Amber checked the seams around the door at the bottom of the stairs and turned the handle. No alarms sounded, and we stepped into the basement. The air was markedly cooler here, damp and tinged with the scent of chlorine. A mop and bucket stood nearby, and I imagined that they had to wipe everything down regularly to keep mold from forming in the dankness.

Fluorescent spotlights lit up the corridor, even with the main overhead lights out. Pipes ran everywhere, moist with condensation. Water dripping into puddles echoed loudly through the concrete space, making me flinch. Amber put a finger to her lips, and began creeping through the maze of pipes and tanks. Every so often, one of the tubes would groan or gurgle. My stomach in knots, I padded silently behind her, trying not to jump at every little noise.

And then I heard it.

The feeble groan that wasn't a pipe. More of a whimper than anything else. The sound of person in pain and afraid. And giving themselves up to it.

Eyes wide, I clamped my hand on Amber's shoulder. She nodded and pointed to where the sound had come from. We continued creeping, a little more slowly now. While Amber scouted ahead, I kept an eye behind us and watched every shadow, making sure no one surprised us.

I really, really, did not want to be surprised.

Finally, we arrived at a large tank. The sound came again, this time barely more than a whisper of agony.

I dared a glance around the side of the tank and saw Rowan, meditating or sleeping with his eyes closed, his back against a pipe. He looked completely at peace.

Alec lay behind him, unconscious on the cold floor several feet away. No. Not unconscious. Dreaming. His hair was tangled, damp with sweat, his face glistening as if with fever.

Amber motioned for me to stay where I was, while she circled around to Alec. I shook my head. I wanted to be the one to go to Alec. Amber silently insisted I stay and stalked off soundlessly before I could protest.

I waited. And waited. Every little sound in the waterworks haunted me, made my heart leap into my throat. I reached down into my boot and drew out the jeweled knife from my father, just in case. Finally, I saw Amber reach Alec safely. She was just reaching out to touch him when Rowan's eyes flew open and a pulse of blue light flashed out from him, knocking Amber and I both off our feet.

"Hello, ladies," Rowan mocked, staying seated on the floor. "So nice of you to finally join me. I was wondering how long I was going to have to sit here. Honestly, Siri, it's not nice to keep your friends waiting."

"Told you it was a trap." Amber said, her eyes glinting as she pushed off from the ground into a round of graceful lasair cartwheels, aiming a kick toward Rowan's head.

Before she could connect, he flicked his hand and a wave of water came up between them, turning to ice as Amber's foot made contact. Her foot shattered the ice instead of Rowan's head, and he made his hand into a fist and gestured toward the ground. Suddenly, Amber dropped to the floor, crying in agony before she passed out.

I ran towards them, halting when he raised his hand to stop me.

"What did you do?" I cried out angrily, gripping my knife tightly.

"Poor Siri. All alone. You know, I can sense what you're feeling. All those fears you have. All your nightmares. I can practically taste them churning around inside of you. Did you forget how sick I make you feel? You should have listened to those butterflies in your stomach, Siri. You should have known I was here. You should have had a better plan." He stood up to face me. "But, as it is, here we are. Now, drop the knife."

I did as he asked, sending the weapon clattering to the floor.

"You knew we were here?"

"Of course. Kick the knife over here. Good girl." He stepped on the blade, as if it might run away on its own. "I am a water fae, stronger than any in my family before me. I could sense you before you even came in the building, your fear was so strong. Really, you should learn to control those emotions of yours. Someday, they're going to get you into trouble."

"What have you done to my friends?" I demanded.

"Them? Nothing much. Just amplified a few of my favorite feelings. Fear. Despair. Kick them up a few notches and a person's worst nightmares will start playing over and over in their head, making it impossible to stay aware of their true surroundings. Pretty cool, huh?"

"Cool? Really, Rowan? Who are you? What the hell happened to the guy I loved, the guy who went out of his way to help people, to make people feel safe and comfortable? The one who greeted customers with a smile, the person who saved me?"

His smile faltered, and for a second I glimpsed the boy I'd fallen for in Falls Depot. And then his face hardened back into a mask of hate.

"You should know. You're the one who killed him. That weak boy died the day the same day as my sister."

"The Shades caused our car to crash, not me. Holly didn't blame me. How can you? I feel so sorry for you, Rowan. You have this amazing gift, and you could use it to make people feel great, to make people happy. You could help so many people. Instead, you do this." I looked away, unable to bear looking at him anymore. My heart felt like it was breaking into a million pieces. "Please. Don't. Let us go. Let our friends go."

Deviant laughter bubbled up behind me, rasping and breaking through the pipeworks like a rusty saw.

"Why, Siri, you simple, sweet girl. Your friends are of no consequence. It isn't up to Rowan to save them. It's up to you."

"You." My fear fled the room, replaced by anger.

"Who else?" The Morrigan clasped his hands behind him as he stepped into view. "Now, it seems to me, that we are in a unique position to help each other."

"As if I would ever help you," I growled.

175

"Siri, Siri, Siri. Don't you want to help your friends?" He signaled to Rowan, who flicked his hand. Alec and Amber both began to writhe, moaning in fear. I tensed and scowled at Mikael.

"What do you want?"

"The same thing I've always wanted, dear girl. You are the key to perfecting my beautiful anti-serum. Of course, I would prefer it if a girl with your talents would join the Dark, but really, just a few minutes of your time is all I need. If you prefer to link your fate to that of the Light, so be it."

"I'm not like you. I'm a healer, not a killer. I'm not doing it. No way."

I stepped forward, ready to launch myself at Rowan and his fists flew open. Alec's eyes rolled back in his head, glowing an ungodly shade of yellow and he arched off the floor, screaming.

"No!" I ran to Alec, cradling his head in my hands. The moment I touched him I was assaulted with pure terror. I could literally feel his soul shredding apart in agony.

"He's only got moments left. Rowan is a rare talent, and he's been practicing for weeks. Think carefully, Siri."

I could feel it. Mikael was telling the truth. Alec was losing everything he loved, everything he was. Rowan was literally destroying him from the inside out. Soon, he'd be nothing but a shell, and the man I loved would be gone.

"Come on, we haven't got all day," Rowan snapped.

Next to me, Amber's eyes flew open, crying out as Rowan targeted her, too. I reached out for her, trying to lend some comfort while I kept one hand on Alec. Instantly, I was assaulted by more pain and suffering than I would have ever thought possible.

I had to stop it. Through the haze of pain, I could barely think. I knew I couldn't sacrifice the world for Alec and Amber. I knew it was selfish. My mind struggled to reach for a solution, and suddenly in the turmoil a pulse washed through my body. My ankle throbbed, and the feeling pushed everything else away. I could breathe again. I remembered my feeling that only love could save us from the Dark, that the only way out of this would be not to fight. Not to hate. Not to be like them. It would take an immense amount of faith and bravery. Could I do it without Alec, without Amber? I wasn't sure.

As terrible as it was, I would have to believe that fate had a plan for me, and follow love.

"I'll do it."

Instantly, my friends' eyes closed and their bodies relaxed. Amber sighed and practically looked blissful.

"Wonderful. I am so glad you saw the light. Pun intended. Rowan will keep an eye on your friends. Come here, girl."

"What do I have to do?"

"It's actually quite simple. All I need is a drop of your blood, and a little of your power."

"My blood?"

"Yes, the Heart of Life isn't just a quaint fairy tale. The Heart is a person who holds the original DNA that was needed to jumpstart the terraforming process of Aeden. You are a perfect union of bloodlines, an exact recreation of the Red Queen, the original Heart of Life, the Ancient fae who saved the fae race and designed our ship. You hold the key to creating all life, and the key to altering it. Or ending it."

"Ending it?" I drew back in horror.

"Yes, your blood sings to the sun itself. If you wanted to, I suspect you could destroy Anansanna. But, even I don't wish to end the world. Where would be the fun in that? No. All I want are a few simple tweaks to the system. The humans have had their fun. Look what they have done to the world. And you! No one's raised a finger to stop them. The humans piss wherever they want, and the Light stays safe and golden down in Aeden. It's disgusting. It's time for someone to take control of the situation and bring the humans to heel."

"Let me guess, that person is you?"

"Why not? I've worked hard to get where I am today. I'm not so bad. The world will thank me in the end. You'll see. Or, maybe not, since you'll be sleeping your life away with the rest of your friends. But, I promise, I will keep Rowan away from your dreams, so at least you will all be at peace."

"What if I stop you?"

"You can try, dear Heart, you can try," he laughed.

"Before I do this, answer one more question so I can understand. How have you been making the anti-serum? How does it work?"

Mikael lit up like a little kid about to show off his Pokémon collection.

"Ah, now that was a truly ingenious idea from one of my colleagues. Her daughter exhibited minimal abilities after her Choosing, but was able to connect with all the elements. We combined her blood with some of the Darkest Druid magic, and inoculated a virulent human strain of Mono, one of the Epstein-Barr viruses. Did you know that all Epstein-Barr viruses are actually triggered by a Light deficiency in humans? That's why vitamin D deficiency presents as a risk factor. It was all quite simple really, a matter of timing and opportunity. It was almost

178

as if nature herself was handing us the solution to the pandemic of humanity."

"But how did you deliver it to a whole town at once? And if you can do that, why even bother with me?"

"We had to deliver the anti-serum slowly, tainting food and water supplies throughout the town, which changes how the virus behaves. When it isn't injected, the anti-serum requires something to trigger it – it took our labs months solve that part of the equation. Finally, we hit upon just the right frequency of EMF waves. One pulse, and a whole town can be brought to its knees in moments. Still, it's not a reliable system. Too many people in too many countries are off grid." He looked at me with a manic light in his eyes. "We need you Siri. Only you can make this a global phenomenon."

"Great," I muttered under my breath. "So how come it doesn't affect you? Aren't you worried this plan might backfire on you and your people?"

"Oh, no." He laughed. "We've taken care of that. Technology really has come so far. Another of our branches has been working on perfecting nanotech implants for the pharmaceutical sector. Of course, our initial idea was to create tech that would seem to be helping humans, making us rich, while in fact it was slowly killing them off one by one. But the human immune system is actually remarkably resistant to nanotech. So we started experimenting on ourselves. Soon, we realized that the nanotech could restore our lifespans to that of our Ancestors. And then, we realized it could be used to destroy the anti-serum in our body even as it spreads."

"Really? I thought maybe it was just because you had no light left in you to destroy." I didn't bother keeping the disgust out of my voice.

"No, sorry Siri. We couldn't exist without the light, much as I hate to admit it. We don't thrive in it the way you do, we gather our strength from the Dark, but still, it's there. No. All we need to stay immune is a simple implant in the hand."

"How very biblical of you."

"Yes, isn't it? I do so enjoy a small dose of irony now and then. Now, enough of this talk. Are you ready to help me?"

My mind raced, but I couldn't see any other way. I had to trust that I would eventually figure out a way to stop him. The solution would come. Right now, all I could do was say yes.

"I'll do it."

"Give me your hand."

I glanced at Rowan, who was standing over Alec, smirking at me. The stars in his eyes had gone dim. I steeled myself and held out my hand. The prick on my finger came sure and swift.

It surprised me. I had been sure someone like Mikael would pull out an archaic Bronze Age blade to slice across my palm. But no. A simple pin prick and he was squeezing a drop of my blood into a glass vial, quickly capping it and giving it a shake.

"That's it?" I couldn't believe it had been so simple.

"Not quite. Place your hands over mine." He held the vial in his open palm. How hard would it be to smash it, I wondered?

But I knew it would only buy me a moment, not a lifetime. Not a world of lives. If I didn't help him, Mikael would find another way. It was better to know what we were up against, than battle the unknown.

"Channel your healing energy into the vial. Awaken the virus. Love it, breathe life into it. Nurture it like a child."

He sounded reverent, loving even. It made me sick. I fought to choke back the bile in my throat and called up my healing powers. It was so easy now, so effortless. I wondered if I had been this strong when Holly was fading, would I have been able to heal her?

A useless question. I couldn't turn back the clock.

I tried to see the vial as something I would want to heal, and remembered Miko, so small, so sweet, dying in my hands before I saved him that first time. My power flared and pulsed. My hands twitched, and slowly the vial changed from clear to pink, starting to emit its own glow.

"Thank you. It's done." Mikael snapped the vial into a case and put it inside his coat pocket before I could blink. "Rowan, release the Guards."

"But-"

"We made a deal. Do it. Your time will come, I have no doubt."

Rowan sighed and stepped away from Amber and Alec. Right away, color began to come back into their cheeks and their breathing eased.

"They should wake up in a few minutes," Mikael said as Rowan grabbed his hand and they both disappeared from sight. "Enjoy your time together, while it lasts."

Laughter echoed off the walls at the far side of the basement. I would never find them now. With Rowan's masking ability, they'd be long gone before I could rally the troops.

Alec moaned, and I knelt beside my friends, considering their prone forms. In a few minutes, if Mikael had been telling the truth, they would open their eyes.

How would I ever explain what I had done?

CHAPTER 22

Alec opened his eyes first. His pupils were dilated and violet eclipsed emerald green. He blinked.

"Siri? Is this...Are you real?"

"Yes, of course. I'm right here, Alec." I caressed his face staring into his eyes. "You're okay."

I really, really hoped that was true. I could feel the confusion emanating from him. Relief and disbelief, warring against each other.

"You were dreaming. Rowan took you, used his powers to keep you in a dream state."

"Those were dreams?" He struggled to sit up and I gave him a hand. He pulled me into a fierce hug, burying his face in my hair. "It felt more like a nightmare."

"Yeah, well, Rowan isn't exactly into the warm and fuzzy feelings these days," I laughed weakly, trying to joke.

"Rowan," Alec growled. "I'm going to kill that kid."

"Let's worry about him later, okay? A lot's happened since you went missing."

"Where are we, anyway?" He looked around the room, running a hand through his damp hair.

"The waterworks building in Timber Valley."

"How long was I out? How did you find me?"

"I–" What could I say? "I'll explain everything, I promise. But right now, I just want to–"

Someone tapped me on the shoulder and I jumped.

"You guys going to sit there all day, or you gonna help me up?"

"Oh my gods, Amber!" I turned and helped her into a sitting position. "How do you feel?"

"Crappy. Your ex really packs a wallop with his powers." She shook her head as if to clear it. "Those were some really crap visions he socked me with – every bad thing I've ever imagined came to life and happened, over and over, like a bad movie on a loop. Ugh. Talk about a hangover. My head is killing me."

"Me, too," Alec said ruefully. "But you're okay?"

They both looked at me.

"Yeah, um, I'm fine. I convinced him to let you guys go."

"Just like that?"

"Um. No. We need to talk. But let's get you guys somewhere more comfortable first, okay?"

I looked away, afraid they'd see the truth in my eyes. I had no idea how I was going to explain any of it, never mind what I was supposed to do next. Just how did one eighteen year-old save the whole world? Some kind of play-book really would have come in handy right about now.

I stood up and gave them both a hand. I leaned down and picked up my knife, slipping it back into my boot. Alec stumbled and I wrapped his arm around me, propping him up as we walked.

"You've been out for two days. I think it's taken a lot out of you." As we walked, I tried to channel some healing energy into him, but it was like filling an ocean with a teaspoon. I knew he needed more than I could give. It wasn't physical damage he was suffering from. There was a sadness and hole inside of him, eating away at his emotional well-being that my healing couldn't touch.

Amber seemed okay. She walked in front of us, holding the door for us and then scouting ahead for danger. I had a feeling there wasn't any. Mikael had no reason to stick around now.

"What is it you're not telling us," Alec whispered in my ear as we slowly climbed the stairs. "Something bad happened, I can feel it. You're afraid."

"It doesn't matter. Don't worry about it."

"Siri." He stopped. "What did you do?"

I looked up the stairs. Amber was already outside. Waiting for us. It was just me, and Alec.

"I did what the Morrigan wanted. I altered the anti-serum."

"What?! Why? How? What the hell were you thinking?"

I cringed internally, but held my ground. "I did what I had to do. They were going to kill you both. I couldn't let that happen."

"But now we're all going to die anyway. Or sleep forever, which is basically just as bad. You've doomed us all."

"No. We'll figure it out. I needed to buy us some time. And I know how the Shades are staying immune. We're going to stop them, I just need time."

"How, Siri, how are we going to stop them? I just spent days dreaming about you dying. Now I'm awake and you tell me it's all going to come true? Maybe you should have just let me die."

"Don't you dare say that to me!" I stabbed him in the chest with my finger. "I saved your life. We are going to figure this out, I promise. But I can't be the Heart of Life without you. I just can't." Angry tears welled in my eyes and he folded me into his arms.

"Dammit, Siri. I'm sorry. But I just don't know about all this." His deep voice rumbled through his chest against mine as he spoke. "No one knows if the Heart of Life wins or not, Siri. The song says 'to save or shade Aeden and begin again.' What if the new beginning is a world ruled by the Shades?"

"No, I won't believe that. I'm not going to succumb to fear and doubt. We are going to get through this, I swear. I just...I know it."

I looked up into his eyes, searching for understanding, and I found it. Relieved, I leaned up and kissed him, a gentle reminder of how much I loved him. The surge was weak, dampened by the damage he'd sustained.

I remembered the remedy that Airmed had given me and dug through my pockets. Yes, the little honey pot was still there. I brought it out and uncorked it, its sweet aroma tickling my nose. I dipped a finger inside and held it out for Alec to taste.

"Here, have some of this."

"What is it?" he asked, and sucked it off my finger before I could reply.

For a moment, I had trouble thinking.

"Oh! Ah, it's honey."

"Obviously," he grinned, a gleam in his eye. Already, a bit of color was returning to his cheeks.

"From Airmed, it's honey from a special rose. She gave it to me, in case you'd been tortured."

"Mmm, well, it tastes wonderful. Not sure it's going to make me feel okay about what's gone down, but I certainly do feel a bit better. Can I have some more?"

I looked in the tiny pot and thought about it. "We should give some to Amber first. You can have whatever's left after she gets a dose. She wasn't under as long as you, but..." I trailed off, remembering her screams.

"I get it," Alec said, squeezing my hand. "Come on, let's go. She must be wondering what we're doing in here."

"Probably thinks we've been making out."

"Mmm. Well, let's not prove her wrong then, eh?" He pressed me back against the wall and gave me a kiss that made me go weak in the knees. This time, the surge was strong. Filled with passion, love, and confidence. There was some fear there, like he was trying to prove with one kiss that everything was going to be okay, but mostly there was just love.

"Stop testing me, and kiss me back," he murmured, nibbling along my jaw.

I hadn't even realized I'd been doing that. I stopped worrying about how Alec was feeling, and poured all my heart into that kiss. I thought about how relieved I was that he was in my arms again. How much stronger I was with his love filling me up. I remembered that feeling from Tyr's mark, the bravery that had filled me before, and

187

channeled it to him. We were going to be okay. There simply wasn't any other option.

Finally, we broke apart.

"Amber. Honey." I said, feeling exhilarated and short of breath.

He laughed, giving me one last peck on the forehead, and took my hand to walk up the final steps.

Outside, I gave Amber the honey and watched her skin warm up under the street lights.

"So, you going to tell us what happened down there?" She asked, handing the pot back to me. I gave the small jar to Alec and launched into blow-by-blow explanation of what had happened.

This time, no one interrupted me, even though it was a pretty long story. I didn't leave anything out. Amber and Alec looked at each other excitedly when I got to the part about the nanotech – I didn't think that Mikael had planned to give me that bit of information. He was probably regretting it already. But, who knew if we could replicate the tech before he launched the anti-serum.

"So, it's airborne?" Amber looked at me. I could tell she was hoping I'd say no.

"Yes. The next time they infect someone, the anti-serum will spread like wildfire. It'll be a global pandemic. No one will be immune, unless they are chipped."

"You mean marked by the Devil," Alec muttered.

"Yeah, pretty much," I agreed.

"Okay, so maybe they still have to chip some of their people. Maybe we have time," Amber said with forced cheer.

"Maybe. I sure as hell hope so."

"How quickly does it affect fae?"

"If it's like the original anti-serum, it takes a couple hours."

"That's not a lot of time. We've got to get as many people as we can underground before the Dark launch their attack."

"What if people are infected? What if they bring it down with them?" I asked.

"I don't know. I mean, it takes a pretty long time just to get through the tunnels." Alec shrugged.

Amber snorted. "Great, so we'd have infected fae dropping from the sky on their gravicycles, or crashing in the tunnels. "Thanks, but no thanks."

"I don't know. Can the Druids help us alter the barriers so that no infected can get through?"

"Maybe. But that's a lot of magic to mobilize on short notice."

"Okay, what if we told everyone to wait by the barriers for four hours before passing through?"

"That could work."

"Alright. So we have a plan." I clapped triumphantly and forced a smile.

"We need to let everyone know. We've got to tell Bran. There's no time to waste."

On the walk back to the village center, I pulled out my phone and called Rose. We needed Druid magic on our side, and Rose and Vala were my first choices.

"Hello?" Her groggy voice reminded me that we were in a totally different time zone, and it was the middle of the night in Vermont.

"Rose, it's Siri. I'm sorry to wake you, I totally forgot how late it is there. Listen, the anti-serum has evolved, it's gone airborne. The Morrigan hasn't released it yet, but I don't think there is much time."

"What? Oh my gods! That's terrible. What are we going to do?"

"We need to get as many fae as possible down below, but we can't let in the infected, or else we'll never have a chance at reversing the effects. We need to strengthen the portal barriers to keep out the infected, and to do that we need Druids. Lots of Druids."

"We'll be glad to help...but Siri, we can't come with you. We can't pass through the portals."

"I know. But you'll be okay. I'm going to find a way to stop it, I swear I will. As long as I'm uninfected, you know I won't stop looking for a cure. We need your help, Rose."

"Okay. Okay. Where are you? How soon can you get here?"

"We're in Montana. We'll need to catch a charter out to Bennington, so probably not until tomorrow morning."

"Okay, fly in to William Morse Airport. It's a tiny strip but it's the closest place to land. Oh, get this – I just found out Cooper's been staying at Vala's for over a week, since Rowan told his family he might Choose the Light. It's winter break here, and he told them all he was going skiing with friends, but really he's been hiding out. His Choosing is tomorrow. A team was coming to pick him up and bring him to Aeden, since his family is probably going crazy now that he didn't show up at home for the ceremony. If you guys are coming, should we tell the other team not to come? Or do you want the extra backup?"

"Hold on, let me see what the others think."

190

I told Alec and Amber what was going on, and they both agreed we should keep as many teams in Aeden as possible.

"We'll be there soon. Tell the others to stay in Aeden. If you can, go to Vala's now."

I heard Rose blow out a shaky breath. "Alright. I'll contact Bran when I get to Vala's, and I'll see you soon. And Siri?"

"Yeah?"

"Stay safe."

"You, too, Rose. You, too."

CHAPTER 23

"I ought to throw you in jail along with the rest of the Shades." Dorian was fuming. I'd left out a lot of details from my story, but he'd heard enough to know one thing.

I had voluntarily used my own blood and magic to transform the anti-serum into an airborne virus.

"What you've done, it's treason! It's a crime against all of Aeden, not to mention humanity. What were you thinking?"

I didn't have a chance to answer. I didn't even bother trying. Dorian had been ranting at me, pacing back and forth, for a good ten minutes. Everyone had left the room, even Alec. It was just me and Dorian.

"Were you even thinking at all? Were you?"

He stopped pacing and lasered me with his eyes.

"Well?"

"Oh! Oh, you want me to talk. Sorry, I just, I mean, well, you've been...Never mind. What was the question?"

"What. Were. You. Thinking?"

Somehow, I knew the words "saving my friends" better not come out of my mouth. No. Dorian was only about duty and service. Not friends. Not family. Nothing came before the safety of Aeden.

"I was thinking that I'm the Heart of Life, and there has to be a way out of this. I thought Choosing the Light would make everything better. I thought that then the Morrigan would leave me alone. I was wrong. Tonight, I saw that he will never stop. There's no point in fighting him."

"No point in fighting him?" Dorian ran a hand over his face in dismay. "Please tell me you are joking. A good soldier never gives up the fight. Never. A Guard always stands and fights."

"But I'm not a real Light Guard, or a soldier. I can fight, but I'm a healer. I like seeing how things work together. And I learned something this year. Fear and anger are toxic. They compromise every decision we make. I see it in Rowan. I see it in the Morrigan. I've seen it in Flynn, and Alec. I even see it in you. If we keep fighting, we're going to become just like them. We're going to become Dark."

"How dare you speak like that to me? What do you know? You've never fought in a war. Sometimes, you have to fight fire with fire."

"Really? Are you sure about that? Because I think when you do, you lose part of what you're trying to save."

Dorian opened his mouth and I held up my palm. "Don't you dare say the words collateral damage, because I might just have to punch you if you do."

"I thought you said you're not a fighter," he scoffed.

"Yeah, well, sue me. I'm still a growing girl. Sometimes I get temperamental."

"Fine. Look, you can't just give in and give up and hope that everything is going to work out okay. War doesn't work like that."

"Maybe not. But maybe peace does. Has it ever occurred to you that the reason we're still at war with the Dark is that we're still fighting?"

"No." He put his hands down on the table across from me and leaned forward. "Please, enlighten me. Tell me how I've gotten it wrong all these years. Tell me, so I can tell your father and the Council."

I swallowed.

"Look, this is how I see it. Whatever you push against, pushes back. When I was living in Phoenix, one of my Native American friends told me a story he'd heard from his grandfather. He said we all have two wolves living inside us. One good, one evil. One made of pure hate and fear. The other, made of love and kindness. They are always at war with each other. And it's up to us which one wins. Do you know which one always wins?"

"Let me guess, love?" he said sarcastically.

"No. Not love. Whichever one we feed. If we keep feeding the evil wolf with hate and fear, it gets bigger. Stronger. The only way to make sure it loses is to starve it, and feed the other wolf. You have to feed the love. Otherwise it dies."

"And this is supposed to help us win a war? Seriously?"

"I think it is. I'm called the Heart of Life, Dorian. Do you really think I'm supposed to go around being angry or afraid?"

He didn't answer, just stared at me stonily.

"Well, I don't. Frankly, I'm tired of being afraid. I'm tired of worrying. It's time for me to stop feeding the bad wolf. And it's scary as heck, and I'm not sure I'm doing the right thing, or even what the right thing is, but I'm trying my best, okay? I have to trust that I'm doing the right thing. I can't move forward any other way."

"Fine. Let's just assume for the moment that you did the right thing." He raised a finger as I started to smile. "I'm not saying that, but let's just assume you did. Now what? What do you want me to do?"

"Well, we did come up with a plan, of sorts, to keep as many fae safe as possible. We need to call all Light fae in – everybody needs to go down below. I've already put out the word to the two Druids I know, and they are gathering more Druids to help bolster the barriers in the tunnels. They should be able to add an extra layer of protection so that no infected fae can pass through. Until the wards are fixed, though, we figured that everyone can just wait by the barrier for a few hours before crossing. The anti-serum, when injected, takes about two hours to knock a fae out. Now that its airborne it might take a little longer, so if people can wait three or four hours by the barrier, we hope that will be enough."

"You hope."

"Well, yeah. That's sort of what I do, remember?"

"And if it's not? Then what?"

"What would you rather do? Seal the borders now? Leave everyone at the mercy of the Shades?"

"No. Our people need to be safe. On that, you and I agree."

"Okay, so next step, we book a flight to Vermont. I need to see some Druids, and there's a Choosing tomorrow that I can't miss."

"Please tell me you're not going to try and stop another Darkling from going Shady," he said, sounding at the end of his rope.

"No, not this time." Dorian relaxed and sank into a chair. "I'm going to watch a Darkling Choose the Light."

Dorian groaned. "I swear, you'll be the death of me. I don't know how Bran does it. Is he punishing me? He must be punishing me."

"Aw, I'm not so bad. You'll see. I might even grow on you after a while."

"That's what I'm afraid of," he moaned. But he smiled when he said it. "Anything else you want to tell me?"

"Well, um, the darkling's parents don't know he's Choosing the Light, obviously. If they find out..."

"You think there might be trouble?"

"I don't know. Anything's possible," I said brightly with an enthusiastic grin.

"Alright, get out of here. I've got to contact your father and bring him up to speed."

"Are you sure you don't want me to stay? I can talk to him if you want."

"No, I think I've had just about all I can take for the moment from you. Go on. Spread the word, tell everyone we're heading out."

"What about the Shade prisoners, what will you do with them?"

"Them? They can rot in their cells for all I care."

I leaned back in my seat and quirked an eyebrow at him.

"You have a better idea?"

196

"The people here are all infected, right? And they just sit around doing nothing, unless you tell them what to do?"

"Yeah, perfect, mindless slaves."

"Okay, well we're going to have to give them instructions before we leave, right? I mean otherwise they'll just sit around and starve to death? So while we're telling them to go about their daily routines, how about we tell one to let the Shades go after we've left? I mean, we can't bring them back to Aeden."

"Aren't you worried they might hurt the humans?"

"A little. But I think they're more likely to run off back to their HQ."

Dorian tapped a finger to his lips.

"What?"

"Quiet...I'm thinking. I might have an idea. But I need to talk to your father first. Alright. Get out of here, I need to get to work. You, see about re-programming the humans, and spreading the word that we're pulling out. Take these keys – you'll need to give them to the human to release the Shades." He tossed me a heavy set of keys and I caught them in midair.

"Okay. Oh, hey wait! Rowan said the Shades are all chipped with nanotech implants in their hand, something that keeps the anti-serum from affecting them. We need to get one of those chips, send it back to Valhalla. Maybe Tower Seven can replicate it."

"Yeah, I caught that part of the story. On it. Now beat it, kid."

I looked at Dorian curiously, wondering what else was going on in that brain of his. "Tell my Dad I said hi, okay?"

197

"Mmmhmm." Already pouring the silvery Aeden water into a bowl, he didn't bother looking up from the table.

"Alright then, I'll just see myself out," I said under my breath and walked into the chilled night air.

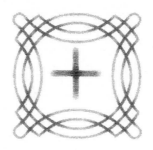

Chapter 24

Flurries of snow swirled through the dark lending the night a magical quality. I hadn't see snow since the year before. I should have been in the mountains, snowboarding by day, drinking hot cocoa by night. Instead, I was embroiled in a war between the Light and Dark, trying to find the path to lasting peace.

Every eighteen year old's dream, right?

Yep. This was the life. At least it had gotten me out of school for the last few months.

Alec was sitting at the bottom of the steps, waiting.

"Where's Amber?" I asked.

"She went to grab some food. You hungry?" He stood, putting his hands in his coat pockets.

I nodded. "What about you? You must be starving."

"Getting there. I don't think Rowan fed me at all while I was out, but I'm not sure." He pulled his hood up over his face and looked away.

"Do you want to talk about it?" I asked in a low voice.

"Not really. Not yet. Eventually." He shrugged and started walking toward the glowing dome down the street. "It's still kinda raw, you know?"

"I can imagine." I threw an arm around him and gave him a quick squeeze as we walked. "I'm so glad to have you back."

"Me, too."

I let go, warming my hands in my own pockets and we walked the rest of the way in silence.

In the large hall, I gathered all the fae and quickly caught them up on what was happening. Once everyone was up to speed most of the Guards dispersed, finding the rest of their teams so they could begin preparations to return to Aeden. That left me with Dorian's group, and a room full of humans. Some of them were sleeping, but many were still sitting up, muttering quietly or just staring off into space.

I shuddered, thinking of how Mikael had abused and abandoned this town. If he had his way, soon the entire world would be like this room. Quiet. Obedient. Enslaved.

I shook off that thought and climbed up on a table.

"People of Timber Valley. Wake up and pay attention!" I clapped my hands and stomped on the table for good measure. Several hundred pairs of eyes looked to me.

I waited until everyone was sitting up, and then I continued.

"Pretty soon, my friends and I are going to be leaving. You need to get back to the task of living. When I climb off this table, you're all going to go back to your homes. You're going to do everything you've always done. You're going to eat three meals a day, take your showers, go to work, feed your families and your pets. You're going to open your stores and take care of your farms. I repeat, you are going to do everything you normally do. Is that understood?"

All eyes were on me, devoid of emotion, and chins all over the room wagged in agreement.

I started to climb down from the table, but then I had another idea and scrambled back up before they could start leaving.

"If anyone else tries to tell you something different than what I just said, you will ignore them. No orders can override mine. Your top priority is to take care of yourself and your families the way you always have. Kids, go to school and laugh and play and learn. Grown-ups, go to work or stay at home, if that's what you usually do. You are your top priority. No one else. Now go home.

I hopped down off the table and bounced over to my friends.

"Whatdya think? Think it'll work?"

"We'll find out."

"I really hope it works. It's not like I could give them orders for every minute of every day." I bit my lip, watching the humans stream out of the dome. Almost too late, I remembered about the Shades.

I spotted a massive young man, probably one of the town's star football players considering the letter jacket he was wearing and his sheer bulk. I ran over and stopped him.

"Hey! My name is Siri. What's yours?" I stuck out my hand.

"Tom," he said, shaking it and giving me a blank look.

"Great. Tom, I have a special job for you. Tomorrow afternoon, after all the soldiers and strangers have left, there's going to be just one trailer parked up by the north end of the green. Have you seen the trailers, Tom?"

He nodded.

"So, after we leave, I need you to do me a favor. You and a couple of friends are going to need to open that trailer, and let out all the people who have been sleeping in there. Don't talk to them, and don't get in their way. Just let them go. If they talk to you, just ignore them."

"Wouldn't that be rude?"

"No, not at all," I said, patting him on the shoulder. It was like talking to a toddler. "It's just what they'll be expecting. You don't talk to them, and they should just leave you alone. If they ask who sent you to let them out, you tell them the Morrigan sent you, and that they need to go back to Headquarters. Do you think you can do that?"

He nodded again.

"Perfect. Here are the keys you'll need to open all the doors. Don't lose them, okay? Great." I patted him again. "Alright then, well, you can go now, get some rest, okay? And remember! No one else can give you any orders. Only me."

He walked away, his head bobbing up and down, up and down. I really hoped the Shades wouldn't hurt him or his friends, and that my instructions would work. If he forgot about them, who knew how long they would last stuck in those cells. And I definitely didn't want them running around town without orders. No, at least if they went back to the Morrigan they'd be out of our way for a while.

I walked back over to my friends and saw that everyone was eating.

"Here, we saved you some." She pushed a bowl of soup towards me with a hunk of bread floating in it. Behind her, people were already packing up the food, breaking everything down.

"Dorian doesn't waste any time."

"By tomorrow, no one will be able to tell we were even ever here. Not that it matters. We'll be long gone," Mari said, and took a long gulp of soda.

She didn't seem fazed by recent events in the slightest. I idly wondered if anything ever ruffled her feathers. And then, something did. Oh, it was slight, barely even a reaction, but when her eyes widened a fraction of an inch over the rim of her drink, it was enough to make me turn around.

"Flynn," we said at the same time. My voice held the flat hint of ambivalence that I felt. Hers sounded almost reverent. A bit of hero worship maybe?

Alec twitched when he heard the name, but he kept eating. Flynn came to an abrupt stop behind Alec, his face an unreadable mask.

"Ward," I greeted him. His hand paused in midair, stopping just before it could rest on Alec's shoulder. "Nice to see you finally."

He looked at me, and his eyes looked bright, almost feverish with a sheen to them. Then he returned his attention to Alec.

"Son," he put his hand on Alec's shoulder and forced him to turn around. Alec jumped at the contact, and swiveled in his seat.

"Father." He eyed his father uncertainly, and then flinched when his father rushed to hug him. He looked over his dad's shoulder at me, eyes wide, before reciprocating the embrace.

Flynn stood back but kept his hands on Alec's shoulders, examining him from head to toe.

"Are you alright? Did they hurt you? When you disappeared, I feared the worst. I was sure the Shades had taken you in for retraining, or worse. I never imagined that you were still right here, under our noses."

"I'm alright, Dad. I don't remember much of it, but I'm okay." He looked at me and smiled. "Siri and Amber found me."

"I know, I came right back when I heard. I am so grateful to you," Flynn said gruffly, clasping my hand. "I know I haven't always been the best father, but I'm not ready to lose my son yet."

"I know just how you feel, sir." I patted his hand and pulled out of his grasp, feeling embarrassed. He didn't know what I'd done to get his son back, and I wasn't sure he'd feel the same when he found out.

"How did you find him?"

"It was luck, mostly, talking to the right people. An elderly woman remembered seeing two boys go into the waterworks building the night it happened. I didn't really believe it could be that easy though. Then, I talked to the prisoners and one said something about Rowan being in his element now that he was a Shade. Rowan's a water fae – once I remembered that, it all sort of clicked. I figured it was worth checking out." I blushed as I finished my explanation, realizing everyone was listening.

"Well, thank goodness you did. Anything I might have said before, I take it all back. You've got a fan for life."

"Yeah, well, about that..." I cleared my throat nervously. "Life is a pretty endangered commodity right now. We're evacuating Midgard."

"What?"

204

"All Light fae are being urged to return to Aeden. The Morrigan has awakened the viral potential anti-serum. It's only a matter of time before he releases it somewhere public, and after that, it will spread throughout the entire world in a matter of days, weeks if people are lucky."

"But that's-"

"Terrible." A terse voice interrupted from behind Flynn. Dorian had entered the mess without anyone noticing. "We know. I just finished talking to Bran and several members of the Light Council, and everyone agrees that the plans Siri and I have come up with are our best hope."

"You? I knew you were up to something." I looked at Dorian with respect. "What have you cooked up?"

"I know you've already made plans to release the prisoners tomorrow-"

Protests of "What?" and "You can't" chorused around the table. Dorian held up a hand and everyone fell silent.

"As I was saying, I talked it over with Bran, and he thinks it's a great idea. He wants a team to stay behind and follow the Shades back to the Headquarters. Chances are, they might split up, especially if they suspect they are being followed, so I think we'll need at least five people for the job. It's a dangerous mission. If the virus is released too soon, the team might never make it back to Aeden. So it's on a volunteer basis only."

"I'll go." Flynn stepped forward.

"Me, too." Mari stood up, not looking at Flynn.

Kye and Jonal both volunteered, along with Ryker and Cleo from Flynn's team.

"Alright, that's six. That'll do. Kye, take Taini's Durango. He won't be needing it in Aeden." He tossed him the keys. "Mari, Ryker, you go with Flynn in his car. That way, you can split up if you need to. We'll make sure we leave some abandoned vehicles outside near the trailer, gassed up and ready to steal, fully outfitted with several GPS trackers each. Hopefully the Shades will take the hint. Come with me, and we'll go over the mission profile."

The seven Guards stalked out of the room and everyone dispersed, leaving Amber, Alec and me behind at the table.

"I guess that means Dorkian will be sticking around with us?" Amber sighed.

"Come on, he's not so bad. He's the one who kept me from losing it when Alec disappeared. If it wasn't for him, my dad probably wouldn't have let me come here. Not that he could have stopped me, but coming with a sanctioned team sure made the trip easier."

"Mmm," Alec said, throwing an arm around me and nuzzling my ear. "I guess I'll have to start being nicer to him, then."

"Definitely," I sighed, leaning into him. "You should."

"Aw, you two are so sweet," Amber perched her chin above her hands and batted her eyes at us. "Can I puke now?"

I laughed and stuck my tongue out at her, but didn't move away from Alec. "You think we can get a flight out of here this late at night?"

"You can count on it. We should probably get our gear together so we're ready."

I yawned, fatigue finally starting to creep in at the edges of my consciousness.

"Don't fall asleep yet, you'll have plenty of time to rest on the plane." Alex's fingers teased at my waist, gently tickling.

"Hey, some people haven't been sleeping for two days." I giggled.

Alec's face paled and his hand went still.

"Crap. I shouldn't have said that. I know, you weren't sleeping. I can't imagine what you went through. That was stupid of me."

It took a moment, but he lost the faraway look in his eyes and smiled at me. "It's okay. Keep making your jokes, don't change. Someday maybe, hopefully soon, I'll be able to laugh at what happened."

"Still. I'm sorry."

"Shhh." He kissed the top of my head. "You have nothing to be sorry for."

"That's great to hear." Amber smirked as she stood and stretched. "Because I have a whole bunch of ways I've been waiting to make fun of you."

"Keep 'em coming, Ambs, keep 'em coming."

CHAPTER 25

"You know, Alec used to be dark and handsome, too," Amber said thoughtfully as she applied a deep cherry lip gloss. "When it was dark, he was handsome!"

Everyone groaned.

The flight from Montana had been mercifully silent while we all slept, but as soon as we'd climbed into our new rental car in Bennington, Amber had started cracking bad jokes again. Most of them were at Alec's expense, but she wasn't sparing anyone from her hackneyed jibes.

"Aw, come on guys! Don't take life so seriously, you won't get out alive." And then she honest to goodness cackled.

"Ugh, Amber, how can you be so alert after less than five hours sleep?" I moaned.

"Well, I can explain it to you, but I can't understand it for you," she mocked.

"If I throw a stick, will you go away?" Dorian growled.

"Ooooh, now you're getting it! Though it sounds like someone really needs a coffee. So I'll go easy on you, Dor.

Just relax, focus on your driving, and if you can't laugh at yourself, don't worry, I'll do it for you."

He pretended to smash his head against the wheel while Amber patted him consolingly on the back.

I bit my lip, trying not to laugh and looked over at Alec. He was smiling, too, the dimple back in his cheek. God. It seemed like a lifetime since it had made an appearance. I'd missed that dimple.

Amber was a genius.

"After all," she was saying, "it would be the height of rudeness to have a battle of wits with an unarmed person."

Dorian adjusted the GPS and cleared his throat. "So, anyway. It looks like we're almost there."

"Yeah, you'll want to turn off at the next road on the left," Alec looked ahead and pointed. "Vala's driveway is the last one on the street."

I glanced at my watch. We'd been able to arrange a last-minute charter from a tiny airstrip near Timber Valley just before three a.m. After stopping to get a rental car in Bennington and then driving for close to an hour, the local time was now pushing 11am. I really wished we'd gotten some donuts or breakfast sandwiches to go with that coffee Amber was on about. At least we could look forward to some good food at Vala's. I was sure she would have a spread all laid out for Cooper's Choosing, even if she hadn't been expecting a big crowd. When Vala had guests, she went all out.

As we pulled into the narrow dirt road that led to Vala's, I remembered the first and last time I had been here. The dirt eventually gave way to an immaculate gravel driveway circling a massive stone fountain of children frolicking under an old oak. The colonial house sat atop a small hill overlooking a lake. Snow lightly dusted the grounds, giving the winter gardens a romanced look. I'd loved the energy here when I'd visited before. It had made me feel vibrantly alive.

Miko had told me then that the lake acted as a conduit to other lakes and wells throughout both Earth and Aeden, allowing Vala to talk with the fae and Druids in those locations. I knew that the property Vala's family had always protected was considered special by the fae, Shades and Light alike, but I hadn't realized just how amazing it was.

Now, with my heightened earth senses, I could feel so much more. See so much more. Even in the dead of winter, the land teemed with living energy. Trellised vines that looked bare were actually pulsing with a radiant aura. Pulses of silvery energy shot out of the lake every once in a while, glimmering through the air. I'd never seen anything like it, even in Aeden.

"Siri, you coming?" Totally absorbed in the scenery, I hadn't noticed the rest of the group already walking towards the house.

I pushed a loose strand of hair behind my ear and jogged to catch up. I'd ask Alec later if he could see what I was seeing, but now I was too excited to see my friends.

I finally caught up just as everyone was going inside. I bounced up the stairs and inside the door, blowing on my hands to warm them up.

"Why sweet Brigid, you four must be freezing! We'll have to dress you a little more warmly before you leave, don't let me forget to find you all some gloves and hats, at least. Now come here and give old Vala some sugar." She laughed, her rich voice pouring over us like warm honey as she pulled Alec into her arms. She mussed his hair and looked over his shoulder at me, a twinkle in her eye.

"And you! My, look how you've changed."

"I have?"

She came around Alec to grasp my hands in hers. "You can't fool me, sweetheart. You've got a river of power flowing through you, the likes of which I ain't never seen before."

She stared at me, like I was a book she was reading. Not sure what to do, I just stood there appreciating the warmth she radiated. Even in the light of day, I was able to see the subtle glow of her aura, a brilliant green circle with sunshine yellow and deep persimmon. High cheekbones and tawny complexion broadcasted her mixed Celt and Native American heritage. Her family had been watching over this sacred land, an ancient place of power and earth energy, for countless generations. With no direct heirs, when Vala passed, Rose would take on her mantle.

"You are like the Tree of Life herself. You share her energy."

"You've been to Aeden?" I asked, surprised. I didn't think any humans had ever been there, Druid or no.

"No, dear child, of course not. But I have been to the Tree of Peace, and the Tree of Enlightenment. I told you before, they are seedlings from the world tree, and they exist to this day. Other seedlings, too, if you believe the stories. But stop changing the subject. You, little one, are like a child of the great mother tree herself. I don't think I've ever seen anything like it. Like you."

"They're calling her the Heart of Life," Alec said proudly, putting an arm around Vala's shoulder. Her white hair clashed softly against his wild black knots. They couldn't be more different, and I loved them both dearly.

"Are they now?" She appraised me. "Well, yes, I can see why they would. Interesting. But come now, where are my manners? Amber, Dorian, why don't you take the rooms at the top of the stairs? Siri, you can stay in the same room as last time, and Alec, you're going to have to stay in the guest cottage, since Cooper is in the other guest room. Unless you'd prefer the couch?"

"No, that's alright, I'll take the cottage."

Dorian cleared his throat. "Actually, I don't think we can be staying. It's a seven-hour drive from here to the tunnels. We should leave as soon as the Darkling has Chosen."

"Nonsense, Dorian. You'll be driving in the Dark if you do that, and you won't get to Aeden for hours after that. You've been traveling for days. I know, Bran told me everything. The Commander himself told me to say you've been ordered to rest here."

"Dorian's right," I said. "It's probably safer for everyone if we leave."

"No. You'll rest. Then you'll travel. You can leave at first light."

"But-"

"The world isn't going anywhere, Siri Alvarsson," she admonished. "If you don't take a moment for yourself to rest and recharge, you're not going to be of much use to anyone. Now go on, settle into your rooms and meet back here in half an hour. You wouldn't want to miss Cooper's Choosing, would you?"

"Okay, but what about-"

"Rose and Cooper went outside for a walk. I sent them on an errand to collect some herbs and flowers for me. I'll send Rose on up to you if she gets back."

212

Seers, I thought. They really did know everything. I blushed, wondering what else she had read in my thoughts. In everyone's.

I gave in and hefted my pack, heading up the stairs behind Dorian and Amber. They went into their rooms and I walked on, opening the door next to Amber's. The last time I had been here, I'd been with Miko. I glanced at the window where he had curled up to nap, half-expecting him to be there.

It was empty, of course.

Sighing, I flopped onto the bed. A deep sleep would be a blessing right now. No nightmares. No worries. No, just quiet and peace.

The house felt so safe, like the space wasn't just warded, but blessed. For the first time in days, I gave myself permission to really relax. I closed my eyes and started to drift off, trance-like images darting to and from behind my eyelids, beckoning me to sleep. To dream.

A gentle tapping pulled me out of obscurity. I opened my eyes, not sure how long I had been there for.

Movement drew my attention and I saw the tell-tale vermillion strands of Rose's hair coming around to door.

"Siri, are you awake?" she whispered.

"Yeah, come on in," I said with a slight croak to my voice, propping myself up on my elbows. "What time is it?"

She glanced at her watch, sitting down next to me on the bed. "It's 11:40. I guess I just missed you guys coming in."

I'd only been sleeping a few minutes, then. My body protested, wanting to rest longer, but I sat up and hugged Rose.

"I've missed you! So much has happened since I last saw you."

"I know! Bran told us everything. I can't believe you and Airmed almost got infected with that lab tech. You are so lucky to be okay!"

"Yeah, that was pretty scary," I agreed. "Not as bad as what happened in Montana, though."

Rose bit her lip, considering. "I heard the Morrigan forced you to awaken the anti-serum. You must have been so scared."

"Scared?" I thought about it, remembering. "Not really. Not for me, anyways. I was terrified Rowan would hurt Alec and Amber. I just couldn't let him do it. Really, I think I was more angry than anything else."

"Do you think you made a mistake? Giving in?"

Only Rose would be open enough to ask me that point-blank. That's why I loved her. Well, that, and her awesome Rainbow Bright sense of style. Today, for instance, she wore faded jeans with patches of clouds and rainbows sewn up and down one leg. A tiny applique of Rainbow Dash, everyone's favorite pony, hovered over the cloud by her knee. On top, she had accessorized with a deep indigo turtleneck sweater, fingerless rainbow gloves, and a grass green scarf. Signature perky pigtails and moonstone ear studs shaped like stars completed the look.

"A mistake? No. Vala told me I needed to learn to trust myself, so I'm trying. It just didn't feel right to sacrifice anyone, not even to save everyone. When I did what the Morrigan wanted, he actually told me how they've been making it, and how they stay immune to it. Can you believe it? It's like he couldn't wait to brag all about it."

"Typical," Rose rolled her eyes.

"Right? I figured even if I refused to do what he wanted, they were going to go ahead with their plan. They were still going to infect the whole world, it would just have taken longer. And I still would have had to figure out how to stop him."

"But wouldn't it have been better to have more time?"

"I thought that, too. But then I realized without Amber, without Alec...I think I would have shut down. Everyone is saying I have all this power, and that I am the Heart of Life. But Alec, he's my heart. I don't know what would happen if I lost him. If I lost any of you. I can't do it anymore. There has to be another way."

"Okay, I get that. Vala told me all about the legend of the Heart of Life. So, you really think it's about you?"

"Well, everyone else does. Some crazy things have been happening, that's for sure. I don't know if I'm actually some reborn ancient queen from another planet or anything, but I do know my powers are really growing since the Choosing."

"I wish I could have been there," she said wistfully.

"I know, me too," I squeezed her hand. "It was kind of embarrassing, actually, I totally collapsed in front of everyone."

"No way, really? That's crazy! What happened?"

I filled her in on everything that had happened on the stage during my Choosing, showing her the new tattoo around my ankle.

She giggled, tracing the mark. "Wow. And you say everyone saw you glowing red? Like Rudolf?"

"Not my nose, you jerk! No, my grandmother says it was like I lit up the entire room, like the sun in Aeden."

"No wonder they think you are the red queen."

215

"Yeah, well, I-"

An alarm started beeping and Rose glanced at her watch. "Ooops, sorry. That's the five minute warning – we'd better get outside for Cooper's Choosing."

We both stood and I stretched.

"I have to grab something from my room, I'll meet you out back in a minute, okay? By the lake."

"Okay," I hugged her again. "It's so good to see you, Rose."

"You, too, Siri. Think Cooper's going to start glowing, too?"

"I sure hope not," I laughed.

Chapter 26

I went outside, where the others were already gathered. Vala stood wearing a simple white cloak, a matching scarf draped over her head, while she talked quietly with Cooper. He looked nervous, but his eyes lit up when he saw me.

"Siri, hi!"

"Hey, Coop," I laughed as he picked me up off my feet in a fierce hug. "I'm so glad you were able to come. It means a lot to have some friends here today."

Looking at him, I could see circles under eyes. "You look tired. Everything okay?"

"What, you mean other than the fact that my best friend is acting like a psycho, Holly's gone and my parents have no clue where I am on the most important day of my life? Yeah, everything's great," he gave a hollow laugh.

"Oh crap, that was a stupid question, I'm sorry," I hugged him again. "It's going to get better, Cooper, I promise."

"Well, it can't get much worse," he said, smiling one of his signature Cooper clown smiles. "So, I hear you're the Messiah now?"

"Shut up," I laughed, punching him lightly on the shoulder.

The smile fell from Cooper's face and for a moment he looked scared again. But he wasn't looking at me. I turned, and saw Rose approaching across the lawn. Like the twins at my Choosing, she wore dark gray in contrast to Vala's gleaming white. The long cloak dragged on the ground over Rose's small frame, and the deep hood hid her face. The only reason I could even tell it was Rose was because of her rainbow gloves, peeking out from the wide sleeves of her cloak.

She walked up to Vala and stood silently at her side, head bowed as she held a tray with several items on it. Upon closer inspection, I saw that it held the same things that the creepy twins had used at my own Choosing: some green herbs, a bowl of water, a piece of pumice, a lit candle and a mortar and pestle. The last was hand carved from a dark green stone, rather than handcrafted from silver, but otherwise, the tableau was identical.

Vala spoke. "Cooper, please stand before us. Alec, stand here and hold the tray. Girls, Dorian, stand behind Cooper, and bear witness."

We all moved into position, the Druids standing with their back to the lake where black ice glittered in the midday sun.

"Cooper Dunkel Hyde," they began in unison, speaking as one without hesitation, "you come to us on the day of your Choosing, a faeling untested and new."

"Today, we awaken your powers, your birthright, and you embrace your future by Choosing your present. Who you are, who you will be, who you have always been, will

218

rise tonight. Your powers have always been within you. Now, tonight, you will align the elements both outside of you, and within."

"We begin with light, just as life on Earth was born from Anansanna, the red sun."

Vala held up the flame for everyone to see, and Rose began mashing the herbs in the mortar while Alec held the tray steady. I should have been paying attention to the ceremony, I mean, it was the first one I'd ever watched as an outsider, but the way Alec's veins were standing out on his forearms while he held the tray? It was a little distracting. Why wasn't he wearing his jacket? What kind of idiot came outside in a Vermont winter wearing only a tee-shirt and a light sweater pushed up to his elbows? Honestly.

Vala was talking, I really needed to pay attention.

"Fire to life, we come together to birth reality."

Rose held up the mortar of crushed herbs, and Vala set the blades of grass on fire with the flame. When the plants had burned to a crisp, Vala set down the candle on the tray and took the vessel from Rose. She smiled warmly at Cooper and picked up the stone from the tray, dropping it into the mortar.

"The earth we stand on is made of the same star-matter as our own bodies." She crushed the stone into the herbs. Again, I found myself transfixed by Alec's arms, holding the tray steady under Vala's ministrations. I swear, I could actually see the Light flowing through his blood. I looked up, trying to focus, and made eye contact with Rose. She grinned at me, and I blushed, returning my attention back to Vala. Of course, that just brought me back to Alec, and I lost track of time again. His aura pulsed, subtle in the light, but the radiant lights emerging from the items on the tray were truly captivating. Each item had its own color. The water shimmered, the herbs billowed brown and green. The lights, they wafted up from the items like visible aromas, drawing me in. I started to take a step forward, and then Vala's voice brought me back to the present moment and I froze, hoping no one had noticed.

"The waters of life bring us together, calling up the past and guiding us into the future through our intuition."

Vala and Rose lifted the bowl of water together, inviting Cooper to drink. I gazed at the bowl fondly, wondering if Cooper would taste the same things I had. Warmth and sweetness, earth and candy. I looked at Alec, remembering. I still hadn't told him that when I had tasted the water, I had tasted him. The intoxicating flavors of coriander and pine had been a shock in the middle of my ceremony, and yet, it had felt so right. Like, other people navigated by true north, and the center of my compass would forever be Alec.

Was I just a lovesick teen, your typical girl in love? Or had it meant something more? A Choosing seemed so personal. So individual. Was it normal to connect so strongly with another person during a ceremony? As if my powers were somehow inextricably linked to his, to him? Who could I ask? Amber might know, I thought, she had Ewan, and she'd met him before her Choosing. She could tell me. I vowed to find out more before the night was over.

"Cooper, you must Choose. Will you serve the Light or chase the Shadows within you? Will you choose to shine your inner light and blaze brightly, or burrow into the slice of Darkness everyone holds within? Do you Choose the Light? Or the Dark?"

"I Choose the Light," Cooper said boldly.

What happened next was nothing short of pure beauty. I saw the lights of all the elements on the tray rise up to race towards Cooper. They swirled around him frenetically, merging into a rainbow stream before they pierced his heart. I felt a strange ache in my own chest, as if it was answering his own, as if we were connected, and flushed with warmth. For a moment, pure white light flashed around his entire body, and then it faded to silver, a tight aura of purity hugging him like an etheric armor.

"Did you feel that?" I breathed to Amber.

"Feel what?" Amber looked at me strangely.

"I...nothing. Later."

I turned back to the Choosing.

"Congratulations, Cooper. You have Chosen." Vala smiled and took the tray from Alec.

"Congratulations, man," Alec clapped Cooper on the shoulder.

"Welcome to the Light," Dorian said solemnly. "We're glad to have you."

"Thanks," Cooper said, shaking his hand. "That means a lot."

His eyes were shining, and a tear rolled down his cheek, despite his wide smile.

"Dude, are you crying?" Rose teased him and he nodded happily.

"I just can't stop smiling. It's like...I've never felt like this before. I feel so good. So full of life." He looked at Dorian. "When we shook hands, it felt so right. I got this rush of comfort, of peace. Is that normal?"

Dorian flushed and I decided to rescue him. "It's normal. What you are feeling is what all Light fae feel when we touch. It's the light within you recognizing the light in him. Here, check it out."

I held his hand and he went quiet, closing his eyes for a moment to take it all in. Then his eyes flew open and he frowned.

"Wait, you said all Light fae. What would have happened if I had Chosen the Dark?"

"It wouldn't be the same. From what I understand, you would feel the energy, but it wouldn't be as strong. And once you went through Shade training, you would have learned joy is a weakness, so the feeling would be distracting, annoying even."

"And if a Dark fae touched me now?"

"When Rowan and I were together, I felt good around him, a connection, because we were both faelings, but touching him, or any of you, also made my stomach flip over. When I met his Dad, a Chosen Dark, it was ten times worse. Touching Sullivan was like touching ice."

"So that's why you ran out on us that night at dinner with his family."

"I didn't know what was happening at the time, and it totally freaked me out. I'd only just found I was fae, and I had no idea about the rest of you. But Rowan says that was the night Sullivan figured out what I was."

Car tires crunching on gravel broke through the moment of quiet, and we all tensed up.

"Are you expecting someone?" Dorian asked Vala in a hushed voice.

"No. No one. Quickly, into the woods, all of you. I'll go see who it is. Don't come out unless I say it's okay."

She gave the tray back to Alec and stripped off her clock, handing it to me.

"I'm coming with you," Dorian said. "It's not safe."

"No. You stay with the younglings. Rose, take off that cloak. Quickly, come with me."

Rose shoved her cloak at me with an apologetic look and ran off after Vala. A car door slammed, and then another, and Dorian held a finger to his lips, ushering us towards the woods. We slipped into the forest as quietly as we could, snow and leaves crunching under our feet as we disappeared behind a crop of boulders.

"Who do you think it is?" I whispered to Alec.

"I don't know. It could be anyone, Light, Dark, Druid. Whoever it is, there's more than one of them."

The longer we waited, the thicker the tension in the air seemed to grow. Even the woods had gone quiet, the animals sensing our nerves.

The back door banged shut and I heard voices.

"No one else is here, I told you." Vala's voice held a warning, though whether it was for us or for the visitors, I couldn't tell. Crows from a nearby tree took wing through the wood, cawing loudly at the disturbance. In my mind, their warning rang loud and clear.

Shades! The Dark ones are coming! Take refuge! Hide!

"Sweetheart, you heard the Druid. He's not here." A man said calmly.

"But where could he be? How could he have missed his Choosing? Seer, you must be able to sense something. Isn't there anything you can tell us?"

"Crap," Cooper swore, his eyes round and wild. "It's my parents."

Dorian shushed him and put a hand on his shoulder, making sure he stayed out of sight. Cooper folded in on himself, suddenly looking very young, and very lost. I reached out and took his hand, trying to channel some reassurance into him. A bit of the lonely look left his eyes, and he blinked, exhaling in relief.

"I see nothing. Spirit has not given me any visions on this. I am sorry."

"But where is he? He could be hurt. I knew we should never have allowed him to go camping in the winter. What if he's freezing somewhere, or wounded?" The woman's voice ached with pain, and I knew that despite her Dark alliance, she cared for her son. Not all Shades were as cruel or twisted as Sullivan Carey and the Morrigan. I wondered how much she knew of Mikael's plans.

Cooper's eyes were still locked on mine, anguished. I knew he wanted to go to her. How could he not. It was his mother. I knew I would have wanted the same thing. I shook my head no. Even if she loved him, they would surely send him to one of the Shade facilities for reprogramming. I couldn't let that happen. If not for Cooper's sake, then for Holly's.

"You know," I could hear Rose talking quietly, "he's still pretty ripped about Holly's death. Maybe he went somewhere special to them? Somewhere they used to go?"

"I don't know," the father began and was interrupted by the mother.

"Yes! The Carey's cabin by Lake Champlain. They used to go there all the time. Cooper thought we didn't know, but Sully told us he had found things of Cooper's there a couple times. That must be where he is."

Voices receded and we heard the door to the house slam closed again.

"That was close," Amber muttered, slumping against the rock.

"That was quick thinking on Rose's part," Dorian said in a low voice full of respect. "You have good friends, Siri Alvarsson."

He patted Cooper on the back and I raised an eyebrow, unable to suppress a grin.

"That's high praise, coming from you, D."

"Indeed," he agreed. "A Darkling Choosing the Light. I never would have believed it if I hadn't borne witness with my own eyes."

A car engine turned and the unmistakable sound of tires driving away carried through the cold air. I sent out a mental call of safety to the birds and animals, letting them know the lands were clear of Shades.

Almost immediately, birds started chattering about what had happened and chipmunks came out of their dens for a much needed snack. Just like Miko, they were totally into stress-eating.

Even though it seemed safe, we waited until Vala came back to get us.

"That was close, but Rose has bought you all some time. I doubt the Hydes will be back here anytime soon. I know you all are probably hungry, but I think Cooper would probably like to burn off some steam first. Why don't you all take a walk in the woods while I go help Rose finish preparing lunch? We've got quite the feast planned."

She walked back inside, leaving us on the edge of the woods.

"Now what?" Cooper bounced on the balls of his feet, looking excited. "I know I should be worried about my parents, but I just feel so, so..."

"Energized? Hyper?" I offered.

"Like a ticking bomb," Cooper agreed.

"It's normal," Alec said. "Everybody gets that way after their Choosing. It's the powers being released through your body on a cellular level. Takes some getting used to."

"Yeah, Ewan wouldn't have anything to do with me back then, and I was so horny, I thought I was going to die." Amber giggled, and Cooper's eyes popped out of his head. Not literally, obviously, but you get the idea.

"Right, well." Dorian coughed. "Classy as always, Miss Slaight. No wonder your uncle is already going gray. Are we going to stand here all day discussing your sex life, or are we going to walk?"

We started off down the trail around the lake. Winter seemed mild this year in the Northeast, and the lake glittered in the crisp sunlight.

"Hey Cooper, what kind of fae are you, anyway?" Amber asked.

"Huh? Oh, fire, I think. At least, I should be. Both my parents are fire fae. But I've never been able to light so much as a match."

"Why don't you try now?" I urged, picking up a dry leaf. "How about this?"

He stared at it concentrating. Nothing happened.

"Maybe try using your hands?"

He held his right hand over the leaf and squinted at it. Still, nothing.

"See? I suck."

"Give it time," Alec said gently. "My friend Loch could barely float a feather for five years, and now all of a sudden he's calling up tornados as will."

"Five years?" Cooper whined.

226

"Dude, you're concentrating on the wrong thing. Tor-na-do," Alec emphasized.

"Yeah, but five years? I don't want to wait that long."

"I doubt you'll have to," I reassured him. "Hey, when we get back to Aeden we'll introduce you to my friend Claire. She's a fire fae, too, and she's amazing. She's been practicing calling up lightning, can you believe it? She uses it like a Taser," I gushed.

Amber snickered. "You should have seen her knock out Siri on the plane last month. I thought her grandmother was going to have a heart attack."

"She practically did," Alec laughed.

"Yeah, yeah, it was ha-larious. Jerks." I stalked ahead.

"If you can't use your element to burn off some of that energy, I think we should make this walk a little more exciting," Dorian proposed. "How about we play a little forest tag?"

Dorian's idea found favor with everyone, and we quickly established some ground rules. We'd start with one "it" and each time someone was tagged they would join the hunt for the remaining targets. No bases, no hiding, you had to stay on the move at all times, and you had to remain within sight of the lake.

"That way," Alec explained, "no one gets lost in the woods. This property is massive, and I really don't want to go on a manhunt today. Well, not a real one, anyway."

CHAPTER 27

It felt so great to run free. The light was brighter here than in Aeden, even though it was winter. With so many trees barren of leaves, and the cool yellow sun above hitting the dusting of snow on the forest floor, the forest gleamed.

I jumped up and kicked my right leg out, striking a tree and sending my body into a side flip before landing on my feet. I paused, cocking my head to listen. According to the gossiping birds in nearby, Amber and Cooper had already been caught by Dorian. Only Alec and I remained untagged.

I wasn't really in any hurry to evade the others. Caught or not, I would be running. After the rigors of travel over the last several days, the exercise was a balm for my soul. Often, if I went too long without running or training, I would get antsy, even irritable. My body had been trained to move hard and often from an early age, and it was addicted. The steady steps and breathing of jogging were my favorite forms of meditation. So it didn't really matter to me if I was capturing or evading the others.

Besides, I had time. Everyone else was on the other side of the lake, while I had doubled back towards the beginning of the trail.

I laughed and jogged closer to the shining water, sparkles visible through the trees. I hopped over a fallen tree, sprang up, ran a few more steps and rolled under another. When I came up, a flash of bright movement caught my attention. Two red squirrels chased each other, spiraling up around a thick tree.

Apparently, we weren't the only ones in the forest today enjoying a game of tag.

Their image seemed to blur for a moment, and I stopped in my tracks. I squinted. More movement flashed ahead of them higher in the tree, and I stepped forward, trying to get a better view. The palest blue light glimmered along the path they were following. As fast as they leapt and scampered, so did the light. They ran so fast, but the trail disappeared almost as fast as they caught it, fading quickly in their wake.

Were they chasing each other, or the blue trail? I couldn't tell. I wanted to know more. No. I needed to know more. If Miko had been here, maybe he would have told me what was going on. As it was, I would have to see for myself.

Before I even knew I was moving, I was already at the bottom of the tree. I had never been the best of tree climbers, having lived only sporadically in climates that grew trees of good stature. Still, how hard could it be? I eyed the branches above me, contemplating my next move. Already, the squirrels were well ahead of me. And then I saw it.

A glimmer of blue spinning along one low limb.

I hopped and reached, grabbing the rough branch in both hands, kicking up and using my momentum to swing myself onto it. The blue trail slithered along the branch, racing up the tree to another branch. I didn't hesitate. Crouching and steadying myself with one hand on the trunk, I followed the path of energy to the next branch, and then to another, and another. Before I knew it, I was standing in the top boughs of the tree, staring out across the forest at the sky.

Bemused, I pondered how I had gotten here so easily. The squirrels had long ago hopped to another tree to continue their race and I was all alone. The blue light was gone from view, having stopped and pooled around my feet moments ago. If I looked down, I could just barely make it out, pulsing a faint silver light now around my boots.

I closed my eyes for moment, enjoying the crisp clean smell of winter. It was so different from Aeden, so different from

the hot humid heat that ruled the underworld of the fae. At least here in the shelter of the thick branches of the pine it was a bit cooler. I paused for just a moment, catching my breath and watching the blue glimmer gather and pool ahead of me, patiently waiting for me to catch up. To climb, ever higher. Down below, all I could see were boughs of green, no hint of ground.

My hands were burning, the palms scraped ragged from falling in the tunnels. But I couldn't stop. This had to be finished. I had to try. Reaching up, I used my arms to pull myself onto the next branch, gritting my teeth against the pain. Sweat dripped into my eye, and I blinked, focusing on the light. Following it. Ignoring everything else. Branch by branch, I would do this. I wasn't sure what waited for me at the end, but I knew I had to get there.

Gods, what I wouldn't have given for a little snowfall right now. A cool breeze...

With a start, I realized my tree was swaying in the chilled winter wind, my hands turning numb in the cold. Shouts of laughter far away reminded me that I was supposed to be playing a game, not hiding out in the cradle of a tree. Rule number one had been you have to keep moving, and right now I was breaking it. I could think about the vision later.

I carefully lowered myself into a crouch and peered below. Shoot. Just how was I going to get back down? Somehow, I had a feeling it wouldn't be as easy as climbing up. It never was. I wished the squirrels were here to show me the way. What was I supposed to do now?

No sooner did I have that thought, when the light around my feet flashed blue again and zigzagged around the tree to another branch on the other side.

This one looked a little easier to drop down from, so I followed the light, trusting whatever the heck it was to be helpful. In my vision, I had certainly been trusting it to lead me somewhere. Somewhere even higher than this.

Limb by limb, I lowered myself towards the round. The light made it easy. At last, I jumped to the ground and rolled to ease my landing. Leaves crackled beneath me and I heard a shout nearby.

"Go South!"

I wasn't sure if they were talking to me or not, but I figured either way it would lead me away from them. I ran, ducking limbs and vaulting over boulders, and just managed miss being caught by Cooper when he jumped out from behind a tree.

Grinning, I darted around some stones to find myself suddenly exposed on Vala's lawn.

"Oops!" I paused, not sure which way to go.

"Ha! Gotcha!" Small arms tackled me around the waist, slamming me to the frozen grass.

I'd been abused by those hands enough times to know who it was.

"Amber!" I used our momentum to flip us both over, and sit on her chest. "Ha! Now who wins?"

"Actually, we all do." Dorian laughed quietly, stepping out from the woods. "You were the last one to be caught."

"Finally! Lunch had been ready for over an hour! Y'all must be freezing. Come get yourselves in here and let's warm up those frozen tushies." Alec helped Amber and I up while Vala held the back door open, ushering us all inside.

The dining room was lit with white candles along the mantle, table and sideboard, making the large room cozy and inviting. Rose came out from the kitchen carrying a giant casserole dish filled with acorn squash drizzled with maple syrup and almond slivers. Already on the table were baskets of cheddar biscuits and cornbread, bowls of fresh cranberry sauce and stuffing, platters of green beans and asparagus.

"Everything looks amazing," I said, sitting down after Vala had taken her place at the head of the table.

"Smells amazing, too," Alec agreed.

"Young Cooper here tells me his favorite dish is acorn squash, so our main course is in honor of him, on this very special day. But first, let us bless our food." She looked down the table at Dorian, who led the prayer.

"We accept this feast today with gratitude to all the beings who contributed to its bounty and beauty, the animals and plants, the farmers and the land, and of course, our beautiful hostess. May this food fill our hearts, bodies and minds with the blessings and the radiance of Aeden, aho-em."

"Aho-em," everyone repeated.

I looked across the table at Cooper while I helped myself to some beans being passed my way. "So, was it as weird for you as it was for me, learning a new way to say Grace?"

Cooper laughed, looking at me conspiratorially. "You know, it really, really was? All my life we've said grace before dinner. But never like this. Vala has been teaching me the different ways of the Light fae all week. Talk about a crash course!"

"I'll never forget how surprised I was when I heard Alec say grace. It was so different than the time we had dinner at the Carey's. Of course, both times really made an impression on me since my mom never really said grace at all. Except at holidays, of course."

"Not at all?" Dorian sounded shocked.

"No. I suppose it was part of her rebellion against my grandmother. Doing everything differently, you know? Our home was way more relaxed than Jade's. Although I always loved visiting her."

Rose looked thoughtful. "You never did tell me much about your dinner at the Carey's. Frankly, I'm surprised the Shades pray over their food. No offense, Cooper, it's just...well, you know. They don't seem into the whole idea of blessings."

In true, Cooper fashion, he just grinned and speared a piece of asparagus, popping the green twig in his mouth.

"None taken. Our blessing is different. More about the power we can take in from our food, less about giving thanks. Here, I'll show you." He placed his hands on the table and dropped his voice a couple octaves, intoning, "We accept this feast today with thanks to our Lord who has given us dominion over the Earth. May it give us strength, so we may live blessed in His abundance and power and glory forever and forever, amen."

"What about the bit about finding the light? Sullivan had thanked the food for helping him find the light," I remembered.

"Ah, I think he threw that bit in special just for you. Exactly the weird twisted sort of humor Rowan's dad always enjoyed." He shrugged, chewing his food. "Or maybe it's because he works with the council helping them do just that. I don't know. My parents are a bit lower down on the totem pole than the Careys, not really so into politics."

"Oh. Are they going to get in trouble? You know, with you defecting?"

Rose choked on her water, and Cooper had to pat her on the back.

""Jesus, Siri!" she exclaimed. "Can't you think of something better to talk about?"

"Sorry," I blushed. "I don't know what's gotten into me lately. I seem to have no filter anymore."

"You had a filter?" Amber smirked at me.

"Not a very good one." I said ruefully. "But lately it seems to have entirely disappeared."

"Don't apologize, Siri. What you're experiencing is natural."

Vala's words surprised me. "It is?"

234

"Are you sure?" Dorian teased, pointing a fork at me. "Not sure anything about that one is natural."

"Easy there, big guy. That's my girl you're pointing at."

"Like I said," Dorian laughed and went back to eating.

"Hush, you two. You're not helping any. Siri, I think what you are going through is natural. After any fae goes through their Choosing, they become more than they were, more of who they are. All their natural powers and tendencies are amplified, heightened. Not just your senses, but everything that makes you, you. You're the Heart of Life. I suspect that means you are going to feel the truth of things more deeply now, and also find it harder to hide from that truth. So it's no surprise you aren't wasting time beating around the bush anymore."

"Huh. I never thought of it that way."

"Oh my God. I'm doomed." Alec mock-sobbed and put his head in his hands. I swatted him with my napkin.

"Shut it, you."

"See what I mean?" He looked up and wiped a non-existent tear from his eye.

Vala laughed heartily. "Well, you certainly won't be bored, Alec, that we can be sure of."

I scrunched up my face, pretending to sneer at them both.

"Fine, I get it. No filter, no problem. Still, I'll try harder, okay guys?"

"Siri, what I'm trying to say is that I'm not sure you should even bother. While not everyone may want to hear what you have to say, the fact is that you're picking up on things that need to be discussed. Trust yourself. Trust your heart."

"You're always telling me that."

"I tell everyone that. Do you know why?"

She didn't wait for me to answer.

"Because it's important, that's why. If everyone really trusted, and listened to their souls, the world would be a much better place right now."

"But," interrupted Rose, "how do you know what your soul is saying? How do you follow something you can't see?"

"Oh honey. The soul may be invisible, but every emotion you feel is a message from yourself. When you're happy, that's good, do more of that. When you are afraid, either you are thinking bad thoughts that are going to get you into trouble, or you are doing a wrong action that is leading you away from your heart path."

"What the heck is a heart path?" Dorian broke in. "Sounds like some Druid mumbo jumbo to me."

Vala sighed. "Don't they teach you fae anything anymore? Your soul is in constant communication with your mind, your body, and it's always trying to lead you the right way. The way that will take you to the best possible outcome, the way that your soul is cheering you on. We don't always follow our heart paths, but when we do, life is usually a lot more fun and filled with serendipitous coincidences that bless our way. Miracles, even," she winked.

"Okay, but I'm with Rose." Amber threw up her hands. "Emotions aren't always clear enough. I need signs. Like, hand-printed, big lettered signs. Billboards would be good."

Vala chuckled. "I can't help you there. Unfortunately, emotions are all most people have got. Sometimes auras

236

can help, or animals will work with Spirit to show us the way."

"Wait, auras?" I looked up from my plate. "How could they help?"

"Well, some people say they can see the energy of different paths, or choices, and that a good choice might look brighter, or have a different tint to it. Or, if you are a seer like me sometimes you can have a peek at the future and examine possible outcomes. Legend says that long ago, people could actually patch into ley lines to connect their souls better with this physical reality, and find their way."

"Wait a minute, what's a ley line? Now you've totally lost me."

"Oh, I know this one!" Amber bounced in her seat, pigtails swishing back and forth.

"Enlighten me, Obe Wan."

"Ley lines run all over the earth like fine meridians or channels of energy. Some of these lines are huge and wide, and people have built holy sites like churches and temples along them for centuries, tapping into that extra power."

"Exactly, Amber," Vala nodded. "And as earth fae, Alec, Siri, you can tap into these lines, too, to amp your power."

"But how do we tap into them to see our heart path?" I asked, feeling more confused than ever.

"First, you need to learn to sense the power, even see it. Most people see the lines as currents of electric blue that runs over everything, sort of like a wireframe grid of the earth, like in those 3D programs that create the effects for Hollywood movies these days."

I gasped. "Blue light?"

"Yes, but it could be other colors. I have a friend who sees everything in shades of pink. Of course, it could have something to do with the fact that she always wears pink sunglasses." Vala shook her head. "Such a strange duck, that Iris."

"But blue? I think I've actually seen it."

"You have?" Rose looked at me, surprised. "Lucky. I've been trying for months to see a ley line."

"Today, out in the woods. I was watching these two squirrels chase each other, and it was like they were chasing their auras, running up the trees. Then I decided to follow them, but I wasn't sure how. I had just decided what I really wanted, and wished that I was better at climbing trees, when the same blue light flashed out in front of me and before I knew it, I was following it from limb to limb, all the way to the top of the tree."

"No wonder we couldn't find you," Cooper said through a mouth full of food.

"Close your mouth, beast." Rose elbowed him.

"You guys were still pretty far away, I could hear you across the lake. But yeah, once I remembered about our game I decided I'd better head back down and the light showed me the easiest way down, too."

Vala looked at me, considering.

"What?"

"Siri, I think you didn't just tap into a ley line. Dear girl, I do believe you were following your heart path!"

"No way," I scoffed. It couldn't be that easy.

"I don't know any other way to interpret what you are describing. I suppose the best way to know for sure is to keep at it, and see where else it takes you."

238

"Yeah, and when you've mastered it, maybe you can show the rest of us," Cooper sighed. "I know I could use some help in that area."

"Me, too." Amber nodded.

"When I figure it out, I promise, you'll all be the first to know."

"Yes, you will have to tell us all. Who knows, maybe you could become a teacher, bring back the old ways. Or maybe you could write a book." Vala winked, rising. "But for now, how about you help me clear these plates?"

We carried everything into the kitchen in just a few short trips, Cooper having jumped up to help as well, claiming he couldn't sit still any longer. Vala eyed him when we were done, noting the way his fingers were tapping against his leg.

"You look just about ready to jump out of your skin, boy. Why don't you go out there and see if anyone will take a walk with you, burn off some more of that excess energy."

"Really? You don't mind? Thanks, Vala!" He shot out of the kitchen before we could say another word.

"Poor boy. What about you? You want to go, too, I expect."

I thought about it. Normally, I would jump at the chance for some more activity, but today I felt relaxed. Comfortable in my own skin.

"You know, I think I'd kind of like to watch a movie. I haven't seen any TV in forever. You think there's anything good on?"

"I'm sure we can find something, between live TV and my recordings. What would you like to watch?"

"A comedy? Or a chick flick maybe?"

"Sounds good to me. How about you and Rose see what's queued up on the DVR. I'll whip up some hot cocoa to go with the desserts and meet you in the living room."

I watched her pull out several stamped boxes from a local bakery.

"Ooh, what's in there?" I reached for the box and she slapped my hand away.

"You might be the Heart of Life, missy, but this is still my kitchen and you will wait until everyone is served. Now shoo."

"Yes, ma'am." I turned to leave. "But don't forget the whipped cream!"

"Brat." She snapped a dishtowel at me and I fled the room, giggling.

CHAPTER 28

After plopping a tray overflowing with chocolate dipped pretzels, dried fruit and cookies down on the coffee table, Vala hunkered down into a worn but comfy looking armchair. Amber, Rose and I had already gotten cozy on the couch under a huge starburst quilt and selected the cult teen classic "10 Things I Hate About You" to play on the TV.

Outside, occasional shouts and grunts could be heard. The guys had foregone the suggested walk in favor of bringing Cooper up to speed on fae fighting techniques. Apparently Cooper had a little bit of experience from some classes he had taken with Rowan as a kid, but he'd dropped out in favor of joining team sports. Now, he was getting his butt handed to him by two of Valhalla's most elite Guards.

I felt for him, I really did.

Still, based on the laughter going on out there, I guessed Cooper was having a fun time. All that energy from his Choosing had to be burned off somehow, after all. No one here was a fire fae, so there wasn't really anyone to help him access his powers, though I hoped they would spark up on their own soon.

Watching the movie, seeing how torn up the main character was about her mom being gone, and how much it had changed her, I couldn't help seeing some parallels to Cooper's current situation. It couldn't have been easy, losing your girl and your best friend in the space of a weekend, and then having to leave your parents behind a month later. Yet he was still managing to keep a smile on his face, still acting like the same old goofy Coop. I'm sure a lot of people had underestimated him over the years because of his easygoing ways, but I knew him well enough to understand that in some ways he was probably stronger than us all. He may have been born a darkling, but he radiated nothing but Light.

I sighed. Too bad some of it couldn't have rubbed off on Rowan.

Amber looked at me quizzically. Right. Movie time. Not mooning time.

I reached for some more apricots and dark chocolate pretzel sticks, dipping the later into the whipped cream on my hot cocoa.

Chocolate made everything copacetic. Like the night sky, the darker the better.

I allowed the food and couch cuddling to work their magic. I relaxed into the sofa, watching scenes roll by on the screen. The boys came in about halfway through the movie, groaning when they saw what we were watching. Dorian didn't even pretend to be interested, grabbing a book off a shelf and heading upstairs to shower and read.

"We're heading out early, so don't stay up too late," he reminded us as he left the room.

No one answered, except to mutter "goodnight." Cooper started raiding the dessert tray, while Alec sat on the floor in front of me and leaned against the couch.

He propped my sock-covered feet on his lap and started to massage one foot. Amber nudged me and mock-leered. I nudged her back and shoved a cookie in my mouth, stifling a moan as Alec worked a knot out of my arch.

Before long, we were all laughing together at Heath Ledger serenading the girl he loved on the football field.

Not that that would ever happen in real life. Not at any high school I had ever been to. But it sure was adorable.

The closing credits rolled and I looked down, realizing I'd been absently playing with Alec's hair the whole time. The back of his head had been braided and twisted into a zillion tiny queues and spikes. I started to work them out, but Alec put his hand on mine.

"Leave it." He leaned his head back on my leg, looking up at me. "It'll give me something to remind me of you tonight while I'm sleeping all alone out there in that cold, spooky cottage." He batted his eyelashes and flashed his dimple at me.

"Oh, you poor thing. However will you survive?" I whispered.

"Oh, he'll survive alright," Vala quipped. "That cottage is as warm and cozy as could be, I'll have you know. And don't you go thinking about sneaking out to see him, either. Your father would have my hide."

"I hadn't even thought about it!" I protested, following her out of the kitchen with the empty dessert platters. And I hadn't. Really.

Now though? It was like she'd dangled catnip in front of a kitten.

"Good, because you know you'll have to wake up with the sun tomorrow morning. Dorian's offered to make breakfast at dawn. You won't be able to sleep much past that. You should probably follow Dorian's lead and turn in early."

"Mmm, that sounds perfect," I said, stretching and pretending to yawn. "Goodnight, Vala. See you in the morning."

Rose breezed through and kissed us both on the cheek.

"I'm heading out."

"Aren't you staying over, too? I thought you'd be coming to Canada with us."

The idea of leaving Rose behind, at the mercy of the anti-serum, gave me palpitations.

"Oh, I am. But I have to pack a few things, say goodbye to my parents, too. They aren't practicing Druids, so they can't help us, but I can't just leave without telling them. I'll be here in the morning bright and early."

Relief flowed through me and my chest loosened up. "Lucky you. You get to avoid breakfast with Dorian."

"Aw, I don't know. I'm kind of curious to see what he cooks up." She winked at me and walked out, calling back over her shoulder, "Sweet Dreams!"

I followed her toward the hall and walked up the stairs to say goodnight to the others. It seemed everyone really was hitting the hay.

A shower and some sweats had me feeling ready to relax, too. But I wasn't tired yet. I flopped on the bed, going through my phone. Of course, there weren't any texts. Pretty much everyone I knew was either in Aeden or here. One old school pal from Colorado had written me an email, so I shot him a line about warm winter and moderate snowfall here in the northeast. Like most of my old friends, he had no idea who or what I really was. The fact is, most of my old friends had barely known me, anyway. That was the real reason I had so few texts. It was hard to bond with people when you hardly made it through the school year in one place.

I puffed out my cheeks and hit send before I put the phone in sleep mode. Then, I remembered our early start the next day, and decided it would be nice to see the sunrise, start the day right. Who knew? If the Shades had their way, it might be the last sunrise I ever saw.

But I couldn't think like that.

I set the alarm on my phone for 7:00am and closed my eyes. If I tried to sleep now, I'd get at least nine hours of rest. Too bad I wasn't tired, and my eyes flipped open of their own accord.

Screw this.

No way was I going to sleep yet.

I hopped out of bed, slipped back into my hoodie, and wrapped a scarf around my neck. Holding my boots in one hand, I peeked out into the hall. Even though it wasn't even 10pm yet, the corridor was pitch black. Apparently, everyone else really was sleeping, even Dorian. No light shone from under any doors. Still, it wouldn't do to get caught.

In movies, people always tiptoe. But here's the thing. Tiptoeing doesn't work that great. If you step on a creaky board, all your weight is on that one point, and you wind up waking the dead. When I was a child, my mother had taught me how to creep like a ninja. First, she'd taught me how to breathe: you had to breathe normally to be quiet. If you held your breath or tried to breathe softly, in the end you would just end up breathing more heavily. And then you'd get caught. Then, she taught me how to move the right way. Crouching low so that my weight would be evenly distributed, I moved forward, keeping my arms still and gently making contact with my heel on the floor, rolling the rest of my foot along its outer arch to land flat on my foot. It was all totally counter-intuitive, but it worked. My mom had made me practice until I could do it without thinking. And then she told me if I ever used my new skill to sneak out of the house I'd be grounded for life.

Luckily, she wasn't here right now.

Guys said if you were in another state, it didn't count. Well, I figured if my mom was in Aeden, and I was here, then I wasn't really breaking any rules. Well, not hers, anyway.

I crept down the stairs and through the house to the kitchen, the only room with a door that didn't open near any bedroom windows. Hopefully, it didn't creak as loudly as the other doors, either.

Damn.

It did.

I held my breath, breaking ninja rule number one. Any moment now a light would turn on somewhere or Vala would jump out of the pantry with a flashlight and yell, "Ha, ha! Gotcha."

None of that happened.

I exhaled and sat down on the step to slip on my boots, not bothering to tie them. I looked up at the stars, pondering my next move. I wasn't even sure where I was going. I just knew where I wanted to be.

Alec. Wherever he was, that's where I belonged.

I looked around, trying to remember if I had seen any guest cottages on the grounds. I drew a blank and sighed.

Now what, I wondered. It sure would have been nice if that blue light would show up again.

I stared at my feet, wondering how to turn the power on. Vala had spoken about ley lines.

I sent my power down into the earth, testing, inviting, and tried to hook into the slow, dormant energy I felt sleeping below the snow. I thought about Alec, and wished that I could see the way to find him.

A pale glow seemed to seep up out of the ground, pooling around my feet. I reached out and made contact, trailing a finger through the dense energy. I could feel it tugging on me, rather like dragging a finger through maple syrup. Like it had a physical mass to it.

Again, I thought of my destination. This time, the light shot off to the right, heading across the lawn, around the side of the house and through some flower gardens.

Slowly, I followed the light across the lawn. Rather patient for a zig-zagging beam of sentient, gooey light, it waited for me. The snow crunched a bit under my feet since the boots weren't as flexible as they needed to be. I figured the noise was too slight for anyone to notice and kept going, taking care to stick to the shadows just in case. No way was I going to walk in the frost with just socks on in Vermont in February.

Finally, I arrived at what was hopefully a tiny guest cottage near the woods among the rose gardens. When I had seen it before, I had assumed it was more of a garden shed, the kind of place you kept lawn mowers and tools, given its size and location. Right now, the lights were off inside, and I wondered if anyone was even inside.

Maybe I'd been wrong about coming. It wouldn't be the first time. I was sure it wouldn't be the last.

I raised my fist to knock on the door but it opened before I had a chance. Pale hands shot out of the darkness and pulled me inside, slamming me into the door so it shut behind me with a dull thud.

I squeaked with laughter as a hand came over my mouth.

"What the hell are you doing? What if Vala caught you?" Alec grumbled, his face inches from mine.

"Mmpfh," I tried to answer, but his hand still covered my lips.

"Hmm. Speechless? Is this really possible? I didn't know it could happen."

He removed his hand, gently placing my freshly washed hair back over my shoulder.

"Alec-" Before I could say anything, he was kissing me. I'd known it was him the moment he'd grabbed me, of course. Even if I hadn't known he was sleeping in the cottage, I would have known his touch anywhere. The surge slammed into me, raging like a river after a heavy rain, carrying me and all my thoughts with it. I ran my hands along his arms, reveling in the strength and power there, even as I felt the depth and softness of his emotions rolling over me.

I hooked my fingers into the waistband of his boxers and pulled him closer to me. Between the onslaught of his emotions, I had a moment to idly wonder if the surge would ever diminish between us, if my love for him would ever feel commonplace. Right now, with my stronger abilities, it felt as if the earth itself was surging along with us, sending power up along my feet and legs, up into my body. I felt invigorated. Alive.

If the sun could sing, why not the earth?

"Do you feel that?" I asked, while Alec buried his face in my hair.

"Feel what?" he said, nuzzling my ear.

"The earth, it's..."

"Yes, I know."

"Is it like that for everyone with the surge?"

"I don't know," he said, leaning back to look at me. I shouldn't have been able to see him at all in the darkness, but our auras swirled and mingled, casting a bright glow of silver, blue and pink throughout the room. Right now, he was grinning at me, his dimple deep and daring in his cheek. "Should we call your parents and ask them?"

"Alec!" I protested.

He pulled me by the hand to the bed, sending us down on the mess of blankets to land in a heap.

"Come on, into bed with you. I assume you couldn't sleep without my reassuring presence?" He moved to lie on a pillow and tucked me in against him.

"More or less, yeah. I didn't bother trying." I laid my cheek below his shoulder, listening to the thump of his heart beneath his t-shirt. I was so worried about you when you were gone. I know you can take care of yourself, but I'm not quite ready to let you out of my sight."

"That's okay. I'm not really jonesing to be anywhere else, either. I saw you coming, you know. If I'd wanted to keep you out, I could have locked the door."

"No way."

"Way. I was lying here in the dark, trying to get comfortable when all I wanted to do was sneak into the house and find you. And then I caught this flicker of light outside. My first thought was Shades, and I snuck to the window to see. Instead, I saw you, sneaking like a Manga hero across the lawn. Except, of course, you weren't too sneaky since you were lit up like a freaking Christmas tree."

"Hey now!" I giggled. "If you couldn't see auras, you would have had no clue I was there."

"True. But I can, so I did. Don't forget, I'm not the only one who can, either. Some other Earth fae can do it, too. And water fae can sense your emotions when you get close. And air fae can sense when you exhale. And a good Fire fae can see heat signatures."

"Seriously? What's the point in having powers if that's true?"

"Well, first of all, I don't think our powers evolved so that we can fight each other. I think we're all supposed to balance each other out. You know, like in a game of rock, paper, scissors. Everyone is equal. Everyone is strong, but everyone is weak, too. We're all the same. Just fae, really."

"Oh, that's deep," I teased. "So, did you see the blue light, too? The ley line or heart path or whatever?"

"Heart path? No. I've never seen what you described. I have seen ley lines a couple times, though I have to really be in the right state of mind to see them, I guess. But they don't move or lead me anywhere. I guess that's why yours is a heart path, not really a ley line."

"Mmm," I said, feeling drowsy despite my best intentions to stay awake.

"Sleep now, doll." Alec whispered and kissed the top of my head,

"G'night."

After that, it was just darkness and peace and dreams and nightmares.

So, pretty much my life.

CHAPTER 29

In the dark, dark night, the insistent crooning of George Michael sliced through the silence.

"Arrh," Alec growled, pulling a pillow over his head. I sat up and stretched, dancing a bit with the song. A moment later he swatted me with the pillow. "What the heck is that noise?"

"Wake me up, before you go-go? Come on, this is a classic." I beamed at him and leaned over him to turn on the lamp.

"Ah, why?"

"Wow, this is a whole new side of you. So, you're not a morning person, huh? Cute. Now get your lazy butt out of bed and come on." I gave him a quick kiss and hopped out of bed to slip on my shoes.

Alec eyed me suspiciously. "Where are we going?"

"Outside. If you don't want to come, fine, but I'm going."

"Alright, alright. Just let me use the bathroom, okay?"

"Yep." I bounced up and down on the bed, feeling excited. It was a whole new day. A whole new sunrise. Who knew what the day would bring. "Come on, Alec," I sang. "Don't leave me hanging on, it's time to go now!"

He came out of the bathroom half-dressed and leaned against the doorjamb brushing his teeth, eyes twinkling.

"Sing it, baby," he mumbled around his toothbrush. At least, that's what it sounded like.

So I did.

He snorted, drooling a little while he tried not to laugh, and walked back into the bathroom.

Damn. I really did love him.

I walked to the door, opening the heavy handmade oak panel and looked at the sky. Stars still glimmered up above, but the horizon was beginning to turn pink and lavender. The colors made me think of the clouds of Aeden during a heavy rain, and I felt a strange pang. Homesickness? Was I doomed to miss both lands, above when I was below, and below when I was above? I frowned. Did it even matter? Who knew when I would be in Midgard again, after today? My sense of urgency grew.

"Come on, slowpoke," I called softly over my shoulder. I pulled up my hood to ward off the morning chill and set off across the lawn towards the lake. The sun would be rising soon and I wasn't going to miss it waiting for Alec.

I didn't have to. Soft footsteps on snow warned me, and then his arms were around my waist, pushing me forward slightly with his momentum. We walked together clumsily for a few steps, and then he moved to my side, clasping my hand and swinging our arms together.

"So," he said after a moment, "where are we going?"

"Here." I stopped at a bench by the lake. "We're going to watch the sun rise."

"Oh, okay. That's cool. I don't think I've watched the sun rise in years. Seen it, yeah, but never just had time to sit and watch it."

I checked my phone, noting the time. We had about ten minutes before the sun was set to crest the horizon. Plenty of time.

"I didn't want to miss this. Just in case we never get to come back here, to see another sunrise, in case...Well, you know. Anyway, since you're here, I have something I want to show you, too."

I sat and patted the bench. Alec sat and I leaned against him as he wrapped an arm around me. The frosted wood of the bench was cold through my pants, but I didn't mind. It might be the last time I would be cold, too.

"So, when I was in Ireland, Miko showed me this amazing thing, something that happens when the sun rises. Did I ever tell you about it?"

"No," Alec shook his head and rubbed my arm to warm me. "What did he show you?"

"We were out running, first thing in the morning, and he told me that the sun sings the world awake every morning. I thought he was messing with me, but he wasn't. He thought I'd be able to hear it because of my ability to talk to animals, and animals can all hear it. He said that everyone used to hear it, fae and humans, but that over the years we had lost the ability. "

"And you think I can hear it? I don't know." Doubt laced his voice.

"You can see ley lines. You're an earth fae. And you have me. I think I might be your secret ingredient."

"I don't get it. What do you mean?"

"It's just a theory, but I think the surge might help amp up the abilities we share. Come on, let's try. Hold my hand. Good. Now, watch the horizon and tap into your earth energy. Draw it up into your legs, up through your body."

I took a moment to do the same. All around us birds were singing, already responding to the barest hints of the sun song.

"Okay, now just gaze toward the horizon. Just relax, let your eyes go unfocused."

I could already hear the music rising through the trees, a low whistle building, a hum along the ground like a thousand bees under my feet. The sky lightened before us and the sound of bells and angelic tones drifted over the lake towards us.

"Siri-"

"Shh." If he couldn't hear it now, there was nothing I could do. At least he had the sunrise to look at.

And rise, it did. The sun crowned the rise across the lake, reflecting on the still black water, and I could see the light racing towards us in waves of sound, flashing past us and stirring birds into flight.

For a moment, the world went still. Quiet. And then the birds sang their song of morning celebration and the trees purred in contentment and all was well with the world. For a moment, anyway.

I turned to Alec, ready to apologize for waking him for nothing. His eyes were closed, and he seemed to have stopped breathing.

"Alec?" I shook him carefully.

He turned to me and opened his eyes. I gasped. A sheen of tears covered the orbs of his eyes, but that wasn't what shocked me. His irises had gone completely violet, so that not a hint of green remained, and they glowed fiercely in the gentle morning light.

"Holy- Alec, your eyes!"

"I saw it, Siri. I could actually see the sun connect with earth energy. I could see the waves of energy colliding." He stood up and whooped. "Did you *see* that? That was freaking amazing! And the sounds it made. How come we haven't been out at sunrise before this? How can you not want to see this every day?"

"So you heard it?" I leaned back, watching him happily. I felt as proud and amused as a parent must feel when their child experiences snow for the first time, or takes their first steps.

"Heard it, saw it, felt it!" He grabbed my face in both hands and gave me a kiss of victory.

"That's great, Alec! I'm so glad it worked."

"We have to show more people, soon. I don't know how much is dependent on being an earth fae, or the surge, but it's worth figuring out. Wow. This is so amazing!" he said again. "If everyone could experience the sun like that, I bet there wouldn't be any more Dark fae. No more polluting. No more air pollution. Everything is so, so alive."

"I know, right? This is the first time I've been topside and had time to enjoy a sunrise since we visited Ireland. I'm glad we had a chance to do this."

Alec looked at me and I noted that his irises were still gleaming purple, just the barest ring of emerald shining around their perimeter. Usually they only flared like that in low lighting. The change was confusing, an anomaly.

I didn't have time to think about it though, because Cooper was at the back door, calling us inside.

This time, it was me dragging Alec somewhere he didn't want to go. It was hard to get him inside, only the promising smell of bacon wafting through the open door seemed to finally lure him to breakfast. We went to the sideboard and grabbed plates to serve ourselves. Vala had really outdone herself, frying up eggs and toast to go along with the bacon, and setting out platters of fruit, sweet pickles and jams, juice and tea. I heaped my plate with fruit and bacon, spreading honey on slices of warm bread, and sat down with a giant mug of breakfast tea.

"This looks fantastic, Vala. Thanks for cooking!"

"It wasn't just me." She peered at me, a reprimand in her eyes. "I woke everyone up to help half an hour ago. But you weren't in your bed. In fact, your bed didn't look like it had been slept in."

"Oh," I blushed, not sure what to say. "I-"

"Siri woke me up ages ago. She wanted to take me for a walk and see the sunrise," Alec beamed, sounding like he had drunk some sort of magical happy hippy potion. Any minute now I feared he might break into song like some hokey twentieth century musical. Not that I didn't like musicals. I really, really did. But I didn't want to date one.

"She had to drag me out of bed," Alec continued. "But I'm so glad she did. It was a sunrise to outshine all others."

It struck me that he had managed to tell the complete truth without hinting that I had broken Vala's house rules and spent the night in his cabin.

"Oh, please." Amber rolled her eyes. "What the heck have you done to him? He's ruined, I tell you."

Dorian snorted, clearly agreeing with Amber.

"And why are his eyes so purple?" Cooper asked, sounding bewildered. "Do his eyes always change color like that?"

Alec just smiled and winked at him, eating bacon and acting totally unperturbed. Okay, seriously. What the heck? Where was my wise-cracking boyfriend? Had the sun body-snatched him at dawn?

"Siri?" Cooper said.

"Right. Um, no. Or, yes? I don't know. The purple does come and go, it flashes in the dark, or if he's excited, that sort of thing. But it never just stays...on...like it is now. I showed him how to hear the sun rise this morning, and they've been like that ever since."

"Hear the sun?" Cooper sounded even more confused.

Vala interrupted before she could ask more. "Are you saying that you can hear the song of the rising sun? And you helped Alec hear it, too?"

"Yes, exactly. Miko showed me when we were in Ireland. Before he... You know. I wanted to see if I could hear it again, before we go back to Aeden. I couldn't help thinking it might be our last time." I shrugged, apologizing for being all doom and gloomy.

"No need to be sorry, I can imagine how you are feeling. But you must fight to keep the faith, Siri," Vala reminded me. "You must continue to trust in your path, in your heart. If you don't, all is lost."

"Gee, no pressure, thanks."

"You'll be fine." She smiled at me brightly. "So. You hear the song of dawn. Amazing. So few have heard it in recent centuries. You may be one of the only people alive who have. What a gift. If you don't mind me asking, how did you help Alec hear it?"

"Well, Miko had me gaze towards the horizon and connect with earth energy. He thought since I could hear him, and the other animals, that I would be able to hear the sun, too. And he was right."

"Can we back up a minute? What the hell do you mean, you can hear the sun?" Dorian barked, making me jump in surprise.

Alec answered for me, his voice sweet and happy. "It sings, Dor, can you believe it? Like angels on the wind. It wakes up the whole earth when it rises. I wonder if Anansanna does the same."

"If it does, I haven't heard it."

"Hmm. That's another interesting topic you should explore when you return below. But back to Alec. What did you do this morning?"

"The same as I did with Miko. He gazed at the sun, connected to the earth. Oh, and we held hands. I figured maybe the surge would help him see."

"Ah." Vala's face lit up. "I think I may know what has happened. You are both earth fae, but between the surge, and the sun's power to connect with your light on a cellular level, I believe you may have awoken Alec's full earth abilities."

"I don't get it."

"Alec is half human. His mixed eyes are a sign of his heritage. The purple flares when he is using his earth powers, correct? Looking at auras? Seeing in the dark?"

"Yes."

"Well, I think Alec is experiencing a cellular shift, an unlocking of his full fae potential."

"His father's eyes are purple. They get brighter too, when he's angry."

"When did you see that happen?" Amber asked, raising an eyebrow.

"At my Choosing. I kind of pushed his buttons, and he got pretty angry."

"She told him he was empty, like a Shade, and he didn't deserve a son like me," Alec said proudly, popping several berries in his mouth.

"You didn't," Dorian said, sounding aghast. Amber, true to form, was cracking up, although at Dorian's glare she ducked behind her napkin. "You told Flynn Ward he was like a...a...I can't even say it. I'm surprised you're still alive."

"Yeah, well, we were all pretty surprised. It wasn't like I meant to say it. He just ticked me off. But it's okay. We've made up." I winked at Dorian and he went pale, as if I had just insulted his childhood hero. I don't know. Maybe I had.

Time for a change in subject.

"So, Vala. Do you think Alec's eyes are going to stay this way, then?"

"What's the matter, gorgeous?" he laughed. "Are you dissing the Vye?"

"No!" I protested, chuckling. "But now we know you're off your rocker, if you're making jokes about that nickname."

"Don't worry," Vala said. "His eyes may well stay like this. But he should come down from this high within a few hours. He's just riding the effects of the boosted light in his system. I suspect he'll be fine."

"I'm going to hold you to that, Druid." Amber pointed her fork at Vala. "I don't think I can take too much of this new and improved Alec."

Alec shrugged and smiled, looking contented, while the rest of us shook our heads.

Somehow, I had the feeling it was going to be a very long day.

CHAPTER 30

The drive up north was quiet. I rode in Vala's Subaru with Alec and Rose, since Dorian and Amber didn't seem to be able to stomach Alec's new sunny demeanor. Alec lay comfortably across the back seat with his head in my lap, watching the sky rush by through the windows while he traced designs along my arm. He didn't speak, except to note the occasional bird or cloud flying up above. The rest of us spoke about everything except what was really on our minds.

I asked Vala about what she'd been teaching Rose, about the history of the Druids, their role in the world of men, how they'd become connected to the fae. We avoided all mention of things dark and shady.

Native American flute music played quietly through the speakers, easing the underlying tension. After we'd run out of magic to talk about, we turned to other topics. The snowfall that year, what it was like to work on the mountain checking lift tickets all afternoon, how the boys were just as bad as the girls when they gossiped.

Rose started talking about school, telling me who was dating who, what the drama of the week was, everything I'd missed in class.

"Emilie is dating the captain of the lacrosse team. He's a total jerk, they're perfect for each other. I think she was hoping to make Rowan jealous, but he hasn't been in school since his Choosing."

We'd managed to avoid anything Dark for hours, but it had to come up eventually. I couldn't think of anything to say, and looked out the window.

"Awk-ward," Alec tittered, and tapped my lightly on the nose.

"Shhh." I hushed him and stroked his hair, as if he was a small child. He sighed and closed his eyes, nestling against me. Maybe he'd sleep. Maybe when he woke up he'd be normal.

Or at least, Alec.

I leaned back and closed my eyes, thinking this might be a good time to meditate. I had a feeling I was going to need to be on my game sooner rather than later.

Vala and Rose continued talking among themselves, discussing various Druid lore and methods of warding, determining what might be best suited for what they had to do. I tuned them out.

I focused on breathing, my hand on Alec's hair still now, and focused on my mantra. Months ago my mother had started teaching me a meditation technique that helped me sink into a hard and fast trance state. At least, that was the idea. I was supposed to repeat my mantra, over and over, silently or out loud. If thoughts came into my head, I was to ignore them. Focus on the mantra. Over and over. My mother had assigned me my mantra – apparently it was tradition for your teacher to give you a word or set of words that was both easy to remember and empty of personal meaning.

Mine?

Katana Core.

I'd pondered the words a lot in the beginning, but eventually, said enough times, they really did lose all meaning.

The voices slipped away and I sank into oblivion.

The best part about trance meditation? You had no idea how long you'd been out. Okay, I suppose that could be viewed as bad by some people, too. But for me, having the ability to comfortably check out, to be at peace and not worry, to not count the passing minutes? It was a rare luxury. My natural tendency was to move, to run, to experience life. I never really sat still, not unless I had to. Meditation had gifted me with a whole new way of being.

It could have been minutes, it could have been hours. I could have been asleep, or trancing out. Once the mantra faded away and I floated into the quiet, still, kernel of stillness within myself, it all became the same thing.

Peace. Pure and simple.

I should have known it wouldn't last.

Pain lanced through my shoulder and I considered my options.

I could run, and hope to escape. I could take the offensive, and bring the Shades into Aeden myself, as previous visions had warned me I would have to do. I could use my Earth powers to bring down the tunnels around us all, removing the key players from the fight. Including myself. Including Alec. Rose. Amber.

The tunnel shook again, and I knew I couldn't do it.

No.

"No!" I came to, already pushing Alec away even as I realized he was trying to rouse me. "Sorry, I didn't mean-"

"It's okay. You were tossing and turning, moaning. Nightmare?"

I nodded, looking into his eyes. Still purple. But he seemed more like himself.

"Where are we?" I looked around, noting the car had stopped.

"We're in Montreal. Amber called a while ago, said she had to grab a few things from the apartment and meet up with Ewan."

"He's here?"

"Yeah. Apparently he refused to go back to Aeden with Mitch, said he wouldn't go until Amber got here."

"Stubborn idiot," I said fondly.

"Always," Alec grinned.

"Where are Rose and Vala?"

"They went to use the bathroom. We're just around the corner from the apartment. How about you? Need some food? Bathroom? A jog around the block?"

"How well you know me. Bathroom would be good, maybe something to drink."

"Alright, come on then." Alec climbed out of the car and gave me a hand, pulling me up against him before letting me go.

He took off running backward, his hair bouncing madly in the wind. He beckoned me towards him with both hands.

"Come on, who's slow now?"

I shook off the fatigue of the car, and jogged off after him. Before I could catch up, he turned and began to run in earnest. I sprinted, trying to catch him, but as usual, he evaded my reach turning our jog into a race to the apartment.

Inside, Amber and Ewan were nowhere to be seen. Dorian sat stiffly on the white couches drinking coffee, while Vala and Rose stood talking quietly in the kitchen.

"Hey, sleepy head," Rose greeted me. "Welcome back. Want some coffee? Food?"

"Sure, thanks." She poured me a mug and handed it to me. I added cream and sugar, enjoying the rich, sweet taste. Alec pulled some chocolate croissants from a bag on the counter and handed me one.

I liked that he didn't even have to ask if I wanted one. Chocolate? Why, yes. Yes, indeed. Thank you very much, sir.

I went and perched on the couch next to Dorian.

"So, how was your drive?"

"Please. Just, don't. No more girl chatter. I don't think I can take anymore."

I barked with laughter before I sipped my coffee.

"That bad, huh?"

"Any chance we can swap rides? I don't think I can handle being in the car with Ewan and Amber for two hours. The way they carried on when we got here..."

"I know. It's embarrassing. At least they're not as bad as my mom and dad."

"This is true," he agreed. "Still."

"Mmm. I feel for you, buddy. But I'm not leaving Rose in anyone else's hands. No offense, but Rose is like family. I feel like I need to stay with her. Protect her. And I'm pretty sure Vala wants to keep an eye on her, too."

"I figured you'd say something like that," he sighed.

Just then, Amber and Ewan came out of their room. Amber's long pigtails were askew and Ewan's shirt was on inside out, and they both had a healthy flush to their cheeks, indicating they hadn't just been having a private conversation. Ewan carried a huge duffle over his shoulder, while Amber was carrying a large camping pack.

"More weapons?" I asked.

Amber snorted, fixing her hair in the mirror by the front door.

"No. Just some of my most valued possessions."

"Clothes?" My eyes widened. I wasn't sure if I was amused or confused. "You're making Ewan carry your clothes?"

"No. Of course not. I have clothes. Ewan's carrying my collection of Demonias."

Dorian sputtered, spitting coffee out over the table.

"You've got a demonic collection? And you're bringing it to Aeden?"

Amber and I looked at each other, trying not to laugh. We only made it about three seconds before we were both

268

cracking up. Ewan took pity on Dorian and enlightened him.

"Bag's full of boots, man. Amber's favorite brand."

"Ah, ok." Dorian said, nodding sagely, but still eyeing us as if we were strange, unknown creatures that might suddenly begin spitting and hissing at any moment.

I couldn't blame him. Truth was, you never really knew with Amber.

Amber sobered up and approached me, whispering "How's Alec?"

I looked around, not seeing him in the room. I figured he'd gone off to use the bathroom, maybe get a few things of his own. We had a moment to talk quietly. Still, I led her away from the others and kept my voice low.

"His eyes are the same, but he seems to have chilled out a bit. Actually, I'd say he seems pretty normal."

"Time will tell, I guess," she bit her lip. "I'm glad he's doing better."

"Me, too. I think we're all going to need to be at our best when we go into those tunnels."

Amber examined my face, seeing more than I wanted her to. "Have you had a new vision?"

"Just more of the same. Dark tunnels. Falling rocks. The freakin' Morrigan. Nothing is very clear, except that the barriers are going to need some serious mojo if we have any hope of keeping them up."

"Well," Amber said over-brightly, "that's what they're here for, right?"

We both looked at the Druids. Rose hadn't even finished her training. Vala was strong, but she was just one person. Would they be able to stand up to whatever forces Mikael was mustering?

Not for the first time, I wished that the Song of Light had come in the form of a long, detailed instruction manual. With pictures. Ikea could have taught the Ancients a thing or two about writing prophecies.

"Right," I said, matching Amber's positive tone. "Actually, this last vision didn't specifically show the barriers falling, so maybe that part has already changed, just by us including them."

"I sure hope so."

"Me, too."

I decided now was a good time to use the bathroom and excused myself. I was almost there when an arm shot out and pulled me into a room. The room was dark and unlit, sheer curtains muting the afternoon sun. I squealed and a hand went over my mouth, stopping me in my tracks. If it had been any other hand, I would have used a palm strike to the collar bone followed by a kick to the ankle to disable my abductor. Instead, I welcomed the warmth against my skin, soaking it in.

Just as quickly as it had come, the hand disappeared.

"Well, hello there." Violet eyes burned into mine. The purple was flaring so brightly in the dim room that it actually reflected off his lashes, making them shimmer in the radiant light.

I leaned my forehead against Alec's. "You surprised me."

"Really? I hadn't noticed. Do you remember the first time you were in this room?"

"I do," I breathed.

"I knew then that you were the one. You had no idea still. I knew you had no inkling of the surge and what it meant. I wasn't ready for it, but I didn't want to leave you alone in here, either. All I could think that night was, my room. My girl. Mine."

He kissed me, and showed me what it felt like to be his. I wondered if he was experiencing the same, because all I could think was that he was mine. All mine.

The moment I had that thought, he pulled me tighter, running his hands up my back to fist his hands in my hair. Yes. He knew what I was thinking. Always. I could never hide from Alec.

Which reminded me.

"Were you waiting by the door for me?" I broke our kiss with the question, and for a second Alec just stared at me, looking dazed.

"What?"

"Were you waiting for me to come down the hall?"

"No." He blinked. "No, I saw you coming."

"Saw me? But weren't you in here? With the door closed?"

"I was." He scratched his head, and walked away, over by the bed where some clothes and books were laid out. "I was packing. I turned, like this, and then I saw your aura coming down the hall. Through the wall. I walked to the door and your footsteps confirmed it. I didn't think about it. I just opened the door and grabbed you. Damn."

He sat down on the bed, stunned.

"What the hell is happening to me, Siri?"

"I don't know."

"How could I have known it was you?"

271

I sat down next to him, holding his hand, rubbing my thumb over his. "Vala thinks we woke up your earth senses when I used the surge to help you hear the sun song."

"What do you mean?"

"I'm not surprised you don't remember everything, but you were acting pretty loopy after the sunrise. You're acting more normal, but your eyes...Well, Vala thinks some of the effects might be permanent. That now that your fae DNA has been fully activated, they'll stay that way."

"What do you mean, my eyes?"

"You haven't seen?"

"Seen what?" He asked nervously. I got up and led him toward the closet, opening the door to show him the mirror hanging inside.

His eyes widened, and he stepped forward. "But that's...they've never..."

"I know. I've seen them flare. In tunnels, at Zora's, and when you're, um, excited. But I've never seen them get this bright. And definitely never for this long. Alec, your eyes have been like this since dawn. Vala thinks it's a side effect of the light being boosted in your system. She thinks this might be permanent."

"So seeing you coming then?"

"Was a new ability? A side effect of your power? I don't know. You can see auras, we both can. You're barefoot right now – what if as an earth fae you can sense sound, vibrations in the ground? Maybe your mind translated the vibrations into something you can understand – like my aura?"

"I've heard of something like that before. Hang on." He stalked to the bed and picked up his phone, tapping on the keyboard screen. I peeked over his shoulder.

"Chromesthesia or sound-to-color synesthesia is a type of synesthesia in which heard sounds automatically and involuntarily evoke an experience of color," I read. "Synesthesia?"

"Yeah, it's this crazy rare condition where people taste sounds, see smells, hear color. All their senses get mixed up."

I frowned. "I don't think your senses are mixed up. I think they are working together."

"Still, it's good to put a name to it, right? Who knows, maybe the humans with this condition are part fae, too."

"Maybe. Or maybe part of them is trying to be. Maybe humans and fae aren't so different as everybody thinks. Maybe it's just a degree of the light."

CHAPTER 31

We didn't share Alec's new ability with the rest of the group. Alec wasn't sure if it would last, or if it would evolve into something else entirely. For now, we agreed to keep it between us.

Unable to take Dorian's desperate, pleading eyes, I'd talked Rose into coming in his car with Alec and me, leaving Vala to escort Amber and Ewan. Ewan offered to drive Vala's car, and Amber climbed into the back seat so I knew Vala would at least have control of the stereo. All in all, she was getting a good deal.

Alec sat up front with Dorian, while Rose and I sat in the back. I'd been right about Dorian's musical taste, which centered on classic rock and smooth jazz. At least he didn't listen to any improv bebop – the jolting and screeching of that entire genre usually made me crazy, and not in a good way. Van Morrison, Pink Floyd, Steely Dan weren't really my thing, but they were easy enough to tune out while Rose and I quietly gossiped in the back seat. The weather outside was brutally cold, but the roads were clear and the car's heater was blasting so that was a blessing.

Rose took off her outerwear, stripping down to a t-shirt, but the rest of us sat cozily in sweatshirts and sweaters. Despite my love of snowboarding and having spent so much time in colder climates, my body really preferred being warm. Looking at Alec and Dorian, I wondered if maybe that was a fae thing. And if so, was it a holdover from our ancient origins on another, perhaps warmer planet? Or was it something that had evolved over time, living under the glow of Anansanna, like ducklings thrive under a warming light?

I asked the boys, but neither had an answer for me. Perhaps Mialloch would know, I thought, and made a mental note to ask him someday.

The woods along the highway grew denser, the cars less frequent. The afternoon sun hung low in the sky, clouds drifting in front of it more and more often as a storm front began to roll in. The closer we got to the tunnels, the quieter everyone became. Dorian put on some Rush in an attempt to lighten the mood. When "Tom Sawyer" came on, Alec surprised me by breaking into a perfect air guitar rendition, setting Rose and me giggling. Dorian joined in, giving us a rare glimpse of his lighter side, something I imagined he normally reserved for the young children waiting for him at home.

Before we could finish the album, we were pulling off the road into some deep woods. Where normally the track was dirt, snowy ruts led the way between the trees. I turned, making sure Vala's car was following. Her Subaru kept pace with our vehicle, heavy snow tires churning heroically.

I faced front, catching a glimpse of Rose's white face. Every time we went over a bump, the freckles on her cheeks stood out more. Remembering the first time I had come to the camp, fearing local bears and harsh conditions, I reached out and took her hand, giving it a small squeeze. Still pale, but relaxing somewhat, she tried to smile.

"Almost there," I said in hushed tone.

"It looks like we must be one of the last groups in," Alec murmured, pointing to the tracks in the road. When we emerged in the large clearing by the rough camp, I agreed. More than thirty cars were tucked around the small wooden cabin. Dorian squeezed into a tiny space between a shiny new Ford Expedition and a vintage Hummer, blocking in another car. Vala parked behind us and we all exited our vehicles. If the cars here were any indication of the number of evacuees, well over a hundred people had already escaped to Aeden through this portal. Dorian said most fae on the east coast of the U.S. would have used a fairer weather entrance down in North Carolina, or else there could easily have been ten times as many cars.

The deep snow should have been impassable, but the many feet before us had made a well-trodden trail, packing the snow down into a slippery path. Winter campers would have no problem finding their way to the tunnels now if they stumbled upon the cabin. I imagined that most people would be more interested in the abandoned vehicles, all unlocked with keys inside, since the fae tended to be communally minded.

Rose still looked uncomfortable as we walked, flinching at every small sound in the woods.

"You okay?" I asked.

"I guess. I'm usually more comfortable in the woods, you know. I feel like I shouldn't be here."

I mulled over her words, and gave her my hand. "Here. Maybe this will help." I pushed out some of my energy towards her, trying to infuse her with light as we walked.

"Anything?"

276

"Actually, I think so. I feel less worried."

"Good." Her cheeks now glowed brightly against her milky complexion. Reassured, I linked my arm through hers.

The cave loomed ahead of us, a gaping maw among stone ledges. Ewan waited by the opening, ready with flashlights for everyone in the group. Alec and I passed, not needing artificial light to see underground. Thank you, earth powers.

"You guys ready for this?" Amber asked, looking at each of us in turn.

"Does it matter?" Rose mumbled, testing out her flashlight.

I nudged her and straightened my back, forcing her to stand at attention with me. "Totally ready."

Amber grinned demonically, nodding at me with approval. "Perfect. Everybody else?"

Everyone nodded and Amber turned, smacking Ewan on the butt before yanking him out of the entrance to follow her into the shadows.

Rose moved to walk with Vala, then Alec and I, while Dorian brought up the rear. Everyone stuck closer together than usual, not knowing what might be waiting within the darkness. Unlike the properties that Vala, Airmed and Jade lived on, this land was neither warded nor secret. The barriers to Aeden stood over a mile away, the only obstacle to a Shade invasion from this point. There was nothing stopping the Morrigan from hiding behind the next corner.

According to my visions, he probably was.

Realizing the danger we could be in, I grabbed Alec's arm. "We should be up front, not them. Come on."

"Okay," he said, letting me lead him past the others. "Why?"

Passing Amber and Ewan, I explained to all three of them at once. "We don't need the torches. We can see and you guys can't. We should be up front. Just in case."

"Good plan. Lead on." Ewan waved us along, allowing us to pull ahead.

I didn't slow down until we had put at least fifty feet between ourselves and the group. As we drew away from the bobbing beams of light, more nuances of the tunnel became visible. Small patches of moss grew along the cracks in the walls. The floors were hard packed dirt, their smoothness marred by the occasional pebble or fallen stone.

"Do you see anything?" I whispered.

"I see the tunnel."

"No, I mean, do you see any aura trails? Like at the apartment?"

"No. Nothing."

That should have reassured me, but I couldn't shake my apprehension.

I shivered, and Alec took my bag, adding it to his own as he wrapped an arm around my waist, drawing me close while we walked. The cold, damp air of the tunnels was warmer than the outside air, yet I felt chilled to the bone.

Another few minutes and we reached the subtle heat of the barrier. Against my cold skin, the warm caress stung. We stopped, standing before the invisible wall without crossing through.

"Now what?" Rose complained when she caught up. Did we take a wrong turn?" I'd forgotten that the barrier looked like a real stone wall to anyone who wasn't fae. Before I could explain, Vala spoke.

"You're using your eyes, apprentice. See with your soul."

Rose closed her eyes, breathing deeply, and I saw her aura flare. When she opened her eyes again she gazed upon the barrier and gasped.

"It's an illusion!"

"Yes. One we must first dismantle it if we are to make it stronger."

"Is that wise?" Dorian questioned.

"It's the only way. The barrier cannot just be strengthened, it must be reconfigured. That requires Rose and I to tap into the energy that is there, pull it apart like a tapestry, and reweave the strands of energy. The barrier won't be destroyed completely, but it will be weaker for a few minutes. Right now Druids all over the world are following similar procedures. They will each put their own spin on the magics they work, but the basic formula remains unalterable."

She dropped her pack and started rummaging through it, pulling out a small, dark polished stick and a bag of coarse salt. She handed the bag to Rose.

"What can we do?" I asked

"You should go. If this goes wrong...You need to be on the other side."

Dorian looked at her, expressionless, and turned. "Okay, you heard the lady. Amber, Ewan, Alec, I want you to take all the gear down to the cavern, get it secured on the gravicycles and wait for us so everything is ready when it's time to go. Siri and I will stay here with the Druids –

on the other side, as you said." He held up a hand to reassure Vala before she could protest.

We crossed the barrier and I watched my friends set off at a jog down the tunnel, flashlights and auras illuminating the stones around them as they disappeared into the distance.

Vala put Rose to work immediately, casting three lines of salt across the tunnel, parallel with barrier. She chanted under her breath, ancient words that had no meaning to me, yet stirred my soul. Vala joined her, increasing the power and volume behind the chant.

"Le geanmnaoicht le croí glan, ó solas mo anama, cearbhaill mo thoil agam, lig isteach mo ealaín gheal."

"It's an old form Gaelic," Dorian whispered in my ear. "She's saying, 'with purity of heart, by the light of my soul, bend to my will, let my white magic in.'"

Vala raised her hands, nodding at Rose to copy her, and they placed their palms in the air above the third line, furthest from the barrier, like two mimes trapped in a box.

The chanting continued on for several minutes.

Their palms crossed to the second line.

I was drawn in, wanting to touch the barrier, to reach through and add my magic to their own. Before I could take a step forward, I heard footsteps pounding behind me, stones skittering past me as approaching feet knocked them away.

Alec arrived panting. I'd never seen him out of breath, and the sight of it shocked me more than anything else could have.

Vala silenced him with a glare, and we moved further from the barrier.

"What's wrong?"

280

"The gravicycles, they're all gone. So many people came through, they used every last one. We'll have to walk."

"Can we call my father, ask him to send someone to get us?"

Alec shook his head. "No. The water doesn't work here so close to the barrier. We'll have to walk for a couple hours before we can call in, less time if we run it, but still a long way. And even then, it will take them a while to reach us. I've sent Amber and Ewan ahead to take care of it."

"Well then," Dorian said grimly, "let's hope that these Druids know what the hell they're doing. The sooner we get moving again, the better."

He padded quietly back to the barrier and crossed his arms across his chest, standing sentry.

Vala and Rose's hands had just reached the first line, closest to the barrier. They chanted for another minute, and then Vala thrust her hands into the barrier itself, continuing her litany. Rose backed away, grabbing the wand, and knelt behind Vala at her feet.

Vala's hands began to glow from within, as if someone was holding a flashlight against them. The brighter the shone, the more translucent they seemed, until they began to sparkle and disintegrate.

"Vala, your hands!" I cried out, unable to stop myself. She gave me another stern look, but did not stop chanting. She appeared comfortable, not in pain, and I could only pray that this magic would not involve any permanent loss of limbs.

Hands gone, sparkles swirled throughout the barrier, like so many fireflies stuck in a pane of glass. The chanting stopped, and she intoned out one word.

"Fearn."

Rose scratched a single long vertical line in the hard-packed earth with four short horizontal lines emerging to the right of the first mark.

The sparkles aligned into a uniform grid pattern stretching from one tunnel wall to the other.

"Straif."

Rose erased the four small lines and drew four more diagonal marks in their place, slashing across the long vertical line. The pinpoints of light fell at once, vibrating slightly above the floor, like someone had shaken them to the bottom of a glass.

"Oghams," Alec whispered in my ear, his breath sending tingles down my spine. "Druid runes."

"What do they mean?"

"No idea. But I think she's just opened up the barrier."

I reached out my hand, and sure enough, the tell-tale heat of warding was weaker, barely discernible. I yanked my hand back, not wanting to distract Vala in any way.

"Ur," Vala called out. Rose inscribed three lines across the vertical mark. Fireflies rose again, whirling in concert to form an open-ended circle that morphed into a loose spiral, back again, and again, on an endless, mesmerizing loop.

"Duir."

Rose erased the three lines, but before she could make a new mark, the earth shook. Rocks crashed down from the ceiling. The sparkles winked on and off, then came together in two quick, bunched masses. They flared once, brightly, and then they were gone. In their place, Vala's hands reappeared.

"Is it done?" I asked, hoping.

282

"No, it's not." Vala's voice shook and she staggered against the tunnel wall. "The barrier is up, but it is weaker than it was before, like a newborn. The final ogham was meant to strengthen the barrier with full power, but now...You must run!"

"What? No!"

Alec grabbed my shoulder, spinning me around. "She's right. I can see them coming. Heart paths, and Siri, these paths are Dark as night. They're closing in fast. We only have a couple minutes, if that."

"I won't leave them here!"

"You have to," Rose pleaded, tears streaming down her face. "We can't come with you."

Dorian laid a hand on my shoulder. "She's right. No one but a Light fae can cross this barrier – no matter how weak it is."

His words triggered a memory, something I'd heard before.

"Miko. Miko crossed the barrier with me, because he was honor bound." Before Alec or Dorian could stop me, I pushed through the barrier to kneel next to Rose. "You have to swear an oath of fealty to me. If you come with me, I'm saving your lives. Swear to serve me for a year and you will be able to cross with me."

Rose and Vala looked at me doubtfully, like they doubted my sanity. "Do it! What have you got to lose? If it doesn't work, I promise, I will leave you."

"You swear it?" Rose asked, clasping my hands.

"Yes."

"Alright." She took a shaky breath. "Siri Alvarsson, I owe you my life. Honor bound, I will serve you until my debt is repaid."

I punched her in the shoulder. "Jerk. That could be forever. You were supposed to just swear it for a year."

"Whatever, it's not like I've done this before. I improvised."

Vala snorted and repeated Rose's oath, this time with the annual limit.

"Great, I accept your fealty. Time to go!" I gripped their hands and hauled them both through the barrier. Expecting more resistance and not getting any, we stumbled into the guys on the other side.

Laughter filled the tunnel and Alec cursed. "They're here."

We all turned to see bright beams of light bobbing down the tunnels, dark auras muddles behind them.

"Go!" I pushed Rose, spurring her into action, and made to follow. Another tremor shuddered through the earth, knocking Vala to her knees. Alec pulled her up and led her down the path as fast as she could go. But Vala was a Druid, not a warrior. She didn't train to run marathons or fight with her hands. She wasn't in shape to outrun an earthquake. Was anyone?

I stood there, watching the Shades approach the barrier. Would it hold?

"Siri, dammit, come on!" Alec yelled over his shoulder.

I ignored him. Beyond the barrier, I could see the Morrigan, lips curled in a snarl. His eyes gleamed in the low light.

He pointed at the barrier and said, "Test it." I could just hear him over the rumbling ground. Rocks had stopped falling, but the earth trembled as if waiting to be released. One of his minions broke from the group and walked into the barrier. He passed through and I gasped.

We had failed.

And then he jerked and fell senseless to the floor. I laughed, surprised and relieved, and waved at the Morrigan. "Catch you later, M!"

He narrowed his eyes and beckoned impatiently over his shoulder. "Sascha, Bethe, hurry. I haven't got all day."

Twin women, girls really, stepped forward and pulled silver daggers from their sleeves. They cut into their left arms and let the blood fall, chanting all the while.

"You aren't the only one with Druid pets, Siri my dear," Mikael laughed.

"You dare defile the barrier with blood magic?" Dorian roared behind me. "May the Ancients curse you for all eternity!"

"Eternity? My boy, I'm only just getting started. Wait until you see what I dare." Mikael laughed, and Dorian cursed mightily.

He moved as if to rush the barrier himself and I instinctively moved to stop him. I played right into his trap. Using classic lasair technique to harness my own momentum, he leaned down and picked me up, tossing me over his shoulder.

"Dorian, you brute! Put me down!"

"Not a freaking chance." He started running, hopping over rocks as he went, holding me securely with one hand.

After a minute, I pinched him, hard. "Can you put me down now? I swear to god I am going to puke all over you if you don't."

Dorian didn't slow. "Are you going back there?"

"No," I grumbled.

"That's all I needed to hear." He plopped me down unceremoniously on my feet.

I glared at him and he raised his eyebrows, pointing his flashlight in my face. For the record, LEDs are crazy bright. Being able to see in the dark made them doubly painful to look at.

"Now run like your life depends on it, because it probably does."

CHAPTER 32

It didn't take long for us to catch up with the others. Vala was limping, having twisted her ankle along the way, so I held her hand as we walked, pouring my healing energy into her. It wasn't a full or instant cure, but soon she was able to jog slowly alongside me.

I filled her in on what Dorian and I had seen and she grimaced. "Sascha and Bethe? I can't believe it. I wonder what he is holding over their heads, that they would help him."

"Maybe nothing," Rose said. "Maybe the Morrigan has used the anti-serum on them."

"I'm not sure that is any better. The power of those two, at the Morrigan's beck and call...The twins come from one of the most pure and ancient Druid lines. Their magic when they work together is more powerful than any I have seen. The barrier won't last long with them chiseling away at it."

"Which is why we need to hurry," Dorian growled. "If you can't pick up the pace, I'll carry you myself, old woman."

"Don't you old woman me, you great lunk. If I need your help I will ask for it, thank you kindly."

Still, she increased her speed and the rest of us matched it.

"The quakes have stopped," Rose said hopefully. We'd just arrived in the massive cavern that usually housed dozens of gravicycles. Now, it was empty. Amber and Ewan were nowhere in sight, and I hoped that they were at a safer distance. "Maybe the Shades have given up."

"Or maybe they just don't want to mess up whatever magic the twins are casting," Vala harrumphed, breathing heavily. I channeled a bit more energy into her, hoping to give her the strength to keep up her "No, Mikael Morrigan is not one to give up so easily. If he can't break the barrier I dare say he'll blast a hole through the earth itself to reach us."

"Can he do that?" I asked.

"He is an earth fae, is he not? But the barrier doesn't just block the tunnel – it extends for a hundred feet in every direction, above and below, through rock and dirt. He'll have to dig far and long to do such a thing."

The ground trembled with shocking ferocity and I reached out to steady myself against the wall.

"It looks like he won't have to," Alec ground out between clenched teeth, positioning himself next to Vala and me.

The earth shuddered with unrelenting force. "It's not letting up. We can't wait. We have to move." Dorian shoved Rose towards the cavern's exit. "Come on. Go. Don't stop for anything."

"Hey! Watch it." She glared, but complied. Vala's eyes shot daggers at Dorian and she hurried after Rose. Dorian stalked off. Alec started to follow, but I paused. As an earth fae, wasn't there something I could do to counteract the Morrigan's power?

"Alec, wait. I have an idea. The Morrigan is powerful, but so are we. What if we can calm the earth, instead of agitating it?"

"It's worth a try. I'm better at working with plants, though, than the earth itself."

"Okay, let's see what we can do. You work your magic, I'll work mine."

We both slipped off our shoes and squatted on the ground, bracing ourselves against the floor.

I reached down deep into the earth, sending out feelers. I could sense the twisted roots of the Morrigan's power, racing along under the floor, angering the earth elements. The Morrigan wasn't controlling the earth so much as he was forcing it to try and buck him off its back. Instead of attacking his magic head on, I flooded the ground below us with mine, reassuring it, bonding with it. Soaking up the strength of its power, and pouring in my love in return. I went so far, I sensed the moment my power emerged on the surface of the mountains of Niflhelf. My power soaked in the radiance of the hot Aeden sun, running along the terrain like wildfire before it returned into the earth. Now, it could battle with the magic of the Morrigan.

It wasn't a conscious decision. I didn't decide to go on the offensive. The light itself was determined to illuminate Mikael's strands of twisted darkness. The moldering hate was a sickness that did not belong, and the light sought it out with laser precision.

His magic began to break apart, weaken and disintegrate. My heart leapt and I knew we were winning. Something brushed my feet and I glanced down, surprised to see that the floor was covered in thick, flowering vines. More vines lined the huge walls and ceiling of the stone hall, weaving in and out of the rock to create a strong, flexible support system from here to the exit. If I was the Heart of Life, if my power was based on the light of the red sun, Alec's magic was life itself. Small tendrils of vine rose up my legs, caressing my skin and anchoring me to the cavern floors.

I returned my attention to the earth. The Morrigan's energy was barely discernible. I followed it back to its source, chasing it with light, feeling it withdraw almost entirely into itself.

"Alec, we've done it. The Morrigan's magic is tapped." I looked at him and he smiled, but I could see sweat beading on his brow and knew he was almost out of energy himself, too.

"That's great. But what are we going to do to keep them out of Aeden? The barrier is almost down, I can feel it. It's weakening by the second."

I looked around the cavern, desperately trying to think of a solution. And then I had it. "You mentioned the Morrigan would tunnel to Aeden if he had to. What if we delayed him? Made him think that he's in a tunnel that leads somewhere – but it doesn't?"

"Make a false tunnel? I don't think I can do that."

"I know. You're running on empty. But I think I can. If you don't mind giving me what you've got left. The same way we helped Jade at her house last month."

"That, I can do."

He placed his hands on my shoulders and his energy washed over me, familiar and similar to my own, yet different. The divine scent of Alec filled my senses, coriander and pine, so welcome in the dank underground. I enjoyed it for a moment, and then I reached once again to the light of Aeden, tapping into the sun at the same time I pulled from Alec. I imagined that the earth was a living, sentient being, and asked it to move a bit to the left, shift a little to the right. Make a new tunnel that twisted and turned to lead nowhere good. The earth groaned again, but this time, it was not the Morrigan who was playing with mud.

It was me.

I saw the rocks singing to each other as they moved, shimmying and shifting to create a wild way that would delay the Shades for hours while they tried to follow it from the cavern. All that remained was for us to follow the right tunnel, its opening only feet away from the false path, and block it as we escaped.

I opened my eyes and grinned, wiping sweat off my own brow. Excavation was hard work, with or without a shovel. Alec looked in bad shape, his face was ashen and his eyes barely shone. Instead of a brilliant violet or even a deep green, they wavered pale silvery lilac.

We had done it, and that was all that mattered.

We helped each other up and began picking our way across the open floor, taking care to navigate around fallen stones and small crevasses that had opened in the ground.

I knew the exact moment the barrier fell. It wasn't dramatic or loud. It didn't shake the earth. It didn't send a blast of light through the tunnel. There was no shockwave.

Part of my energy was still rooted to the earth and I felt the barrier's energy get torn apart, like a veil. The interesting thing was, it didn't just disappear, like I had thought it might. The energy was absorbed back into the earth, welcomed back like family with love. Too bad I couldn't feel that way about the Shades gaining access to Aeden.

"We need to hurry." I gritted my teeth and kicked a rock in my haste, stumbling and then catching myself before I fell. "Quickly! The barrier's down."

Alec grunted, also stumbling and trying to keep up with me. It was the first time I had ever outpaced him, and I didn't like it one bit.

We had just made it into the mouth of the true tunnel when I felt the first rush of Dark power heading for us. It was as if the earth literally hissed and recoiled from the distorted energy. I braced myself for another earthquake, but it never came. Instead, a tsunami of negativity roared into me, stealing my breath and dropping me to the floor. I cried out as my knee jammed into a sharp rock, but the pain was nothing compared the sorrow I suddenly felt. I wanted to curl up on the floor right there and sob like a little girl until the Shades arrived and put me out of my misery. Hope was gone. Happiness was gone. I reached for light, but felt none.

Where was Alec? Where were my friends? The barrier had fallen. We were doomed. I could feel Rowan pumping horror and depression into the air like a transfusion, and I was unable to break free from the depths of despair.

A moan behind me jolted me into awareness. Alec. He wasn't gone. He was right behind me. Knowing he was nearby, reminded me of who I was, where I was. I had to stand up. If not for me, then for Alec. The tunnel had to be closed. Now, before the Shades arrived in the cavern. I didn't know how much time had passed since they broke through the barrier, but I had a sickening feeling that we only had moments left.

I tried to stand and my head swam, nausea bubbling up from inside. Pain rocketed through my knee and I moaned.

I heard shouts and laughter, the familiar voices of Rowan and Mikael standing out as they laughed and called to me. Taunting me.

But I'd already changed my earlier visions. We were almost home. Today, I refused to lead the Shades into Aeden. They might get there eventually, but I was going to do everything in my power to delay their arrival.

Today, we were going to do things my way, not theirs. I'd helped the Morrigan once. I would never do it again.

I gathered the last of my reserves and reached into the earth one last time. I expected my work to be harder, more difficult, after I had already done so much. The emotional attack had shattered me to the core. But as I dipped down into the earth, I was buoyed up by the lingering power of the barrier. It had fallen, yet its traces remained.

Drawing on its power, I understood a little more about how it really worked. Not of the light itself, it was a living, breathing sentry created to know and embrace the light. It whispered of strength and rebirth, of new beginnings and purity of intention, of care and the presence of the gods. Recognizing something in me, ancient blood calling to ancient power, it untangled itself from the earth and pooled around my feet.

The way forward was clear. Rowan ran into the cavern alone just as I was pulling the power up across the tunnel like a curtain, rebooting the barrier.

"No!" He sprinted across the floor, faster than I'd ever seen him move, and dove headlong through the wall of energy just as it locked into place. Too late. He spasmed in pain and fell to the ground in a twisted heap, but I wasn't paying attention. Aeden was shielded once again, but it was just another temporary solution. I still needed to buy us more time. I called to the stone and the dirt and coerced them to dance once more. Rocks skittered together, hiding the tunnel from view. The last thing I saw as the wall closed us off from the cavern was Mikael's foot striding into view, about to step upon the cavern floor.

I could only pray he hadn't seen me, too.

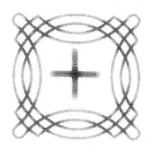

CHAPTER 33

Alec was weak, but with a bit more shared energy, a sample of the surge combined with my own healing power, I was able to rouse him. I'd thought his eyes pale before, but now they were dull, too. Covered with a sheen of pain. Perhaps it was because he'd already been weakened. Or maybe he was more susceptible to the harmful water magic after having suffered its torture for two days. Whatever the reason, the attack Rowan had sent through the tunnels had hit Alec harder than me.

It didn't matter. We needed to get moving. Rowan still lay unconscious at my back. According to what people had told me, he'd be out for hours. Enough time to find the others. Maybe even enough time to get back to Valhalla. Perhaps my father would know how to release him from the thrall of the Dark. Maybe we could reprogram him ourselves. At the very least, he might have an idea of what Mikael was planning next. They seemed to have bonded in their hatred of me, their desire to bend me to their will and punish the light. Mikael had found a willing acolyte in Rowan.

That gave me another reason to keep him close, keep him safe. If Mikael valued his new pet apprentice, he could beg me to make a deal. It was a longshot, but it was a chance. Or maybe it was fate.

On his feet, Alec narrowed his eyes. "What the hell is he doing here?"

"Shh, I don't know how thick that wall is," I said, pointing at the rocks behind me. "Mikael and his people might still be on the other side."

Alec crossed his arms and waited, staring at me impassively.

"He jumped through the barrier, right before I raised the wall. He'll be out for a while, but we really should get moving. It's going to take us longer carrying that dead weight."

"Carry him? You can't mean to bring him with us," Alec hissed.

"Why not? We can't leave him here to cause more trouble. At least if he's with us we can keep an eye on him."

Alex cocked his head, the twitching muscle in his jaw a glaring tell that he was irritated.

"I could kill him, that would keep him from causing trouble," Alec said seriously.

"Not an option." I remembered the collar in my pocket and took it out, showing it to Alec. "Look, I have this. It'll keep us safe, even if he wakes up."

I looped the thin silver band around Rowan's neck and secured it. A small light winked on and off, signaling that the collar had been activated.

"There, now his powers are blocked."

Alec looked unconvinced.

"What? It's a good plan."

He sighed. "I suppose. Can we at least drag him by his feet? Maybe over a few bumps, cause some brain damage?"

"Alec," I warned.

"No, you're right. It wouldn't make any difference. He's mentally impaired as it is."

I laughed, despite our situation. "Come on, jerk. Help me lift him."

We positioned Rowan between us, bearing his arms around our shoulders so we could half drag, half carry them. It was awkward, but it was manageable.

"What if he wakes up before we reach the others? Tries to fight?" Alec asked while we walked.

"You can knock him out again, I promise."

Alec grunted. "Trust me, I will."

We hiked through the unlit tunnel without talking for a long time. I could tell Alec had questions, but I was grateful for the silence. Rowan was getting heavier and heavier, and I knew we wouldn't reach the end of the tunnels for hours yet. Maybe days. I had no real concept of the length of the tunnel. On the gravicycle, riding at 25-50 miles per hour, I knew it took an hour or more. Doing the math in my head, I guessed we still had anywhere from thirty to sixty miles to go. At an optimistic three miles per hour, it would take us close to half a day to walk the distance.

That wasn't counting breaks, or the fact that we were lugging Rowan like a fallen soldier.

The thought of dragging Rowan the whole way on our own was depressing, so I decided not to think about it. There was no sense worrying about something I couldn't fix.

I'd succeeded at not worrying, putting one foot in front of the other relentlessly, when Alec picked up the thread my mind had dropped.

"How long do you think you're going to be able to keep this up?"

"What, you getting tired?" I scoffed.

"Not any more tired than I already was. But in a little while we should at least switch sides."

"Hmpf. I guess."

Honestly, the idea of putting Rowan down and picking him up again was even less appealing than walking for another hour straight. Not something I was ready to admit to Alec.

"You know, a less secure guy would think maybe you weren't over your ex. You know, since he keeps coming between us."

I snorted. "Nice one." I rolled my eyes at his lame attempt at humor. Not that he could see the gesture, with Rowan's head lolling between us.

"I'm trying, Siri, really, I am. But this guy, the things he's done..."

I knew he was thinking of the days when Rowan had held him captive. The lost hours he still hadn't told me about.

"Do you want to talk about it? What he did?" Part of me wanted to know, to understand what Alec had gone through while Rowan had him. But I was scared, too. What if I couldn't forgive him? I knew it was bad. I knew the darkness in Rowan's mind had eclipsed the light in his soul, at least for now. I wasn't a complete Pollyanna.

Alec didn't answer me. Not right away. And then he sighed, a heavy sound, almost like a release.

"I guess now is as good a time as any. I've told you what happened to my mom and sister, how the Shades tortured them before they were killed?"

"Yes. I remember."

"Well, the things I saw that day, when they found them...my mother was literally in pieces. There was blood everywhere. And my sister..." I sensed, rather than saw, him shake his head. "She was only seven, you know?"

"I know," I whispered.

"I've imagined so many times what it must have been like for them that day. How it must have gone down. Rowan's power, it brought it all back, in the worst possible way. You know how I told you a water fae can use their powers to make someone experience their worst fears?"

This time, I nodded, unable to speak. I bit my lip, a terrible feeling of pain rising in my sternum.

"Yes."

"Well," he laughed, a hard, grating sort of sound, completely devoid of humor," your friend Rowan has perfected his art. I saw it all, in vivid detail, over and over."

The pain in his voice made me close my eyes. Immediately, I saw imagined scenes of blood and horror, and I opened my eyes, denying the vision.

Alec went on in a whisper. "Except it wasn't my mother, or my sister. I saw you. Every time, it was you. Being tortured and abused, by Rowan, by Mikael, by every Shade I've ever met. Over and over again. Every time, I thought I would die, and I begged them to take me instead, to spare you, to-" He broke off. "It didn't matter. They would laugh, and I would be helpless, watching you suffer and die. And when you died, a part of me would die, too. I could feel it. The pieces of my soul being chipped

299

away. I would wish I were dead, and everything would go black, and I would be so thankful that it was over."

"Oh, Alec-"

"But then it would start again. Sometimes in my old home in Boston. Other time, other places. But always me, bound and helpless. And you. Suffering right in front of me. People say, 'I don't know what I'd do if something ever happened to you.' But I do. I know, Siri. And it kills me. Killed me."

I didn't know what to say, just let out the breath I didn't know I'd been holding.

"But," he said, and I could hear the hint of smile in his voice, "you saved me. You didn't just bring me back, you saved me. All of me. Whatever happened to me during that sunrise, you brought me back. All of me. I'm stronger than I was before. Whole."

"But...are you sure? I'm so sorry, Alec, I had no idea how hard this really was for you."

"It is hard. Talking through everything has helped. I didn't realize I was still holding onto the things he made me see, not so much. But talking through it, I can see it better now. If you want to bring him in, I will do it, because it's what you say we have to do. And I trust you, completely. And you're here. We're both here. All that fear I had inside me, it's not gone, I won't say that, but it's smaller. And I can identify it for what it really is: fear. Nothing more. Nothing less."

"Thank you, Alec. You know, a part of me died when I saw him using his powers on you, too. I went kind of crazy when I saw him take you. Dorian can tell you all about it, sometime."

"I know, I felt you when you saved me. And that's why I was so angry when I found out that you gave the

Morrigan what he wanted, just to save me. Because I was already dead, but you..."

"I know."

"Tell me we're going to make it through this, Siri."

"We are." I said it like it was a sure thing. Like I really knew we would all be okay.

"Okay then."

We went back to walking in silence. Minutes collected, like drops in a bucket. Drop. Drop. Drop. We couldn't even play "I Spy." The tunnels were monotonous, other than the occasional fluorescent rock embedded in the walls, peeking through the Alec's flowers and vines. Eventually, I knew the rocks would become more numerous, since when we were on the gravicycles they appeared like galactic stars shooting by in hyperdrive. Now though? They were just starting to appear, one here, one there.

Boring.

And just seven or nine more hours to go. Perfect.

"I see something," Alec whispered.

"Really? Because I was thinking we could play 'I Spy', but then I figured there wasn't much to look at."

"No, Siri. I see something coming. Someone."

"Can you tell who it is?"

"No. But it's got to be one of our people, since the Shades didn't break through the barrier before us."

"Hope so. I could go a few more hours without seeing any Shades."

"Um..."

"Except this one, jackhole. I'm not leaving him."

"Yeah, yeah. I know. Time for that break, 'cause here they come."

We stopped and gently lowered Rowan to the ground. Well, I did, anyway. Alec kind of let him drop when he got closer to the ground. I winced and he shrugged, as if to say, *what, it was an accident.*

I wasn't buying it, but there wasn't time to worry about bruised craniums. Footsteps pounded up the tunnel towards us. Out of the darkness, a hulking mass moving surprisingly fast, a tiny LED beam flickering along the dirt floor.

Blonde hair reflected pink highlights from a nearby glowing rock.

"Dorian?" Alec and I said at the same time.

"Jinx," Alec said over his shoulder, stepping forward to meet the Guard.

"Alec, Siri. Vala and Rose are having a 'sit in'," he grimaced, making air quotes. "They say they won't move until they know you are okay."

"We're fine, as you can see. We bought us some time. The Shades should be chasing their tails for a while down some blind tunnels."

"What blind tunnels?" Dorian asked, confused.

"Ones that I made. By the time they figure it out, hopefully we'll be long gone. Better yet, maybe we'll be in Valhalla already."

"Then let's move. We've still got a lot of ground to cover."

"Not so fast. We have a prisoner." Alec stopped Dorian, pointing to Rowan behind us in the shadows.

"What the hell? How did you-"

"Long story. She can tell you all about it. But now that you're here, you can help me carry him."

"You carried him? Are you crazy? Why didn't you just leave him where you found him?"

"He came through the second barrier I erected and passed out, but eventually he'll wake up. We couldn't leave him there to help the Morrigan," I explained.

"What do you mean, the second barrier? Never mind, it doesn't matter. We can't bring a Shade into Aeden. It's treason."

"Well, he's already past the barrier, so he's already in. Now he's a prisoner of war, right? He might be useful. Anyway, I'm not leaving him."

Dorian stepped closer to the still body.

"Isn't that your darkling friend? The one who took Alec? Are you sure this is wise?"

"No. I'm not sure of anything. But he's coming."

"Fine." Dorian exhaled heavily and started pulling off his belt. "Let's secure his hands and feet. Either of you have another belt?"

We didn't, so I undid its knotted end and pulled the thick string out of my hood. Dorian nodded.

"That'll do." He wrapped the webbed belt around Rowan's ankles pulling it tight before he fastened it. Then, he flipped Rowan roughly unto his stomach, tying the rope around his wrists and hands, pressing his palms tightly together. "That should help keep him from using his water power if he does wake up."

We all stood, and Dorian picked Rowan up like a carpet, heaving him over one shoulder.

"I'll take this shift, Alec, you have carried him far enough for now."

"Actually, we were carrying him together, splitting the load," I piped in.

Dorian rebuked Alec with a glance, as if carrying unconscious people wasn't women's work. Alec looked away, running a hand through his hair. Oh my God. Was he actually embarrassed?

"What? It's not like I could carry him myself," I said, annoyed. "And we didn't know you were coming back. You thought Alec should carry him the whole eight hours or whatever?"

Dorian shook his head and started to walk away. "I'm not getting into this with you. I think we've already established you aren't entirely reasonable."

"What do you mean," I yelled, running around him to get in his face. He kept walking towards me, so I jogged backwards. "I am totally reasonable."

"Really? You barged your way into a rescue mission for Alec. You went off on your own when you thought you knew where he was."

"Rescuing him," I retorted.

"Activating the anti-serum," he scolded.

"Whatever. Like you're so perfect."

"Do you have proof to the contrary?"

That actually stumped me. As annoying as he could be, Dorian followed protocol to the letter. And he'd always helped me when I really needed.

"See?" Dorian grinned when I didn't answer right away. "I take it all back. You're totally reasonable."

"Ha. Don't tempt her, Dor. Who knows what she'll do next," Alec warned, amusement rich in his voice.

"She might insist on the Morrigan for a pet," Dorian laughed.

They continued on like that for longer than I care to remember. It was at least another half hour before we reached Rose and Vala. When they saw us round the bend, the women both leapt to their feet, rushing towards us.

"Thank the gods, you're alright!" Vala embraced us both in her arms, and Rose joined in for a warm group hug. "But who's this..."

Dorian dumped Rowan on the ground and Vala drew in her breath in shock, recognizing him instantly. "The young darkling? You brought him here?"

"He came on his own. After the Shades broke through the barrier Alec and I combined our Earth magic to stop Mikael and strengthen the tunnel," I gestured at the vines. "I made a false path for them to follow, and was about to block the way here from the main cavern. Then I realized that some of the energy from the barrier was still there, still in the earth around us. I called it up and formed a new barrier. I had just brought it up when Rowan appeared, running through. The rest of the Shades weren't far behind and I sealed the tunnel at the last second. Right now they should be miles away, thinking they are on their way to Aeden. It will take them hours to figure out what's really happened, and then they'll have to find the right tunnel, and take down the barrier again. Hopefully, by then we'll be safe back in Valhalla. Or at least on our way there."

"You did all that?" Rose asked, astounded. "I knew you were powerful, but...that's amazing. Calling up the barrier by yourself?" She shook her head.

Vala patted her shoulder. "Our Siri is a wonder, indeed."

"Well," I blushed, "I didn't do it by myself. You guys did most of the work. The barrier was there, it just needed to be pulled back up."

Alec threw an arm around me, "See, she's humble, too. That's my girl." He pulled me to him and kissed the side of my head.

A weak laugh sounded behind us. "Ugh, you guys are disgusting. Does the cheese factor ever let up?"

I turned to look at Dorian, but he shook his head, looking down. Rowan.

So, the Dark had risen.

I stared at him, not sure what to say. What words did you use when you were staring at a friend who had done everything they could to hurt you? I should have been mad at him. I should have been pissed that he was trying to hurt not just me, but everyone I knew. I was so sure though, so adamant that the root of his evil and hate grew from an overabundance of love. Love that had been damaged, twisted and hurt. I had promised Holly that I would help him. And I would. I knew her death wasn't really my fault, at least, not the way Rowan thought of it. But I felt like I had a responsibility to Holly's memory to rehabilitate her brother. Maybe it was crazy. Maybe it was unrealistic. Maybe, as Dorian had hinted, it was even unreasonable.

Holly's death had scarred him in ways that I was still having a hard time coming to terms with. Hell, Holly's death had scarred me, too. Maybe it was just part of my own healing process, but I was determined to make things right with Rowan eventually.

Deep down, I guess I felt like his surprise appearance at the barrier was fated. A second chance to get him out of the Shades clutches. An opportunity to fix him.

CHAPTER 34

What is it they always say about girls who try to change their boyfriends?

Right.

It can't be done. I'd read enough magazine articles to know it was stupid to date someone you wanted to "fix." Everyone has their own inherent character and set ways. Sure, sometimes people's attitudes change, but everyone said it was better to find a man you liked, than to try and mold one to your liking.

I knew that. So what was I thinking?

I started questioning the wisdom of my decision to bring Rowan along almost the moment I heard his voice. The sarcasm and underlying hatred I heard stung me, but I didn't let it show.

"Hello, Rowan. Welcome back to the land of the living. So nice of you to drop through the barrier for a visit." He'd always brought out the snark in me. Perhaps I should have taken that as a sign.

"Hey, Serious. Enjoying your last conscious moments?"

"Enjoying my...Are you threatening me?"

Alec and Dorian both moved to step in front of me, and I sidestepped them.

"I would never," he chuckled, sitting himself up against the wall. "Just stating a fact. Last night we sent out ten teams with the virus to infect major airport hubs around the country. By the end of the week, 95% of the world should be infected."

"So why are you here? Why are you chasing us?"

"The Morrigan knows you all won't be content to stay safe down below forever. You might like to pretend you are all lightness and good, but you could never let someone else control the world. You want to be the best, to control the world just as much as we do. You must be stopped. Quarantine isn't enough, you need to be contained."

"I've heard enough of this crap," Dorian strode forward and knocked Rowan out cold. "Siri, you really expect us to lug this trash all the way to Valhalla?"

"I do." Dorian threw up his hands and started pacing. "Look, I know he's unpleasant, and I get how you you're feeling, I totally do. But we don't have a lot of time. You want to waste it arguing about him?"

Dorian grunted and stalked angrily over to Rowan, reaching to heft him onto his shoulder again.

"Wait," Vala said. She'd been staring at Rowan, deep in thought, for the last several minutes. "You don't need to carry him."

"Vala," I sighed, exasperated.

"Don't you 'Vala' me. Hear me out. We've got everything we need right here to make a stretcher for the boy, let's use it."

309

She waved her hand at the vines, just in case we missed her point.

"Great idea," Alec said, and started ripping vines down off the walls. I tried to help, but the vines didn't budge.

"You have to ask nicely," Alec teased.

I shot him a look and sent out a silent plea to the plants, explaining what we needed them to do. I tugged on the vines and they fell away from the walls. Vala gathered them from the floor and began weaving a narrow stretcher, complete with two long, looped handles so that Rowan could be dragged comfortably by two people. Alec touched the stretcher and smaller vines wound between the weavings, strengthening the craft. We loaded Rowan onto the stretcher, head up towards the handles so he wouldn't be jostled as much (despite Dorian's encouragements to do the reverse). Alec stroked the stretcher again and vines shot out around Rowan's body, tethering him tightly.

"He's going to be so pissed when he wakes up," I muttered.

"Right, good point." Alec said with a twisted smile, placing his hand on the vines over Rowan's shoulder. Soft, leafy tendrils looped together over Rowan's mouth, holding it closed. "There. Now you don't have to worry about his head bumping around while we run."

"You have a dark side, Alec Ward," I teased.

"Don't we all?" He grinned, and moved around to the front of the stretcher. Dorian snarled but he joined Alec to take up the handles. "Okay, you heard the darkling. The Shades are on their way and the clock is ticking. We're going to have to go as fast as we can, for as far as we can. This is a marathon, not a sprint, so we'll just be doing a light jog. Can everyone manage that?"

310

We all nodded.

"Great. When you need a break, say something. Hopefully Amber and Ewan have gotten a message to Bran by now, and help is on the way. But we can't assume anything." Alec straightened, assuming the mantle of leader. "Vala, Rose, I know you guys aren't used to running the way Siri and I are, so you two head out in front. You set the pace. We'll follow. Siri, you should bring up the rear. I don't like the idea of Rowan being unsupervised, even if he is trussed up like a Thanksgiving turkey. It's your job to keep an eye on him."

"Don't worry about us, Light Guard," Vala laughed slyly. "We Druids still have a few tricks up our sleeve."

"Good. Let's move out, people."

We started running at a slow pace, the kind of jog I knew I could maintain for hours if needed. Ahead, I could hear Vala leading Rose in a quiet chant as they ran, the throaty accent of foreign words catching my ear. It wasn't Gaelic. It sounded older. More primitive. Whatever it was, I hoped it gave them the stamina needed to carry us fast and far.

My gaze fell on Rowan. The stretcher made moving our prisoner much easier, and I was sorry I hadn't thought of it myself before. He slept soundly, strapped tightly to the contraption.

His face was relaxed, peaceful at rest. The Rowan I had known seemed within reach when he was like this. No anger marring his countenance. No hate twisting his features. No grief shadowing his eyes.

The hate and blame could perhaps be alleviated by some good therapy and reprogramming in Valhalla. But the grief? I wasn't sure there was any cure for the trauma of losing your twin, besides time.

I grimaced and fought off the wave of sadness that always threatened to overtake me when I thought of Holly. It wasn't the way she would have wanted to be remembered. So I turned my thoughts aside to sunnier ideals and found myself thinking of the Ananzi portal. I wished there had been more time to explore and study the ruins. The glittering tableau that adorned the ceiling in the main chamber had been particularly remarkable.

That sun. The seven rayed symbol of Anansanna had become synonymous with Ananzi wherever he went. A god who taught people to get along. To farm. To harness the warmth of the sun to heal the people. In all the stories, cooperation was the key to harmony.

What if it was more than just a story? What if there was a lesson, a message in the ancient folktales?

All at once, I saw a glow pool in front of me, lighting the way before me, trailing alongside Rowan like a caress, spinning around Alec, and shooting up and past Rose.

A heart path. My heart path. I knew it was trying to show me something, but what?

Did it have something to do with the sun? With the Ananzi portal? Or with my friends? The heart path continued before me in the same pattern, beaming past Rose to flow down the gloomy path, trailing out of sight.

I thought back to something Alec had said after the sunrise that morning at Vala's. Less than a day ago, yet it felt like an eternity. Still, his words came back to me with perfect clarity.

We have to show more people. If everyone could experience the sun like that, I bet there wouldn't be any more Dark fae. No more polluting. No more air pollution. Everything is so, so alive.

Easier said than done. I couldn't dream of how to show that many people to hear the sun's song. Somehow, I didn't think the Dark would be interested in learning that new skill, and interest was sort of key to hearing it.

Wasn't it?

The heart path shuddered and withdrew itself back into me, pooling again around my feet, and then splayed out into seven flared rays. It flashed once, twice, seven times. And then it disappeared.

What the hell?

I looked up to see Rowan watching me, eyes wide. Had he seen something? He saw the question in my eyes and narrowed his, spearing me with a look of hatred yet again. I sighed. Great. Just what I wanted to look at while I ran. Feeling childish, I stuck out my tongue at him and gave him a cocky look. I wasn't going to let him rattle me. Maybe some running meditation was in order again.

I fixed my eyes on the empty space above the stretcher and counted my footsteps, breathing in time. One, two, three. One, two, three. One long inhale, one sharp exhale. Breathing in. Breathing out.

I fell into the mindless rhythm effortlessly, zoning out as my boots pounded the floor.

We stood below the Tree of Life. My heart path was radiating out from me, pulsing and weaving among my friends before zipping up the tree. Again and again it flashed the same pattern. Encompassing my family, my loved ones. Ascending the tree.

I had to be right. We were all connected to this, somehow. I had to trust that the solution would be clear if I followed the way being shown.

I looked around. My mother. My father. Alec. Amber and Ewan. Rose and Vala. Rowan and Dorian. Jade and Claire.

"Quickly. You know what to do." I watched the people I cared most about in this world scatter and fan out towards each of the seven towers.

Trusting them to do what needed to be done, I took a deep breath and turned. I stared up the trunk of the great tree, watching my heart path flash among the limbs.

I didn't know what might wait for me at the top, or if I even would have to travel that far. It didn't matter. We'd run out of options. Out of time to think or plan.

It was time to climb.

I stumbled over a root and came out of the vision. I knew now where we were headed, what I had to do. Or at least part of it.

I looked at Rowan, who was watching me again. I suppose he didn't really have a choice, given the position he was in. I appraised him, comparing the Rowan in my vision to the Rowan before me now.

Same clothes. Same dirt on the face. Feet unbound, but arms tied behind his back. Dorian, dragging him away roughly.

For whatever reason, he was part of the solution. We needed him.

I rather wished I knew why.

I tried to reason it out, to understand what my vision had told me, but nothing rang clear. A science-minded gal, it rankled to have to put all my faith in visions and heart paths. But I didn't see as I had any other choice.

Rowan must have seen the consternation on my face, because his eyes laughed at me. He thought he was going to win.

I wasn't going to let that happen.

I lifted my gaze and focused on my friends. We had slowed somewhat, but Vala and Rose were keeping an admirable pace. Whatever powers they had invoked, it had worked.

Suddenly, Alec lifted his free hand in warning. "Everybody, hit the floor!"

Dorian and Alec let go of the stretcher as we all dropped to the ground. Rowan grunted, distracting me for a moment. And then I heard it. A quiet hum, the unmistakable sound of gravicycles approaching fast.

Twelve golden machines burst around the corner and raced over our heads before slowing and turning around.

"Good thing you heard them coming," Dorian grumbled at Alec. "Their rescue mission almost turned into a decapitation party."

"Sorry about that," Amber jumped off her cycle and hugged me. She had been leading the charge. "I never imagined you guys would have gotten this far already."

Someone pushed Amber out of the way to hug me.

"Mom?"

"Yes, darling. I wasn't about to let your father have all the fun." She threw my father a 10,000 megawatt smile, then wrapped her arms around me again. "I've been worried sick about you," she admonished.

"Welcome to the club," I sighed.

"What's this," Bran pointed at Rowan on the floor. He chided Amber, "You didn't tell me there was wounded."

"There wasn't." She shrugged.

My mother's eyes went wide. "That's Rowan Carey. Siri, what have you done?"

"He came through the barrier, Mom. We had to take him with us."

"That's debatable," Dorian argued.

"No, it's not. While we were running I had another vision. We're going to need him."

I filled them all in on what I had seen.

"So you see, we need to get back to the tree right away. There's no time to lose."

"Right, well, it's a good thing we brought some extra Guards. Nix, Barit, Carr, Jackson, Sandra, patrol the tunnel, but stay away from the new barrier. If you see any Shades, you alert me immediately and get the hell out of here. The rest of you, double up."

Dorian volunteered to ride with Rowan. The vines around his body fell away and we unbound his feet, forcing him to straddle the bike while Alec called the vines to secure him in place behind Dorian. The gag remained on at Dorian's request.

My mother hitched a ride with my father, telling Alec and I to take her cycle. Everyone else grabbed a partner and we sped off towards the exit. We flew the tunnels faster than I'd ever dared before, faster even than I had ridden with Amber. None of us wanted to be caught in the tunnels when the Morrigan came through.

We dove through the earth, navigating corridors swiftly, then climbing up for the final leg of the underground journey. We were just finishing our ascent towards Aeden when a loud rumble shook the cavern walls. Alec's vines had not grown this far, so nothing prevented rocks and pebbles being rattled loose. The debris showered down on our heads, pelting us like hail. I looked over at my parents, and saw a large button on the gravicycle light up. I peered over Alec's shoulder to examine the identical button on our bike. It was clear and domed, rather like a small snow globe. Inside, a small air bubble bobbed and weaved. I had always assumed it was a sort of level, something to help fliers navigate the sky. But now I realized it was filled with the silvery waters of Aeden. Bran was shouting over the wind, slowing down the gravicycle while he argued with a voice coming from the water. Barit.

I motioned for Alec to get closer. I wanted to hear what they were saying.

"They've blasted a hole through the tunnel walls and taken us by surprise, sir. A few of us are hurt. I can't see...I'm behind some rocks...Oh gods. He's sprayed Carr with something. He's out..."

"Get the hell out of there, Barit!" my father ordered furiously.

"There's nowhere to go...I-"

"So sorry, the young man seems to have fallen asleep." The unmistakable voice of the Morrigan transmitted gleefully over the water, followed by a dull thud that sounded sickeningly like someone kicking soft flesh.

"Now, now," Mikael reprimanded, "No sense kicking a man when he's down."

Voices argued in a jumble, and then silence.

"There's nowhere to hide now. Nowhere that's safe. We're coming for you. Don't worry, I'll make your transition from power as painless as possible."

Laughter rang manically over the waves and Bran swore, smashing the button. My mother exclaimed as the

317

bike swerved and the glass shattered under my father's hand, water trickling down the side of the bike.

My father turned to look at me, despair in his eyes. "They're only an hour behind us. Whatever it is you're thinking to do, that's all the time you're going to have. I hope it's enough."

He faced forward and sped off, leading us through the tunnels at breakneck speed. My mother looked over her shoulder, her face a mixed mask of encouragement and resignation. She wanted to believe I could do it. That I could fix this.

But how could she, when I wasn't sure myself?

Chapter 35

We didn't bother landing on the gravicycle deck. There wasn't time.

Alec had called ahead and arranged for my grandmother and Claire to meet us in the main plaza. My vision had shown them there, so I assumed it was important.

The area had been cleared, there wasn't a single person in sight. Everyone had been evacuated to other towns and homesteads. If this didn't work, we hoped to make the Shades work as difficult as possible. At the very least, it would give people time to say goodbye to loved ones.

Below the tree, shielded from the red sun by the dark green canopy, stood Jade and my childhood friend. They waited, looking concerned, Claire wringing her hands as we switched off our engines. Quickly, without speaking we unloaded our bags and released Rowan from the vines strapping him to the gravicycle. I walked over to my grandmother, giving her a kiss on her cheek, and motioned for everyone to gather near.

"Mom, Dad, Ewan, Amber, Alec, Rose, Vala, Jade, Claire, Rowan and Dorian." I named everyone from my vision. "I need you here. The rest of you – take a cycle and go to your families. Leave Valhalla. Get to safety, wherever you can."

The remaining Light Guards who had accompanied my father looked to their commander for confirmation. Bran inclined his head solemnly and they saluted him, then dashed for the bikes. In moments their gold machines had scattered in different directions and winked out of sight.

"Okay. This is it then. I told most of you my vision already, but not everyone here has heard it. Basically, I know that there is an answer for me waiting at the top of this tree. And I know that I need at least one of you in each of the towers around me. I don't know why. I just know that's how it's supposed to be. I suppose this is where that whole trust thing is supposed to come in," I smiled weakly at Vala.

Rowan snorted, and Dorian gave him a shove. The two fae glared daggers at each other and I went on.

"I'm not sure, but I think the answer has to do with love, and that's why I need you. Because I care about all of you, deeply."

I looked each of them in the eye, one by one, my gaze coming to rest on Alec.

"I don't know exactly what you are supposed to do in the towers, but I know I am supposed to follow my heart path and climb up this damn tree. So I think the best thing is for you all to climb to the top of your towers, too. Get as high as you can."

"As some of you know, each tower has an observation deck at its highest point," my father interrupted, looking excited. "Access has always been restricted to the decks, and only the Commander of the Light Guard ever has the access code. It's part of my job to inspect the decks once a year, and make sure they are still functional. Otherwise, they are never to be used."

"Can you give us the code?"

"Yes. When I was sworn in, I was given a ledger that said the code has never been changed, that the decks are integral to the continuation of life and light itself. I never imagined I would get to see how."

Rowan made a gagging sound and rolled his eyes.

Dorian looked at me. "Are you absolutely sure we need this one?"

"Completely. In fact, you get to partner up with him. So make sure he stays conscious."

Dorian made a face and grumbled something under his breath but looked resigned.

"Dad? The code?"

"Red Queen. You only have to speak it at the doors, and they will open."

"Okay then. Time's a-wasting. Mom, you take Tower One. Dad, Tower Two. Alec, Three. Amber and Ewan in four. Rose and Claire in Five, Jade and Vala in Six, and Dorian you take Rowan to Seven. Everybody got that?"

Everyone nodded.

"Great. Move as fast as you can, and don't leave your posts until it's over."

Everyone started to fan out, but a question from Ewan stopped them in their tracks.

"How will we know it's over?"

"Well, hopefully it will be something obvious. That, or you wait for someone to come get you."

"Right," he nodded. And with that, the motion resumed.

I waited a moment, watching everyone I held most dear hurry towards the towers. Some walked quickly, others ran. Dorian hoisted Rowan over his shoulder again when Rowan resisted walking.

It was time.

I took a deep breath and looked at the tree, seeking my heart path. Almost immediately, light shot out before me, snaking its way up the limbs of the tree. It was leaving a discernible trail, but it clearly wanted me to hurry.

The Song of Light said I would light the way and rise. Maybe this was what it meant?

Right or not, it was time to climb. Time to see if I would save or shade the world forever. I was really pulling for the first option.

The first limb was well above my head so I gave myself a running start, leaping and kicking off the tree, twisting my body to catch the branch the light had marked. I grunted and pulled myself up. After the first branch, things got a bit easier. I could just barely reach the limb above me, and I settled into an easy rhythm, entering a sort of fugue state as I clambered from limb to limb.

After ten minutes I looked around to gauge my progress. That was a mistake. I could see that I was well over halfway up the height of the surrounding towers and the idea of it made me dizzy with fear. Glancing down, I thanked every Ancient I could think of that I couldn't see past the dense foliage below.

For the first time, I realized that the denizens of the tree were talking about me, singing my praises and wondering what I was doing here.

"That's Mikowa's bond."

"The Heart of Life."

"What is she doing here?"

"Has she come to bring news of Miko?"

My heart sank as I realized that Miko had made friends here, and I had never told them what had happened to him above below. I would have to tell them. But not now. I had to focus on the task at hand.

My heart path was zigging and zagging to and fro on the limb above me as if to say, "*Come on, lazy girl, I haven't got all day.*"

I scrambled up and continued my ascension.

One branch, and then another. The climb went on and on. Ever so slowly, I could tell that the branches were coming closing together, easing my climb.

Another fifteen minutes and I was level with the top of the towers. I could see two of the spires, the distant forms of some of my friends. While they stood out clearly against the gold, I doubted they could make out my form among the branches. I'd made it two-thirds of the way to the top. I was over 600 feet above the ground, higher than the Washington Monument. That may have been the tallest freestanding stone structure in the world, but I was already twice as high as some of the tallest trees in Midgard.

My arms were starting to burn and I was grateful that the branches were now staggered just three or four feet apart, making it simpler to progress upwards. My heart path shimmered above me, glimmering as it darted from branch to branch.

It led, I followed.

While I climbed I went over the visions I had seen in the last few months, what had changed and what hadn't. I thought of the people I had met, my new friends and family, and those I had lost. I went over it again and again in my mind, trying to think of what I might have missed, where I was heading and what I might do.

Clarity eluded me, so I settled on singing with the birds as I climbed. A peace stole over me, calming my mind and relaxing my body. The limbs grew closer and closer, the spaces tighter and tighter. Like a ladder now, the branches of the tree allowed me to go higher.

Until I couldn't.

Surprised, I evaluated my surroundings. I wasn't quite at the top. It seemed there must be at least another ten or twenty feet above me.

But I could go no further.

My heart path winked at me, pooling on the branch in front of me, beckoning me forward instead of up. Curious, I eased my way around the trunk, spiraling across the several limbs. And then it stopped. The light flowed into a smooth knot on the tree and disappeared.

Worn shiny and smooth, the knot was an anomaly in the rough bark. Now what?

I thought of my friends below in their towers, waiting, watching. Perhaps this was another voice activated system?

"Red Queen," I said loudly. Nothing happened.

Among the chatter of the trees a new song was taken up.

"They are coming! The Shadows. They are here! Run. Hide!"

Sure enough, I could hear the low hum of several gravicycles approaching, coming to roost below the tree.

What could I do?

I decided to follow my heart path's lead, and placed my hands over the well-worn knot. I sent all my heart into the tree, furiously trying to connect, to access its core. I sent healing. I sent love. I sent wonder and respect.

At first, I felt nothing. Then, a stirring. A glimmer of acknowledgement. A slow awakening.

And then, I was consumed. Consumed with knowledge. I could see the Ancient home of my people, the land from whence this tree had come, the city where its mother had grown and shed its seed. I watched the ship arrive, the seed unfurling, the tree growing almost as if overnight, the sun awakening. The terraforming, the populating. The divide with the Shades. Oh, that was so painful, the sadness the tree had felt to see its beloved lights splitting apart into darkness. I experienced it all. Through Anansanna, the tree created life, anchored it, blessed it. Even when there was pain, even when there was sorrow, the tree lived on. But it had been so, so sad and lonely of late. It felt the pain of the world it had created and had been calling for help.

For the tree could not work alone. Just as it anchored the red sun, it needed someone to help fix its attention, to guide it, to co-create a new world. It could not be done alone. Fae and tree had to work together, as they had always done.

It felt my own sorrow and perseverance, the love in my heart, and it recognized me instantly. I was its heart. The soul that was needed in the recipe for creation.

That was why I needed the people at the seven towers. We were the power, the tree and I, and they were the ground. My hands felt electrified, glued to the tree. My consciousness grew to fill the tree from the tip of its boughs to the depth of its roots. The roots themselves twined around the spires deep in the earth and our energy raced up the golden towers, connecting everything so that we were as one organism, the towers, the tree and I.

I could feel the emotions of all my friends, my parents, my grandmother, the way that I normally experienced the surge with Alec. Together, we formed a hive of empathy, of love and trust.

The bond was complete. The energy raced back down the spires, falling into the earth and upwards into me, filling me, fueling me.

The tattoo on my ankle burned like a hornet's sting and the muscles in my body collapsed. The tree lifted its limbs to cradle me, to hold me in position. I couldn't have fallen, anyway. My hands were glued to the knot on the tree, immovable.

Light exploded from my eyes and I screamed, throwing back my head as I poured all the healing energy I could draw from the bond with the seven towers, from my friends and family, from the hearts of my heart, into the tree, to heal the sun. To heal the rift of light and dark and re-forge the world.

The sun flashed, a pulse of blue light escaping from the red, sending newly awakened ions at the speed of light through all of Aeden, from the earth's core to all peoples far and wide.

In that moment, I was one with everything. I felt Mikael and his minions fall to their knees on the stairs of the towers, weeping with joy as the veil of darkness dissolved around them. No longer were they separate from the light. I experienced Rowan's reversal of heart and the moment he forgave me. I saw wars around the world stop in their tracks, weapons laid down as if they were poison. Abusers prostrating themselves to beg forgiveness. Executioners lowering their swords.

Hate fled the building as love rushed in. Anger turned to compassion, guilt turned to acceptance.

In an instant, there was peace on earth.

Epilogue

I know what you're thinking.

How boring, right? Nothing to fight anymore. Nothing to lose.

But the world is anything but boring. In the four years that have passed since that day, the world has been reborn.

Fear has been banished from our hearts, so there is no "us versus them" mentality. No one fights, no one steals. No one goes hungry anymore. Corporate greed is a thing of the past. In just several years, most illnesses have been cured, the world has unanimously transitioned to renewable energy sources, and the environment is improving every day.

Relationships are equal, honest and open. People work on what interests them, when and where they want. You would think that might make people lazy, but it has stimulated creativity in ways no one could have foreseen.

The borders of Aeden have been opened, allowing free communication between fae and humans. Bigotry, misogyny, sexism and racism are all things of the past.

Technology is being shared and new horizons are opening up above, below, and in space. Already, a colony has begun on the Moon, and plans are in motion to terraform Mars.

With the amped up ions pumping through the world, everything is changing, even the humans. More and more young adults are awakening every day with elemental powers, and children and babies are exhibiting signs of increased intuition, stamina and regenerative capabilities. All signs point to a shifting of the human race towards fae. It seems that the only thing separating the species really was a degree of light.

Things have changed for the fae, too. Faelings now access their powers at Ascensions, not Choosings, since the only choice now is the Light. And more and more fae are mingling in the human world, falling in love, mating and bringing both species even closer together. More fae are accessing old, rare and forgotten abilities. Talking to animals. Hearing the song of the sun. Flying.

And me? I'm enjoying the ride. My responsibilities as the Heart of Life ended that day on the Tree of Life, when my tattoo burned and the red sun on my ankle disappeared. I still have the ring of blue arrows above my foot, a constant reminder to always be Tyr-wise and Tyr-brave. Otherwise, I am just a regular girl now. Well, mostly. It's not like my powers have gone away. Some people still look at me in awe, or stop to thank me when they see me. But all in all, everything is good.

Just a week ago I graduated from Bennington with full honors, concentrating my studies in the fields of archaeology and biology. Alec graduated, too, getting a mixed degree focusing on forensics and ancient history. We plan to travel the world together, researching the roots of both fae and human cultures. Maybe it's because I was raised knowing so little about the faw world, but I'm interested in learning everything I can about where we came from. Who we were, and what we might be becoming.

My father turned over the Light Guard to Dorian, saying the job was a bit too tame for his taste now that the world is safe. Still, we need to maintain the Guard, the towers and the tree. Who knows when a divide might happen again, when another Heart of Life will arise and need to save the day. The tools of light have to be protected. Dorian was happy to take the job.

With nothing to do, my father has turned his attention to his family. He and my mother were both adamant that I finish college living at home, where they could keep a watchful eye on my relationship with Alec.

It was amazing getting to know my father, having the opportunity to bond with Bran for four years.

And yeah, I am so glad it is almost over.

Graduation day has come and gone, and my wedding day is here. In just a few hours, the guests will be arriving. A few hours after that, I'll be on a plane to Turkey with Alec to honeymoon in the Cappadocia mountains and explore underground citadels that have long been dubbed "fairy chimneys" by the locals. You can safely say that this young budding archaeologist is insanely intrigued.

So, do you think I'm in the guest room at Vala's, doing my hair, getting ready for the ceremony? After all, I promised Amber I would meet her there half an hour ago.

No. I'm grinning happily, sprinting through the forest and leaping over fallen trees.

Deep, husky laughter follows me, making my whole body tingle with anticipation.

Has he almost caught me?

I kick off a tree, spinning 360 degrees in the air, and glimpse Alec not twenty feet away, smiling as he follows.

He is shirtless, just wearing a set of loose green Valhallan shorts. His jet black hair is slightly shorter than usual, showing off his sexy ears. Gods, did I really just say that? Do I really think even his ears are sexy? Let me think about it.

Yeah. I most definitely do.

"You can't lose me, Siri," he calls out. "I'll follow you to the ends of the earth. But it's time we headed back to the house, or Amber's gonna have my hide."

I dart around a tree and double back, tackling him from behind. He spins me around and stares into my eyes. Violet into silver. His eyes never returned to their previous natural color. I don't miss it. He is perfect, in every way. The heart of my heart.

He reaches up and tucks a loose strand of hair behind my ears. My entire body sings at the light touch and I hum under my breath.

"Amber's going to have to do something about your hair," he muses.

And just like that, I want to smack him.

Some things never change.

Instead, I choose the high road and kiss him deeply. I pour all the passion and longing and waiting I've stored up over the last four years into that kiss, knowing my grandmother will die if we kiss like that in front of her friends at the wedding. Alec responds with his own outpouring of gratitude, love and awe, and we surge together in the middle. In our hearts, we are already one.

Today everyone will witness us come together, in the same spot we first met, where it all began.

For a moment, we stand with our foreheads pressed together, just breathing, and staring into each other's eyes. And then he laughs, and gently pushes me away, calling "Catch me if you can!" as he dashes away.

And so I sprint after him.

I run, because there is nothing to fear anymore, and everything good in the world to run towards.

Acknowledgements

Inner Origins has taken me to new and unexpected places in my life and in my own heart. I have cried and laughed along with the characters, and enjoyed every minute of it. They have truly come alive for me, and I am thankful for their presence in my life every day. That said, I have some real life heroes to thank, too!

My heart is full of gratitude for my team of editors and beta readers from Earth Lodge. You guys are a family to me, and your excitement for each new chapter lit a fire under me and kept me going like nothing else. Your encouragement and kind critiques were instrumental in the creation of *Inner Origins*.

The fantastic reception I've received online from fans has been amazing and uplifting, too. Because of you all, I could not stop writing even if I wanted to! New books are churning through the mire of my mind, and on their way, I promise. The only question now is, do we move forward, or backward? Stay tuned, and find out!

ABOUT THE AUTHOR

Ellis Logan has been talking to fairies and writing stories since she was a little girl. She lives a quiet life with her family in New England, where she enjoys skiing, boxing, hiking and eating chocolate...always chocolate!

Follow Ellis on Facebook and Twitter at
EllisLoganBooks

and

Join Ellis's mailing list at EllisLogan.com
to stay tuned for new releases, giveaways
and more!

Want more?

Check out **Heart Ward**, the Inner Origins Companion novella. Experience the love story between Alec and Siri all over again, told through Alec's eyes. Find out what he was doing before he met Siri, and read his struggle to allow love back into his life.

Made in the USA
Charleston, SC
03 October 2016